Learning to Love it

'The thought of being bad turns me on,' said Lissa.

'Tell me about it,' he said. 'You can tell me all your secrets. Every fantasy you've ever had.'

It surprised her – the feeling of release at his words. She *could* tell him; she knew it. And if she told him all the kinky twisted things that had ever made her come, then he might do them – and that was scary and wonderful and exciting.

By the same author:

Strictly Confidential
Sweet Thing
Sticky Fingers
Something about Workmen

For more information about Alison Tyler's books
please visit www.alisontyler.com

Learning to Love it
Alison Tyler

BLACK LACE

This edition published in 2007 by
Black Lace
Thames Wharf Studios
Rainville Rd
London W6 9HA

Originally published 2000

A catalogue record for this book is available from the British Library.

www.black-lace-books.com

Typeset by SetSystems Ltd, Saffron Walden, Essex
Printed in the UK by CPI Bookmarque, Croydon, CR0 4TD

The paper used in this book is a natural, recyclable product made
from wood grown in sustainable forests. The manufacturing process
conforms to the regulations of the country of origin.

ISBN 978 0 352 33535 7 [UK]
ISBN 978 0 352 34149 5 [USA]

Distributed in the USA by Holtzbrinck Publishers, LLC, 175 Fifth Avenue,
New York, NY10010, USA

Contents

For SAM, always

Prologue

'*I*t's a spanking,' Colin said softly to the trembling woman upended over his lap. 'Spankings are supposed to hurt.'

Lissa knew that he was smiling. She couldn't see his expression – not in her current position, with her head towards the floor, long blonde hair falling forward over her face. Still, she felt his eyes looking down at her, could picture the subtle smile playing over his mouth. Colin's smile changed his looks, softened the planes of his starkly handsome face.

'What did I tell you this morning?' Colin asked, still speaking in the same, unhurried tone. Lissa didn't answer. Although her sobs were coming slower now, they hadn't completely subsided. She tasted salt as tears wet her parted lips.

For once, Colin let her get away without responding, patiently answering his own question. 'I said that if I caught you again, it would mean a spanking.' He paused as she shivered. The way he said the word twisted something inside her – *spank*, with a hard 'k' sound at the end. When *she* said 'spank' or 'spanking', her voice trailed upward, as if she were asking a question. But there was no question at all in his use of the word. It

1

had a finality that made her stomach feel weak. 'And when I give a spanking,' he continued, 'there are always plenty of tears.'

As if to prove this point, Colin let his strong hand connect with Lissa's bare bottom five times in rapid succession. The pain came through her hindquarters in a rush and she flailed across his lap, feet kicking behind her, hair trailing across her face, hiding her flushed cheeks. It was as if she believed the frantic motions might cool her burning skin or help her to get away. They did neither. Colin kept her in place with one arm firmly across her waist, her delicate wrists captured easily in his hand. He waited until her thrashings ceased, didn't speak again until she had composed herself.

'We'll start at the beginning, won't we, love?' he asked. His voice remained soft, almost soothing. He never yelled. Never cursed or swore. If anything, he grew calmer in direct proportion to the rising intensity of their encounters. Lissa was unable to recognise his displeasure simply from his tone. 'We'll start with one.'

She couldn't believe it. 'Colin, no. Not one.'

'Excuse me?'

Lissa flinched, even though he hadn't started spanking her again, and remained silent. How could she have told him 'no'?

'Did you say something?' he asked next. It sounded as if he were amused at the thought.

'I'm sorry,' she hurried to say, 'I didn't mean to.'

'There's a price for misbehaving,' he reminded her – it was one of his favourite statements. 'There's always a price to pay. Isn't that right, Lissa?'

Yes, and she was paying it with her own pain. Heat radiated from her and she tried to visualise what her ass must look like. The way his handprints would stand out against her pale skin in bold, purplish relief, like obscenely lush flowers. She squirmed to look over her shoulder, but was unable to see the way he'd decorated her bottom. The mental image came easily enough, however. She'd often stood in front of a mirror after one of their sessions, admiring.

'Like a canvas,' Colin had observed the week before, coming up behind her in the bathroom and staring into the mirror alongside her. Lissa had thought he might chastise her for looking so long at her reflection, but he hadn't. Instead, he'd seemed to approve of her interest in his handiwork, took pride in it like a master artist. 'Your skin is my canvas,' he'd told her. 'I paint you, turn you into a masterpiece.'

Together, they had watched the colours fade, from dark plum to raspberry to a petal pink. Then Colin had backed her against the mirror and made love to her, letting the coolness of the glass penetrate into her heated flesh. He'd been tender at first, but as he'd come, the animal side of him had emerged and he'd pressed his mouth to hers, biting her bottom lip, bruising her with the intensity of his kiss.

'Count for me,' Colin said now, bringing Lissa back into the present, readying her with his words. Her body tensed, but Colin never gave it to her when she was prepared. This time was no different. As soon as she finally began to relax, he struck. The heavy weight of his palm landed, stinging, on her right buttock. He left his hand on top of the mark, letting her feel the pressure. Lissa exhaled the word, 'One,' in a rush of air. How could it be only one, when she'd endured so much already?

That thought made her recall a picture Colin had shown her. It was from a hardbound book of erotic art. Swirls of reds, blues and golds lit the background in a Klimt-like display. A young woman lay sprawled on her stomach on a velvety sofa in the foreground, looking over her shoulder. The viewer could see the rear of her long legs, her ass and back, slender shoulders, sharply drawn chin tilted down. The woman's hair partially hid her face, but her mouth was visible. Her lips were slightly open, full and dark, like cherries. The model's

3

thighs and rear revealed marks that, at first glance, had appeared to Lissa like the delicate imprints of a butterfly's wings. On closer inspection, she'd realised the patterns were handprints, fading to a pale rose in places, still boldly crimson in others. Although the woman's hair cascaded forward, her shining blue eyes could be seen through the strands of her platinum tresses.

Lissa had stared for a long time at the picture, trying to decipher the message on the painted face. The look wasn't caused just from pain, and it wasn't solely from guilt or shame, although all three emotions seemed to be present. There was a glow to the woman's face, as if she'd just had the most intense orgasm of her life. This, Lissa decided, mixed with the obvious hurt from her spanking, was what left the model with a radiant, almost transcendent expression. Lissa couldn't remember the name of the work, nor of the artist, but the picture had stirred her when Colin had stopped at that page, and its image remained with her now as her lover lifted his hand up high and then let it connect with her burning skin for the second time in a row.

'Two,' she said, her voice hushed, her body like one taut electrical wire. She would behave this time, she mentally assured herself, would reach twenty without failing him. She felt secure in this decision, until Colin's fingers suddenly probed between her thighs, checking there for the sweet moisture that awaited him. His fingers slid between the lips of her sex and then started to make a simple circle around her clitoris. One rotation. Two. Three. Circling in perfect rhythm, just the way she liked it. The pleasure was immediate, working deep within her, countering both the pain and the humiliation of being thrust over his lap like a naughty child. All of these feelings flowed together as he played her, coursed through her body in powerful waves. Colin's fingertips were slightly calloused, and the roughness against her most sensitive areas brought an added wave of wetness to her cunt. Flooded her.

'Oh, God,' the words escaped before she could stop herself. 'Oh, please –'

'Please what?' he asked, his voice serene.

There was no way to put into words what she wanted, since even she didn't actually know what it was. Something. *Everything.*

'Please what?' he repeated, his fingers pausing in mid-rotation.

Now she knew what to say. 'Don't,' she whispered, her voice made somehow prettier by the begging. 'Please don't stop.'

He kept going and her body tensed in confusion. Would he let her come? If he did, it would be a break in his rules. Rarely did Colin allow her to reach orgasm until he was through with the punishment portion of a session. Breathlessly, she realised that she was about to climax and, at just the same moment, he withdrew his hand and gave her another spank. Hard. Keeping her on the edge, as always, keeping her unsure of what to expect next.

'My bad girl,' Colin said softly, sounding almost as if he were proud of her for misbehaving. 'Why are you always such a bad girl, Lissa?'

She didn't have an answer. But as the pain burnt through her, she recalled the erotic portrait again, understanding in a mental flash why he'd shown her the picture. It was a way to tell her what lay ahead, in her very near future. For now, this very evening, he was re-creating the painting with her in the role of the model.

Book One:

Adulteries of Art

Robes loosely flowing, hair as free:
Such sweet neglect more taketh me
Than all the adulteries of art;
They strike mine eyes, but not my heart.

— Ben Jonson

Chapter One

The naked man dangled upside down from the second floor of the museum. His body did not move in the breeze, appeared unaffected by the light drizzle. Behind him, in a nook on the same floor, a marble sculpture stared down into the courtyard with stony eyes, as if following the movements of the slender blonde woman below.

Although the courtyard bustled with tourists, Lissa was particularly noticeable, standing beneath a ledge to shield herself from the hazy rain. She had on her favourite ankle-length coat, made of bright red cloth with shiny black buttons running in a row down the front. It was not appropriate gear for the weather, but she didn't plan on staying outdoors for long. Her leather boots, with three-inch heels, made her nearly six feet tall, head and shoulders above the young students who crowded in the atrium like ducklings, following their teacher in two neat lines. She observed them intently, catching their excited energy, the way they hurried after their male teacher. Watching them made her smile, made her forget for a moment why she was there.

'These statues were created by a local artist,' the

8

teacher told the students. 'Can anyone tell me what the work represents?'

Lissa listened to a few curious responses, then moved her gaze from the children back to the suspended, upside-down body. She was captivated by the form and yet it, too, soon lost her attention.

Where was he?

Slowly, she began to walk around the perimeter of the courtyard, stepping over other similar human forms to the one above, not seeing the dark figures so much as the people who were staring at them. She was supposed to meet Colin at the museum but the current exhibit had drawn more tourists than she had anticipated. Colin must be hiding in a doorway somewhere, she decided. More likely than not he was watching her right now, watching as she scanned the multitude of black and tan raincoats and umbrellas for the ones she would recognise as his own. Although his bright red hair usually served as a beacon, she couldn't immediately locate him. This did not mean he wasn't there, only that he was well-hidden. He liked cat-and-mouse games, excelled at them, while she simply floundered, searching for clues.

As she scanned the men clad in various types of rain gear, Lissa realised that she knew Colin's outer attire more completely than the clothing he wore beneath. This was only because their relationship was occurring in London. If romance had found them in her home state of California, she would have memorised his shorts and T-shirts, his beach wear, or the casual khakis and denim shirts that everyone seemed to favour, even for meals in fancy restaurants.

There. She spied him standing at the corner of a building, hiding in shadows just as she'd suspected he might be. He blended in with the life-size, cast-iron figures as innocently as if he'd been positioned there by the artist. I've been here the whole time, his attitude implied. Watching you while you were unaware. She started towards him, but he shook his head, just once, and she immediately stopped, now exposed beneath the elements. The rain, more mist than rain, decorated her white-blonde hair with crystalline drops.

Stopped near a fallen figure, she tried to behave as if she'd been hurrying to this site to see the artwork, a strange exhibit of iron figures, identical to the one hanging from the window ledge above.

What did he expect her to do now? she wondered. She knew only to obey Colin's silent command, to wait for the next one. But if he would not let her approach, how could she know what he desired of her? Lissa's grey eyes flickered back and forth, from the students, now in a semi-circle around the sculptures in the main courtyard, to Colin, who continued to frown. She felt as if she might start crying at any moment, although she knew from past experience that this would not help her, would not draw him to her side, would possibly even make him leave.

What did he want?

Through the windows of the building, she could see workers in the museum offices, unimpressed by the art around them. Or, more likely, accustomed to it. Lissa understood this feeling, although she was constantly surprised at how quickly one could become immune to art. Personally, she found the latest exhibit actually frightening, the remnants of an iron battlefield, the distorted figures, some bent into foetal positions.

She'd been in a similar position recently, in Colin's bedroom, curled with her knees to her chin. Her pale body had trembled all over while Colin observed her in the same manner that he was doing right now, watching and not letting on to what he was thinking. Emotionless in his stares. Yet he *was* capable of exerting his emotions, of forcing them upon her. When he did so, she always found herself surprised at the depth of his feelings, at the manner in which he was able to express himself when he so desired. Although he could be robotic in his ability to hide his emotions, he could also show hurt, and longing, and anger.

Was he angry now?

There was a good chance that she'd disturbed him by walking so forcefully towards him, head held high, sharp-heeled shoes making their clacking sounds on the stone path. When she walked, her entire attitude became one of confidence and defiance. Colin did not appreciate either in their romantic relationship and she, despite her many lessons at his feet, bound and obedient at least for the moment, did not seem able to tone down this side of herself. Or maybe he *did* appreciate this part of her personality, for he would shake his head and look down at her, calling her his little upstart, his defiant one, then punishing her for it. If she did not misbehave, he would have no reason to discipline her.

But would he discipline her here, in public? Her body shuddered involuntarily at the thought. Colin had punished her out of doors before, but never in such a crowded location. In the past, he had chosen places specifically for their quiet ambience. Still, she had learnt not to underestimate him, and the question nagged at her: what would he do now?

Rather than search Colin out with her gaze, Lissa stared at the closest figure on the ground, its head back, legs to chest. She wondered what the artist was saying with this particular exhibition. Trying to decipher the work instantly calmed her, even if she could not immediately discern the artist's intention. Did the work imply that the world was a battlefield or that war was wrong? Were those explanations too simple or not simple enough?

After studying art for many years, dissecting some of history's most important works came naturally to her. But new art was more difficult. With the masterpieces, there were books to study, people to gain insight from, predecessors whose views could be distilled in order to find her own. With newer creations, she stumbled blindly. She found it similar to her attempts at divining Colin's soul, trying to wring truth from the objects. A single brush stroke on a canvas could convey so much, or nothing at all.

Marcus didn't understand this. He felt that anything he could create himself was not art. 'Now, that's a painting,' he would say, pointing to a portrait by Rembrandt or Vermeer, arrogantly showing her the light and the shadows, even though she knew the works better than he ever would. 'But that,' he would continue, motioning to something avant-garde, 'that's just trash.' Then he would shut his ears, refusing to hear as she explained why the modern artists were important. Why any art was worthwhile if it could reach someone. Why people like Rauschenberg or Warhol or Mapplethorpe were able to open venues that had not been available before. These were the explorers of the art world. They charted maps and learnt new languages.

She shook her head to dislodge memories of the old arguments she'd had with Marcus. Those fights were ancient history – going back nearly ten years, to their initial meeting in college. For the moment, she must concentrate only on Colin. If he would not let her approach him, then he most definitely had other plans in mind. He *always* had plans. She looked around, attempting to think as he would, something she never found easy. It wasn't in her nature to control her emotions. When she wanted something, she went after it. When she felt something, she could not hide it. Marcus had often teased her about her inability to play poker, to disguise her hand. She simply couldn't help but give herself away, whether she had cards of garbage or a straight flush.

She looked towards Colin. He wasn't standing in the corner any more. Had he left her alone? Frantic, she spun in a circle, nearly knocking down a young student. Where had he gone? She knew that she was panicking without reason. He might simply have stepped under an awning to shield himself from the rain. Or he might have moved to another side of the courtyard. She circled again, quickly, and then heard his laugh from directly behind her. He was always able to guess her movements, to know what she would do even before she knew it herself.

In this same manner, he had known they would have an affair. He had told her so at their first meeting, at the fiftieth anniversary of the Frankfurt Book Fair, coming into the booth where she'd been promoting her latest art book, sidling in behind her and pressing his lips to her ear. 'You'll be in my bed tonight.'

She had turned around to face him, to strike him, but reconsidered as soon as she saw his expression. Surely, he had mistaken her for someone else. And surprisingly she'd found herself unoffended at his words. His appearance, red hair parted and combed neatly, small tortoise-shell spectacles in place, had made her think of a professor, not some lecherous bastard. He'd been wearing a crisp black suit with a black-on-black shirt and tie, and his dragon-shaped tie tack was similar to one her husband – estranged husband – had owned. For some reason this small connection to a familiar object put her further at ease.

During the few seconds it took for her to assess him, Colin had remained silent. From his appearance, she'd assumed only that he was looking for someone else, that he'd mistaken her for a lover. She knew all about book-fair romances. Many people connected for the seven days, finding a safe haven away from responsibilities at this gigantic book show. He could easily be one of those people. Besides, there were several other women working alongside her in the booth who were young and attractive. Perhaps he'd thought she was Marie. They were both blonde, both slender.

'I'm sorry,' she'd said, instead of 'excuse me'.

'Of course,' he'd told her, 'you would be. That is your nature.'

13

The meeting had confused her and, hours later, when she'd found herself in his bed at the fanciest hotel in town, an empty bottle of fine champagne nearby, half-filled glasses on the table, red roses dripping petals on to the floor, she had remembered what he'd said.

'Why?' she'd asked softly, not entirely certain she wanted to know the answer. 'Why did you say that it was my nature?'

Her wrists had been captured above her head with his black silk tie, her body only half-shielded by the crisp white sheet. Colin had sat at the edge of the bed looking up her bound form, admiring the dips and curves, his head cocked as he stared at her. She'd recognised the look on his face, had seen it often enough at museums and galleries. The expression was international – he'd looked as if he were drinking in a work of art.

'It simply is. You can't help it. Any observant person would recognise your will to submit. You said you were sorry for something you hadn't done, said you were sorry when you had done nothing wrong at all. I was the obnoxious one, coming up behind you, speaking so openly to you. Insolently. You ought to have smacked me.'

'I thought about it.'

That comment had made him smile. And with her tied so securely and unable to escape, he'd leant forward and struck her, slapping the right side of her face forcefully enough to knock her back into the down-filled pillows. She'd sighed. Another surprise. No tears had filled her eyes. It had felt good, somehow, the flush of pain. It must have felt good, because instantly she was wet again, ready for him, although they'd only just finished making love for a second time. None of it made any sense.

As none of it made sense when he put his arms around her in the courtyard of the museum, holding her tightly for a moment before giving her his next command. Then he pressed his lips to her ear, speaking

14

softly and telling her to go to the restaurant on the corner, to order them each a glass of wine, to wait for him there. Another time, the person whom she used to be would have asked why. She was over that now. The lessons had stuck a bit. She had learnt.

Colin watched Lissa leave the courtyard, listened to the heels of the boots that he'd bought for her as they clicked against the slick wet stones. She wasn't perfect. Not yet. But she would be. Lissa had more potential than any of the others. When she turned around to look at him, he had the frown in place.

God, he knew her. Every single move.

Chapter Two

*L*issa ordered the wine but didn't drink. When Colin joined her, they would lift their glasses together. Until he arrived, she took her mind off her worries by observing the decor of the restaurant. Reprints of artwork by the American painter Maxfield Parrish adorned the walls, creating a display of exotic women sprawled on cliff tops, around fountains and under golden-lit skies. The colourful pictures put Lissa momentarily at ease – Parrish's refined art was meant to calm the viewer, and even after so many years, the paintings did their work.

But soon, she turned her gaze from the pictures to the couples nearby. Often she found herself wondering whether other people were enmeshed in relationships similar to hers and Colin's. Lissa focused her attention on a pretty brunette in a crimson turtleneck. Was she like Lissa, bubbling with nervous energy, ready to greet her lover for a secret rendezvous? And if she was, did her lover do the things to her that Colin did to Lissa? Did he spank her, tie her up, torment her in the most decadent manner possible?

Most likely not, Lissa thought as she quickly summed up those around her. The other patrons were probably

16

workers from nearby shops, filling the few moments of their late afternoon breaks with a quick roast beef or cucumber sandwich and a magazine. Lissa caught a glimpse of her reflection in the mirror above the bar. No one else looked as anxious or unsure as she felt. The rain had mussed her hair, adding a slight hint of curl to her fine locks. Her cheeks were flushed, as if she had already drained her glass of Merlot.

Even though the ambience of the café was comfortable, she felt only slightly more at ease than she'd been at the museum. Knowing that Colin was displeased made it difficult for her to fully relax. How long would he make her wait? The suggestion of meeting at the museum had been hers, the site chosen after she'd read a review of the exhibit. She had never dreamt there would be more than a few stragglers in the courtyard, had not expected a hoard of schoolchildren milling about. From the write-up, the exhibit had seemed inappropriate for children. She wouldn't have thought that a teacher might choose it for a Wednesday afternoon outing.

Still, Colin liked to meet her in public, and it had been her turn to choose the location. He favoured playing in places where they might get caught, backing her against the cold, stone wall of some three-hundred-year-old building. Kissing her mouth until it felt swollen, his hands up under her blouse, pinching her nipples, digging his fingernails down her flat belly. He had taken her beneath damp bridges, in the rumbling thunder from cars travelling overhead. He had fucked her at midnight in a poorly lit alley near their apartment. But as a well-known doctor, he had to keep himself under control, did not want to be discovered as the exhibitionist she knew him to be. In general, *he* chose the places to play, knowing the city much better than she did, able to find nooks, alleyways, empty parks with ease. She rarely met with as much success.

'It's your turn,' he would tell her, a smug half-smile

17

in place. 'You find a location and tell me when to meet you there.' This simple request inevitably sent Lissa into a tizzy. She would page through guide books in search of the perfect spot, casually quiz the few acquaintances she knew in London, always couching her questions so that her motive would be unrecognisable. There was no conceivable way for her to state outright, 'I need to find an out-of-the-way place for my boyfriend to fuck me.' Colin, of course, knew the difficulties of his missions, and seemed to revel in Lissa's nervousness almost as much as he did in the actual act when she finally found an appropriate location.

Today's site hadn't worked out, and this was what made Lissa feel so insecure as she watched Colin finally enter the restaurant. Next time, she would work harder. She had several places in mind – the rooftop of their apartment building, the unisex bathroom at their favourite restaurant. Today, she had tried to be clever, and look where it had got her.

She stared at Colin as he stuck his umbrella in the blue-and-white porcelain urn by the front door, then headed slowly towards the table. He had one of his unreadable expressions in place. Lissa didn't know if he were angry with her, although she could guess from past experience. Her insides felt watery and she clenched her thighs together under her tight black skirt, as if warding off an accident. Sometimes, in anticipation of their meetings – and what that simple word might mean – she had nearly wet herself. This time, as his cold green eyes focused on her, she could visualise it, the puddle forming on the glossy wood floor under her chair, the way Colin would laugh at her embarrassment. He enjoyed her discomfort, had said to her once, 'You seem so poised, leading people through museums, explaining what the artist was thinking. But it takes nothing to tip you off balance. Just a puff of air and you fall.'

His eyes, calm as still water, flickered a message as he sat down. Lissa tried to decode it, but failed. Was he angry? *Wasn't* he? Before he said anything to her, he lifted the wine glass and took a sip. Then, delighting her, he smiled. His smile filled his eyes as well as his lips, and she grinned at him in return, foolishly thinking that everything would be all right.

Colin chose this moment to lean forward, ready to impart a secret message, whispering, 'You're such a bad little girl, Lissa. You must like being punished. You must really enjoy it.'

Her smile instantly faded. The rosy flush that had coloured her cheeks turned to a hot blush, and she put one fluttering hand to the hollow of her throat in a nervous gesture, feeling the pulse of heat beating there.

'Do you remember what happens to bad girls?' he asked. Without waiting for an answer, he continued. 'You must remember, Lissa. It hasn't been that long since your last time over my lap, has it?' She nodded without thinking. Then shook her head the other way. Was the correct answer 'yes' or 'no'? She couldn't be sure. She could never be sure. The only thing she could honestly rely on was the fact that he liked to torment her, that he played games and teased and won every single round.

He continued to taunt her now, his voice low, almost soothing. He had a brilliant bedside manner. 'What happens to bad little girls, Lissa?' he queried. Then, even softer, making sure that no other customer could hear him. 'What happens to *my* bad little girl?'

She sighed. She didn't want to answer him. Saying the words out loud always made them seem more real than when they were only buzzing around in her head.

'Tell me,' he urged, and his voice dropped another level, changed in tone, letting her know that he expected an answer. Immediately.

'Bad girls are punished,' she said, hoping that the words would satisfy him, praying silently that he would let her get away with that response. He wouldn't. As much as it was her nature to submit, it was his to push her, to keep her ever on edge. Forever teetering.

'How?' he demanded.

She lowered her head, wishing they were in his apartment, wishing he wasn't so captivated with the idea of playing in public places. Yes, it turned her on to be watched, to be on display, but the act was so difficult for her. She caught her reflection again, this time upside down in a silver spoon, and she could make out the beet-coloured glow to her face. Her skin was fair. When she blushed it showed from her cheeks to the base of her neckline.

'You'll spank me,' she told him, still speaking in an undertone.

'Tell me more,' he urged, obviously enjoying himself. He took another sip of the wine and leant back slightly in his chair, letting her know with this gesture that he expected her to talk at a reasonable level. Although she'd been through the scenario before, it never got any easier.

'You'll take me back to the apartment,' she said. It was only a hope – occasionally he *did* spank her in public, but despite threats to do otherwise, he tended to indulge in that pleasure only after dark. 'You'll make me take off my panties and then you'll give me a spanking.'

'With what?'

Tears formed in the corners of her eyes. She couldn't help it. 'I'm sorry,' she said, unable to stop herself.

'Don't be,' he said. 'You know I don't mind.' He leant forward to touch a teardrop before it could slide down her cheek. She remembered him saying that her looks were enhanced by tears, either imminent or real, coursing down her face. He'd gone on to explain that while he appreciated the tears of anticipation, he preferred the ones that came from pain he inflicted. Those, to him, were more honest because they were earned.

'What will I spank you with?' he prompted her now, returning to their original conversation.

She sighed again, a deep, shuddering sigh. It was almost impossible for her to talk about her needs and desires. Before she'd met Colin, she'd never been able to ask for what she wanted. Yes, she'd written about her sexual urges in a diary, but that was as far as she'd been able to let loose. Never would she have considered telling Marcus what she wanted him to do to her. The thought was mortifying.

Because of her shyness, she had hardly ever experienced an orgasm prior to her relationship with Colin. At least, not the way that women in movies appeared to have them – the flush of colour that rushed to their cheeks, the moans and sighs that seemed to accompany all sex scenes on cinema. The only thing that had given her a similar pleasure was art. It was why, as an art historian, she spent hours in museums and galleries, always hoping to discover a new masterpiece.

Colin treated her as if she *were* the masterpiece.

She found it uncanny how he seemed to know exactly what she wanted. Everything she wanted. He took charge, understanding that her desires always outweighed her fears. Desires of being exposed, being bad, playing dirty. With Colin, Lissa was able to give herself over completely. Give herself as he wanted her to do right now.

'With what?' he asked.

'With a paddle,' she said, still speaking in a hushed tone, her fingers squirming uncontrollably in her lap, her chin lowered nearly to her chest.

'With your *special* paddle,' he said, that smile in his voice now, more sinister than when he'd arrived at the restaurant.

She twisted the platinum band around her ring finger, looked at it as if it held a special fascination, unable to meet his eyes.

Chapter Three

*B*y the time they finished their wine, grey clouds had filled the sky and the sidewalk was a virtual sea of bobbing black umbrellas.

'We'll take the underground,' Colin said, motioning towards the nearest station. Under the safety of Colin's own umbrella and with his arm around her waist, steering her through the crush of people, Lissa felt immensely safe. Even though she knew what awaited her when they arrived at the apartment. And even though that thought made her look down at her feet in embarrassment, as if each passing pedestrian could read her mind and know that she was in for a bare-bottom spanking when her boyfriend got her back to their home.

As usual, Colin seemed to understand her thoughts. 'You remember the first time you got a spanking, don't you?'

A heavy, middle-aged woman overheard the comment and turned to give Colin a shocked look which he ignored. Colin couldn't trouble himself with other people's hang-ups, while Lissa hated to be judged. Even by strangers. Still, she managed to nod in answer to his question. The memory was imprinted in her mind, permanent and unerasable.

'That will seem like a game of pat-a-cake when I get through with you this evening.' He paused, the expression on his face absolutely placid, as if he were simply discussing the weather. But what a forecast it was, Lissa thought: we're in for a chance of heavy tears, with an unexpected heatwave flowing through the lower region of my anatomy.

The tube bustled with the normal activity of a late afternoon commute. Colin found Lissa a seat and then stood in front of her, blocking her with his body, his cock exactly at her mouth-level. He looked down and gave her a lecherous wink, then bent to whisper in her ear. 'I want you to think about that first time,' he told her, 'I want you to remember.'

She waited a moment to see if he would give her any additional instructions, but he simply put one hand on her shoulder, as if for comfort, then looked away.

It was easy for Lissa to recall the first time he'd bared her bottom. Her indoctrination into the world of sexual spankings had been in Frankfurt, on their second evening together. Lissa closed her eyes, her body rocking with the motion of the subway car, dipping swiftly into the memories of an evening one month in the past.

After dining in a restaurant that Colin told her had the worst atmosphere but the best food in Frankfurt, they'd retreated to his hotel room again. Lissa had thought they would make love at once, as they had done on the previous afternoon, falling into each other, stripping off their clothes in such a hurry that she'd got a run in her stockings and had lost a button off her sweater. Instead, Colin had surprised her.

Seated on the edge of the king-sized bed, he had stared up at her, waiting. The look had made Lissa, standing a few steps in from the doorway, feel suddenly naked, even though she still had on her black skirt and lilac silk sweater. Her golden hair was swept cleanly into a French twist, revealing her slender neck. She'd chosen her jewellery carefully, wearing only tiny hoop earrings and a thin chain. It had been her desire to look classy for him, because she had noticed on the previous evening how well-dressed he was. All of his clothes sported the labels of the most chic, yet subdued, fashion designers.

Standing before him, however, she'd felt as if she might have dressed inappropriately, even though he'd seemed to approve of her attire when she'd arrived for their date. Was her sweater too tight? Was her skirt too short? From the look in his dark-green eyes she knew she'd done *something* to offend him. Finally, when she could stand the silence no longer, she'd stammered, 'Is something wrong, Colin?'

Silence.

'Are you angry?'

He'd shaken his head, but hadn't smiled at her. Lissa's hands had begun to move uncontrollably, one on top of the other, as if all of her nervous energy had concentrated into her fingertips.

In the subway, now, her hands mimicked this response at the memory, and when she opened her eyes and looked up at Colin, he grinned at her, as if he knew exactly what she was thinking.

Without speaking aloud, he moved his mouth in an exaggerated manner and she could read the words form on his lips. 'Bad girl.'

Then he looked away, focusing on the back of the newspaper being read by the man standing next to him. Lissa took this as a sign that she should return to her own thoughts, and she shut her eyes again.

That second night in Frankfurt, she had clenched her hands together to stop the sinuous motion, and Colin had noticed the gesture and laughed.

'You're nervous,' he'd said, a half-smile playing over his lips. It wasn't a friendly smile, but one that Lissa

24

couldn't instantly read. (Now, she knew what this expression meant. Then, it had managed to frighten her even more than his silence.)

Of course, Lissa had known that she could leave at any time, simply turn round and walk both out of Colin's hotel room and out of his life. Many of the affairs begun in Frankfurt also ended in Frankfurt. There was no need to keep them up after the book fair ended. At least, not until the following year, when a reunion was often possible.

But she hadn't wanted to leave. She'd wanted to know what she'd done to make him stare at her in such a way. And she'd wanted to experience another night of unbelievable lovemaking as they'd shared the previous evening. Uncomfortable, she'd looked at the floor, focusing on the toes of her shoes while trying to figure out what to do. She had felt like a young kid, a schoolgirl called on the carpet at the principal's office, made to atone for some form of transgression. The silence in the hotel room was almost overpowering. Finally, she moved her head, staring at anything except Colin's face: the clichéd painting of flowers that hung on one wall; the heavy comforter cover, decorated in bold red stripes; the gilt-edged mirror over the bed.

Her gaze had ultimately locked on Colin's tie tack, the same one he'd worn the previous afternoon. It was a dragon made of platinum. After clearing her throat, she'd asked Colin, 'Did you go to university in the States?' It was small talk, but at least she was saying something. Anything was better than being trapped in that odd, icy silence.

Colin had ignored the question, answering it instead with a question of his own. 'Why are you so nervous?'

'I mean,' she'd continued, her voice shaky, 'I know two people who own similar clips. It was the sign of some sort of club they belonged to.' Both Marcus and her ex-boyfriend Beau had been members of the fraternity, which had made it uncomfortable when she and her husband had initially started dating. But they'd lost track of Beau after college, so the awkwardness had faded. She had found herself explaining all of this to Colin, thinking that perhaps if she stumbled along in this inane conversation, he would smile at her.

He hadn't. 'When I ask you a question, I expect an answer.'

That was rule number one. She would remember it later, the way he'd spoken the words, as if she should pay careful attention to what he said. As if she ought not to let him down.

'I don't know,' she'd told him. 'The way you're looking at me.'

His response had been instantaneous. 'And how am I looking at you?'

She'd thought about it for a moment, trying to put her feelings into words, aware of the sound of her heart pounding. It had seemed so loud to her own ears, like a drum beating or soldiers marching, and she'd wondered if he could hear the noise from where he sat. 'You're looking at me as if I've –' She'd let the sentence remain unfinished.

'As if –'

'As if I've been bad.'

Apparently, this was the correct answer. Or, at least, the answer Colin had been waiting for, because he was on her in a second, moving quickly and agilely. She'd realised, somewhere deep in her mind, that although she had pegged him solely as an intellectual, he must also be a fantastic athlete. He was lithe, catlike, standing right next to her, seeming to tower over her. In a voice he hadn't used before to her, he'd hissed, 'Have you been bad, Lissa? Have you been a bad girl?'

She'd been unprepared for her body's response to the questions. Her legs had trembled and she'd wished Colin would hold her, would wrap his strong arms around her and tell her that everything was fine. But she had also realised that her pussy was wet – *drippingly* wet

– and that if he'd wanted to fuck her he could do so, without any further foreplay, without any additional lubrication. She'd known that she was drenched even before Colin bent on his knees in front of her, roughly pushing her skirt up and sliding her panties down. 'You're ready for me,' he'd said softly, two fingers now probing inside her. 'The thought of being bad gets you all excited, doesn't it?'

He hadn't touched her gently. He'd thrust his fingers into her pussy with more force than any other lover had ever used, and it had made her even wetter than before. Then, he'd suddenly switched the manner in which he was touching her, stroking her pussy lips slowly with two fingers, then holding them open between his thumb and forefinger to reveal her clit. For a moment, he'd simply stared at her, as if he were looking at a work of amazing beauty. Then he'd returned to touching her, running his thumb between her parted pussy lips and over that button of flesh that gave her such intense pleasure.

'You adore the thought of being naughty, don't you?'

She'd nodded, her eyes closed, basking in the way he was fingering her. The evening's progression confused her, yet she had not been able to keep herself from responding to his touch. But when she didn't verbally answer his question, Colin had quickly removed his fingers.

'I expect a response to my queries. I won't tell you a second time without issuing a punishment for breaking this rule.'

A punishment. She'd tingled all over at the thought, and when his fingers had returned to her cunt, she'd moaned, unsure if she were responding to his touch or to his threat. *How* would he punish her? Why did that thought both intrigue and excite her? It had been in her mind to be bad just to find out what his punishment might be. Could she do it? No. She was too much of a chicken to test him.

'Yes,' she'd said, her voice soft, almost hoarse. 'The thought of being bad turns me on.'

'Tell me about it.'

'I don't –'

'Tell me all about it, Lissa.' His voice had been a melody, crooning, his lips only a sliver away from the lips of her sex. She'd felt the heat from his breath against her skin and it had made her weak. If he put his tongue inside her, she thought she would slip to the floor in a pool of liquid pleasure.

'You can tell me all your secrets,' he said, his voice so low and soft that she'd had to strain to hear it, 'every secret fantasy you've ever had.'

It had surprised her, the feeling of release at his words. She *could* tell him, she knew it. And if she told him, if she curled up next to him in the king-sized bed and whispered all of the kinky, twisted things that had ever made her come, then he might do them. Might make it his personal mission to bring each and every one of them to glorious fruition.

She had understood this as she looked down, meeting his eyes, momentarily startled by how green they looked in the light from a single lamp. They'd seemed to glow, like a cat's in darkness.

'So, Lissa,' he'd continued, 'what's your secret fantasy?'

Before she had been able answer, he'd nuzzled closer and she'd known that he was going to lick her pussy a second before he did. Oh, Christ, it was good. The feel of it. The warm wetness of his mouth against the secret place between her legs. He'd begun to tease her with his tongue, first flicking the tip of it up and down between the swollen lips of her sex, then lapping in a circle using flat, broad strokes.

On the subway, in present time, Lissa's eyes were closed at this memory, and she let out an involuntary moan. This made Colin, standing above her and looking down, laugh out loud. When she quickly put one hand up to cover her mouth, aghast at having lost control of herself, even for a moment, he gave her a tiny headshake and a grin as if he knew exactly which part of the memory she was reliving. As if she were pleasing him by taking this personal trip down memory lane.

Flushed, Lissa looked at the map across from her to see how many more stops there were until they reached their own. She was surprised to see that they had actually passed their station and Colin simply shrugged and bent to whisper to her.

'We're in no hurry. You keep remembering that first time. I want you to be nice and ready for me when we get home. I want to be able to wring those panties out and watch your juices drip to the floor.'

Obeying quickly, Lissa shut her eyes again and it was almost like re-entering a movie theatre, the velvety darkness surrounding her, the film already in progress on the silver screen of her mind.

She remembered the sensation of Colin's knowledgeable tongue against that most sensitive region of her body. It had made her legs tremble again, but now for an entirely different reason than before. Colin had kissed her clit for a moment before pulling back and repeating the question. While he was speaking, his fingers had thankfully taken over from his tongue. He was good. Oh, he was good. He knew just how to touch her, how much pressure she could handle, working faster or slower as if absolutely in tune with her needs.

'Tell me, Lissa,' he'd demanded before returning to his languid ministrations.

She'd felt his tongue brush her clitoris, just a light tap against it and she'd gripped on to his shoulders to keep herself upright. He'd moved forward and she had felt his soft hair tickling her inner thighs, sighed at the brush of slight roughness from his whiskers. The two sensations were delicious and when he'd added the third,

29

of his lips locked around her clit, giving her a warm, French kiss, she'd again moaned aloud. It hadn't occurred to her that he had asked her a question, that he expected an answer, and that, by simply responding to the pleasure he was giving her she had already broken rule number one.

Colin had spent several minutes with his tongue probing her pussy, making designs with the very tip of it up and down, in and out. He'd seemed to enjoy this part of their lovemaking routine, because he worked at a leisurely pace, taking the time to find all of the ways that Lissa liked to be touched. Then, as if understanding exactly how much Lissa could take before coming, he'd stood, lifted her into his arms, and carried her to the bed.

'Hold your hands over your head,' he'd told her. 'Lock them together. I don't want them loose.' She'd obeyed immediately, watching as Colin stripped off his jacket and shirt, then walked into the adjoining bathroom. Lissa had heard him fumbling with something in the other room, but she'd stayed totally still. She would not disobey him. Not yet. When Colin had climbed back on to the bed with her, he'd held a pair of silver scissors in one hand. He hadn't spoken as he cut through her sweater and Lissa, although she'd felt the protest in her mind, had not told him to stop.

Upon reaching her bra, Colin had cut cleanly through the connecting band in the front and then spread open the white silky fabric. He'd kissed the soft skin of her breasts before moving to her nipples, one then the other, and then pinched them between his thumb and forefinger. Lissa had arched her back and made a soft purring sound as Colin bent to kiss in a long line between her breasts and down to her waist. Reaching her skirt, he'd brought out his scissors again, letting Lissa feel the cold metal against her naked skin as he cut through the fine material.

A thought had fluttered in Lissa's mind – what on

earth would she wear when it was time to leave the hotel? One of the white fluffy bath towels? Colin's red dressing gown? – but Colin had erased the worry easily by replacing it with another one.

'Tell me the first fantasy that comes into your mind,' he'd said. 'And then I'll give that unbelievably beautiful ass of yours the spanking it deserves.'

Chapter Four

Colin stroked Lissa's cheek and she opened her eyes. He was looking at her with a gentle expression on his face and she couldn't help but smile at him. Sometimes, he touched her with such care, it made her feel as if she were made of expensive porcelain. As if she were easy to break.

'We'll get off here and take the next one back to our stop.'

She nodded, in a daze. Colin led her docilely through the traffic of commuters to the appropriate landing, then wrapped his arms around her waist and pulled her back against him. She could feel that he was hard, and this knowledge made her more excited than even the memories had. When Colin was turned on, anything could happen. She looked around the landing, searching for some dark corner Colin might herd her towards. Or a pillar they could hide behind. He was always at least one step ahead of her, but that didn't mean she couldn't try to guess what awaited her. Would he take her in public, just to prove that he could succeed where she had failed?

No. Once the train pulled up, they walked on together, this time finding two seats side by side at the rear of the carriage. He gave her a sly glance, and again she wondered what he was going to do.

It didn't take long to find out. As soon as the train started to move, Colin slipped one hand under Lissa's long red jacket. He quickly sought out the indent between her legs, and then surreptitiously began stroking her pussy up and down through the fabric of her skirt, his secretive movements well hidden by her coat. Lissa sighed as Colin leant forward, whispering to her softly. 'Think back, Lissa. What was it like when I first put you over my lap?'

She took a deep breath, jumping right into the memories, like diving from a high-up board into cool, blue waters.

A spanking. As if he'd known the whole time that's what she wanted. Her eyes had widened but Colin hadn't been looking at her, focused instead on the matter of cutting through the expensive fabric of her black silk skirt. Reaching her panties, he'd made one slit at the top, and then had set down the scissors and torn the rest open with his bare hands, jaggedly ripping them off her. Lissa had felt more exposed for the manner in which he'd undressed her than if he'd simply asked her to take off her clothes herself.

'You're so lovely,' he'd said, staring at her with a reverent expression.

Following his gaze, she'd looked down at the tatters that remained of her outfit and then had looked up at Colin as he ripped her fancy panties into strips. Once again, she'd found herself wondering what she was going to wear on her way to her own hotel. But more importantly, what was Colin going to do now?

She should have guessed, she knew it, as he'd tied her wrists together with the wet fabric strips that previously had been her panties. She'd wanted to tell him that she would have kept her hands locked together without the bindings, but she'd found, as soon he returned to eating her pussy, that she was lying to herself. All she'd wanted to do was reach forward and stroke his fine red hair, to twirl her fingers in it, to press him harder against her. The bindings had kept her from doing that, reminded her to behave for him.

Behave. That word had echoed in her mind. He was going to spank her because she'd misbehaved, and now, in order to avoid disobeying him a second time, she had to tell him a fantasy.

'Or I'll stop,' he'd warned her, lifting his head from her pussy, his mouth wet and glistening with the sweet juices of her pleasure. 'I won't give you any more.'

He *had* to continue and she'd searched her brain for something to tell him. If she had simply said she wanted to be spanked, he might not have believed her, might not have believed that it had been in her mind long before he'd suggested it. Even though it was true. Even though she'd fantasised about this event for years before meeting Colin, before even meeting Marcus or her ex-boyfriend Beau. She'd written about it in her electronic diary while still a virgin, an eighteen-year-old who knew what she wanted but didn't have the slightest idea how to ask for it.

Why she wanted to be spanked, she didn't know. She couldn't conceive of a reason except for the fact that to her it meant letting loose. Being out of control. If a lover put her over his lap and paddled her ass, she would be at his mercy, and that was a tantalising thought. But she'd guessed from the way Colin had looked at her that he already understood this. He wanted something else, something more.

So what could she say? She'd found it increasingly difficult to concentrate with Colin playing those in and out games with his tongue in her pussy. Oh, did it feel marvellous. She couldn't have told him how to do it better. He seemed to know when to work softly, when to speed up. With each flick of his tongue, he sent her spiralling towards the finish line, making it almost impossible for her to obey his command and share a fantasy with him. But this, she'd realised correctly, was his goal. He was going to make it difficult for her in the most erotic way imaginable.

'I want –' she'd started, speaking before she truly knew what she was going to say, thinking that perhaps if she simply began to talk, a fantasy would come to her.

'Yes –' Colin had prompted her, his words vibrating against the tender skin of her sex. He hadn't stopped what he was doing, which Lissa was thankful for.

'I've always wanted –' she'd begun again, rephrasing the statement, aware that Colin was waiting for her to continue. The movements he was making with his tongue suddenly became slower and softer, just as she'd needed him to go faster and harder. He was playing with her, taunting her, and she'd understood that she had to talk to him in order to get what she wanted. A catalogue of fantasies flickered through her mind and she'd considered several before ultimately choosing one. 'I've always wanted to do it in public,' she'd finally blurted out.

Colin had raised his head up and looked at her. 'Do *what* in public?'

He wasn't going to let her get away with anything.

'Fuck,' she'd said, instead of 'make love' which had been on the tip of her tongue. 'I've always wanted to fuck where people might be able to see me.'

'That's not a fantasy. That's a wish. Tell it to me the way you fantasise about it. Give me every little detail.'

She'd closed her eyes and tried to visualise the picture. This fantasy had started for her in her sophomore year at the University of California at Los Angeles. It was autumn and the jacaranda trees were in bloom, their lush purple petals creating a thick carpet over the walkways and lawns of the campus. This created a sort of fairyland in her mind, and it had seemed almost too perfect when she'd spied a couple making out on the grass in the sculpture garden. They had spread a

35

red-and-white chequered blanket next to one of her favourite statues, a nude of a woman standing with her arms folded over her breasts, and they were engrossed in their public display of affection, apparently not caring who watched them. Lissa, who had been sketching one of the statues, remained where she stood, sketching the amorous couple instead.

Back in her dormitory room that night, she had waited impatiently until her roommate had finally fallen asleep, before taking care of herself. With the unsexy sounds of Catherine snoring in the background, Lissa had masturbated to the memory of the kissing duo. This was the scenario she'd chosen to describe for Colin.

'Have you been to UCLA?' she'd asked, wondering if he could understand the words. Her voice had been unrecognisable to her own ears. He was so close to making her come.

'For a seminar,' he'd told her, moving his mouth away from the lips of her sex just long enough to answer.

With yearning in her voice, she'd explained the first part of the story, describing the time of year, the way the sculpture garden had looked in the late afternoon. 'But what I most liked,' she'd confessed, 'was the fact that they didn't seem to care who watched them.'

Again Colin had taken his mouth away from her pussy, and this time he'd smiled at her, letting her know that he understood. He'd replaced his tongue with his fingers, gently massaging her clitoris and the sensitive area around it, keeping her at a plateau without allowing her to climax. Oh, he was good at this. Too good. It was as if he'd possessed a manual on how to touch her, how to give her the most pleasure possible.

'Did you masturbate to an image of them?' he'd asked, staring at her as if he already knew the answer.

'I put myself in the girl's place, and I put a senior from one of my art lectures in the boy's place, and I stripped off our clothes and had us fucking on the blanket.' Fucking. There, she'd said it again. She had

36

found it surprisingly easy to say once she'd started, and she had wondered what else might grow easier over time.

Colin had nodded, as if this was exactly what he had expected. And now that she had succeeded in giving him what he wanted, he would give her what she needed. He'd cut through the bindings that held her wrists and quickly positioned her in proper spanking form over his lap, her bottom ready and waiting for the feel of his hand. He had moved too quickly for Lissa to protest – but then, she hadn't really wanted to protest, had she?

Draped over his knees, her mind had gone blank. The only thing she'd understood was this: he was going to spank her. That thought had come bursting through her consciousness, just as his hand had connected with the bare skin of her ass. He was going to spank her, and *that* was going to make her come.

Chapter Five

Colin continued to stroke Lissa gently through her skirt. He liked the way it felt to tease her in the crowded tube train. Liked the rocking and rolling of the train as it travelled along underground, and the sensation of doing something indecent in public. His cock strained against his slacks, but he ignored it. Stretching out the time before he would finally make love to her was one of Colin's favourite pleasures. In this manner, his methods of foreplay could last for hours – days, even. Although tonight he planned to take care of both of their needs before the morning came.

He looked at Lissa and saw that her eyes were shut and she'd drawn her bottom lip into her mouth, worrying it between her teeth. She was as turned on as he was. For him, the excitement came from the fact that he and Lissa were in the midst of a crowded carriage filled with commuters who didn't know what was going on right under their noses. Most people didn't have any idea of the world around them. It was sad, Colin thought, to go through life so unaware, but it worked to his benefit.

There were two more stops before their own, and during this time Colin allowed himself the decadent pleasure of recalling that first big milestone with Lissa, himself.

It had been a pivotal moment for him, discovering whether they were truly compatible. With the words she had spoken, softly, a sound of subdued fear in her voice, she had instantly won him over.

Of course, the fantasy itself had hardly sparked Colin's interest at all. Fucking in public was definitely wonderful, something he enjoyed immensely, but it was also fairly clichéd. Many people shared the same fantasy. Open any magazine containing readers' confessions and you could find several with the desire to do it in public. No, what Colin most liked about Lissa's fantasy was the fact that she had masturbated to it while her roommate slept only feet away from her. It meant that his new playmate hadn't been able to control her urges. To him, this showed a woman who went after her needs. What if her roommate had woken up and guessed what Lissa was doing? Lissa didn't seem to be the type of girl who would have such strong sexual urges, and Colin revelled in discovering that type of sexuality beneath the surface of a staid-looking partner.

He knew she had a difficult time voicing her desires, but the fact that she had them at all led him to imagine an infinite amount of possibilities. Together, they could work on getting her to open up. He forced her to do so every chance he got, like this afternoon in the café. Made her talk when she thought she couldn't. Pressed her onward when she felt that she'd reached her limits.

The most important thing for him to remember was not to rush. When he'd spanked her, that very first time, he had gone easy on her. What he had wanted to do was introduce her to the world of pleasures that awaited her. He hadn't wanted to frighten her at all, to scare her away from him. But by giving her a taste of the future, he had known he would be able to make her his.

The spanking had been almost routine, a dictionary

definition of a spanking – one given on her bare bottom administered only with his hand. Later, he had understood, they might work up to a paddle, to the black leather belt that he favoured, to a riding crop. Still, there was something sensuous about bare skin meeting bare skin, about feeling her ass heat up beneath his open palm.

And, actually, each spanking partner brought something new to the experience. With Lissa that first time, the way she had tried to hold herself still for him, tried to behave when the pain began to flow through her, was an added sweetness that he hadn't expected. With some lovers, he'd had to hold them down, firmly, from the start – that was the thing that they needed in order for it to work. Lissa had seemed more concerned with holding herself in check, trying to please him until the last possible moment.

He hadn't made her cry, which was an intentional move on his part. There was a special release that came from crying during a spanking. Although he longed to see her pretty face streaked with tears, he had decided to save that for later, back in London, when he was sure that she was committed to being with him. In Frankfurt, he had simply whet her appetite for the smorgasbord of pleasures that awaited them both.

As they arrived at their stop, Colin sensed Lissa was on the verge of coming. Perfect. She would be hungry for the events he had planned for the evening. Without a word, he reached for her hand and led her off the train and up the concrete steps into the twilight.

Chapter Six

*L*issa shivered. The temperature in the apartment seemed even cooler than outside. Walking down the front hallway to the living room, she realised why. Colin had left the windows open, and the thin white curtains billowed inward with the breeze. Although the rain had stopped, moisture glistened on the sill and a small silvery puddle had gathered in front of the windows on the wood floor. It looked like a tiny reflecting pond in the midst of their apartment, reminding her of one of the Parrish paintings she'd seen earlier that afternoon at the café.

Once Lissa had taken off her coat and hung it in the cupboard, she went towards the windows, preparing to shut and lock them. Colin stopped her.

'Leave them open.'

She almost asked him why, but she caught herself before the word reached her lips. Colin didn't appreciate too many questions, always told her that he would give her the answers when he was ready if she hadn't worked them out on her own. 'You're a smart girl,' he'd say mildly. 'You'll grasp it soon enough. If you don't, I'll give you a clue.' His clues were never enjoyable. They always involved some sort of pain. But then, Lissa reminded herself, she had recently discovered her affinity for pain, so in some dark way, perhaps they *were* enjoyable.

Now, watching him pull his heavy leather chair to the centre of the room, she instantly answered the question herself. The building opposite their apartment housed several floors of offices. The floor directly across from theirs held a conference room, its modern wall of glass facing directly towards their own open window. While she watched, Colin fastened the curtains back so that anyone in the office across the way would have an undisturbed view of the interior of their living room. Lissa could see that the conference room was empty, but for how long? The company – a start-up that featured some new Internet product – often held meetings that went late into the night. Colin didn't let her linger on the thought. With a single look towards her, he said, 'Get the paddle, Lissa.'

She moved without thinking, her body following the command automatically. She appreciated the fact that her hands could move, her feet could walk, while her mind remained peacefully numb. It was as if she possessed a type of mental auto-pilot, could send her body down the hall, to the drawer in the bedroom where he kept their toys, her heels clicking on the wood floor as she walked back to him, handed it over, waited for his next command.

He didn't issue one. Instead, he sat in the straight-backed chair – chosen because it was both extremely sturdy and it did not have arms – and pulled her over his lap. He didn't make her strip first, didn't ask her to take down her stockings or panties. She knew that he liked to keep her endlessly guessing. Now, her brain tried to process what was happening, but her heart pounded so loudly in her ears that she felt confused. Actually, there wasn't much to process. He was going to give her a spanking.

And it was going to hurt.

The feel of his hands under her skirt made her tremble. He reached up under the tight fabric and got hold of the waistband of her cobalt-blue panties, pulling them down and letting them dangle from her ankles. She was wearing pearl-grey stockings and a matching belt, as he always demanded. Garters were so much more practical than pantyhose for his purposes. The panties came down over the garters, so he left the stockings on her slender legs. He hiked the rich fabric of her skirt up to her hips, revealing her ass, now framed by the grey lace of the garter belt, framed perfectly for his paddle.

They had bought the lingerie together, Colin choosing the different items and then having Lissa put on a mock fashion show for him in the dressing room. She'd grown wetter with each successive change, draping herself in the type of undergarments she had previously dismissed as frivolous. Now, she could understand their sex appeal. Who wouldn't feel pretty wearing such delightful outfits – sheer nighties trimmed in marabou, garters woven through with satin ribbons, stockings with bands of lace at the thighs, that only a lover would ever see.

Although men generally weren't allowed in the rear of the lingerie shop, the owner had made an exception because Colin was such a good client. Lissa had blanched when she'd seen the total amount spent on the frilly items, her mind doing the instant calculation of pounds to dollars, but Colin hadn't seemed to notice.

Now, upended over Colin's lap in her favourite garter belt, Lissa pondered the fact that there was a moment before he struck that always seemed worse to her than the first blow. The waiting. She knew about it, understood it, but she never got over it. The anticipation of the pain made her think about begging him to forgive her. Forgive what? It wasn't really about an indiscretion, a mistake or faux pas. It was about the fact that he liked to spank her. That it made him hard and it made her wet, and all the begging she might do wouldn't change those facts.

As always, her mind changed with the first blow. The anticipation was nothing compared with the actual spanking. The sting of the paddle brought instant tears to her eyes. It was much, much worse than the waiting. She had this argument within herself every time, but Colin could obliterate those rational thoughts quite quickly by simply continuing the spanking, slapping the leather paddle against her right cheek and then her left.

When she began to squirm, Colin scissored one strong leg over her struggling limbs, getting a better grip on her and starting to punish her with more serious intent. He had chosen to face the office building, and now he told Lissa to keep her head down, to stare at the wooden floor, while he described what was going on in the conference room across the way.

'Just because you can't see them, doesn't mean they can't see you,' he said, in between spanks. 'You're such a lovely thing, and the four businessmen who have arrived simply cannot believe their luck. Oh, wait,' he gave her three spanks in a row, and then continued, 'an adorable young redhead has joined the men. She's staring at you, Lissa. I'll bet she wishes she were over here, next to you, maybe even waiting in line for her turn.'

Lissa pictured the scene in her mind. The men arranging their chairs to face the window so that they could watch the show. The fluttering, bird-like girl trembling behind them. Lissa painted the picture further, gave the woman a smart, pale-blue suit that went well with her short auburn hair. Gave the men tight physiques, sports fanatics, all of them, no paunchy middle-aged businessmen watching her ass get spanked. She almost laughed at herself, at the idiocy of the mental picture, but Colin was causing her too much pain for the slightest giggle.

'The little lady across the way looks so sorry for you,' Colin said, letting up after several blows while he further described the scene. 'She must know the feel of it, herself. I'll bet she's been positioned over at least one

boyfriend's sturdy lap for a thorough, bare-bottom paddling. I can see it easily, her legs kicking as she squirms
with each blow. She probably struggles as much as you
do.'

The story he spun for her was a complete fabrication.
The office across the way remained empty. Still, it didn't
matter whether Colin's tale was true or not. It was true
for Lissa. 'You're a bad girl,' he told her, smiling at the
way she sucked in her breath when he said it. She had
no say. No way to make him stop. 'Such a bad little girl,
Lissa. I wish you could see the way that redhead is
watching us.' He hesitated. 'You know, I think I was
wrong about her. She isn't the kind of girl who would
be in line waiting to get over my lap.' He paused again.
'From the hungry look in her eyes, I think she'd be
waiting to get *you* over *her* lap. Strong little thing. She
could handle you. She doesn't feel sorry for you at all.'

It didn't matter to Lissa. She felt sorry enough for
herself. Teardrops ran down her face in twin streaks.
Although she had not started to sob out loud, her tears
dripped down on to the wood floor. She imagined he
could hear them making tiny splashing sounds between
blows. Little, melancholy pings on the hard wood.

She wondered if Colin would make her cry her own
puddle before he finished with her.

Chapter Seven

Colin could picture Lissa's expression even when all he could see was the back of her tousled mane of blonde hair. The transformation was almost hauntingly beautiful, the way her face changed from only a tiny spark of pain. Her eyes took on a warmth, as if a magic heat source burnt within them, and her full bottom lip plumped outward in a pout, making him want to bite it. Hard.

With an effort, he paused again in the spanking, allowing himself a few seconds to fully appreciate her beauty. Staring intently at her hind-end, he unknowingly pondered the same thoughts that she'd had only minutes before. Which was better, the expectation of what would happen or the actual event? Before one of their sessions, he always felt like a kid on Christmas morning, waiting to see what Santa brought him. Would he get a lump of coal or a stocking filled with toys? Or, better yet, would he get a naughty woman over his lap to taunt and torment.

Sometimes, when Lissa begged him, it made Colin even harder than actually spanking her did. Listening to her pleading excuses while he smacked the leather paddle against the palm of his hand was almost sweeter than positioning her over his lap and pummelling her with it. But, as always, he ultimately decided that the spanking was better. He delighted in the colour that the paddling brought to Lissa's previously pale skin, a happy pink hue that turned a bit darker where he worked the same area repeatedly.

Enough thinking, it was time to get back to the task at hand. Colin gave Lissa a series of quick, hard blows. The sound was like applause – a satisfying noise that was pleasing both in its rhythm and volume. Tonight, he had chosen to use a paddle he'd bought on a trip to Amsterdam, visiting several sex shops before finding a tool he approved of. The paddle had a satisfying weight in his hand and, unlike some meaner supplies he'd viewed in the shops, he could spank her with it for a long time without ever breaking the skin. He had no desire to harm her. Even as he was her punisher, he was her protector.

Lissa suddenly squirmed on his lap, teasing his erection and making him struggle not to moan aloud. It would not serve his purposes to let her know how much control she really held over him. He was the dominant in this relationship and it was up to him to put on a good show.

'Steady,' he told her, getting a better grip on her struggling body and holding her in place. Still, he loved the way her hips felt as they rocked against his groin. A few more good, solid spanks and he would be ready to fuck her. He drew the paddle back again, and then stopped. What a perfect ass she had. The colours he'd brought forth now ranged from a rose to a deep berry. He rested one hand across her bottom to feel the heat. She was going to have a difficult time sitting when he was finished.

No problem.

His plans this evening called for her to stand.

Chapter Eight

On her feet in the highest, shiniest patent leather heels she'd ever seen, Lissa was held upright only by thick metal chains attached to the cuffs on her wrists. Colin had hooked the middle of the silver chain to a loop set in the high ceiling for just this purpose. Lissa had to work to stay balanced, pulled as she was by her wrists, and slightly shaky in the spike-heeled shoes. The chains had been purchased at a basic hardware store, but the handcuffs were specially crafted ones that Colin had seen and fallen in love with in New York.

That trip, one of two he'd taken away from her, had told him how much he'd grown attached to her. He'd spent those few days apart missing her, planning what he'd do to her when he returned, and calling her on the phone at odd hours, needing to hear the sound of her voice in order to get off. After buying the cuffs, he'd put one on his own wrist and jerked off while listening to Lissa describe for him, at his insistence, what it felt like the one time he'd spanked her in public. The cuffs had cost almost as much as the two nights' stay in a top hotel, but he had splurged anyway, visualising the way Lissa would look with them fastened around her wrists.

Now Colin was seated comfortably at the table in

front of her, holding a large photo book open for display. A blindfold kept Lissa in the dark, literally, but Colin carefully described to her what he was looking at.

'You,' he said. 'I have a lovely photo right here of you in this exact position.'

Lissa tried to make sense of what he was telling her. The red ball gag in her mouth prevented her from asking any questions, and it most likely also prevented her from receiving another skin-tingling spanking. Colin would explain in time. Still, she wondered what he was talking about. Aside from a few naughty photos she'd taken with her boyfriend Beau, long before her marriage, she'd never posed. And those photos were tame in comparison to the position Colin had her in now, simple nudie poses that had seemed indescribably sexy to her at the time but were far less revealing than even a *Playboy* spread.

She couldn't imagine being tied up by Marcus. He'd have had no time for this sort of thing. He liked to be on the move, always ready for the next event. On weekend mornings, he would refuse to make love because he had a racquetball date that he wanted to be up for. 'Sex makes me sluggish,' he told her once when she'd pressed him. 'The little blue ball will hit me in the head while I'm thinking about our morning romp. You don't want to kill your husband, do you?' No, she hadn't wanted to kill him. She'd simply wanted to fuck him. In the evenings, he had generally found time for her, but only in the certain positions they'd always used: missionary, spooning. Nothing kinky. It was one of the reasons she'd insisted on their separation, knowing, somehow, that there was more to life – more to love – outside their bedroom door.

'The only problem is your hair,' Colin continued. 'We'll visit a wig store tomorrow and choose an appropriate one.'

The blindfold was suddenly removed, and with it

went all thoughts about her estranged mate. Colin stood before her, holding a thick hardback book of photos from the fifties, Bettie Page in a similar stance to Lissa's current captive position. Ball gag, leopard-print teddy and heels. Lissa had seen the book for sale at a store in London, the pink lettering on the cover, the pose of Bettie on the beach. The collection of photos had stirred her, but she hadn't even considered buying it. Some pompous part of herself hadn't considered it an art book. Now, she wasn't so sure.

'See?' he asked, smiling. 'You could be her twin.'

Lissa still didn't understand. The rubbery taste of the ball in her mouth was bitter and she focused on that, instead. Was Colin going to make her bite down on it? Was he going to punish her more than he already had? Her ass still burned from the evening spanking, but he hadn't fucked her yet, and he generally needed to administer a bit of pain to stir his cock into action. She'd learnt this in their first few weeks together. They never had sweet sex, which was a genuine relief for her. She'd had enough of that for a lifetime.

'It's for my collection,' he went on. 'I like to bring art to life.'

Now, she looked at him questioningly. He was talking about something that interested her. Art played a tremendous part in her world. She had always managed to find a piece of artwork to represent each stage of her life. Whether she was happy, sad, angry, turned on, there was some sculpture or painting, collage or collection that matched her emotions. Did Colin feel the same way?

'You have questions,' he said, still smiling at her. 'I can always tell. They shine, unanswered, in your eyes. But if you keep them to yourself, like a good girl, I'll take off the gag. I prefer the way your lovely mouth looks without it.'

She nodded to let him know that she'd obey, and he removed the ball gag and placed it on the table, where it lay glistening next to the book of photos. The entire collection was of Bettie Page, she could see that now. So the wig comment meant that he would buy her a dark wig. Long black hair cascading down her naked back – she could picture it instantly. But why?

Colin left her with her arms above her head. She'd almost forgotten about the awkwardness of her position, was too interested in what he was doing. Bringing the book closer, he started flipping the pages.

'These poses,' he said, pointing to several, all of Bettie in some form of bondage. 'I want to re-create them. You look quite a bit like her, except for the hair, as I said. I plan on photographing you in each of these positions.' His fingers pointed to the different pictures. Bettie tied to a tree. Bettie in full bondage gear, sneering at the camera. Bettie naked, in cuffs, throwing an insolent look at the camera. Colin motioned to a shot of Bettie over another woman's lap, and Lissa swallowed hard and blushed. Colin watched her intently, and her expression made him laugh. It was a cross between fear and desire, the two emotions fighting a battle on Lissa's face. Her eyes wide with the fright of the concept. Her mouth opening at the thought of being over a woman's lap. 'All of them,' he said again, emphasising the word 'all'. 'I'll get another girl, someone suitable, and we'll take that picture first.'

Of course he'd start her with the most difficult. It was always a test. But by failing his tests she seemed to pass them. That concept confused her, didn't make any sense, yet she knew he enjoyed watching her stumble, watching tears form in her eyes and streak down her face. If she did everything right, he'd have no reason to punish her. And where would they be then?

She looked from the picture in the book back to his face, then lowered her head. The muscles in her arms were beginning to ache.

'Just a few more minutes,' Colin said, undoing the button fly of his trousers and letting her see his cock. It

51

was hard, and he stroked it lazily with one hand while he continued to explain his plans. 'I want to watch that beautifully tortured expression of yours while I jack off.' He wasn't going to let her come. Not tonight. She gave him her best doe-eyed look, the closest to begging that she could muster after the ferocity of her afternoon paddling, but he simply slapped her face for it and began to work his hand a little faster.

'Life imitates art,' he said softly, his hand moving rhythmically up and down, his eyes staring at her heart-shaped face. 'Just remember that,' he smirked. 'It's going to be on the quiz later.'

Colin had planned to simply take care of his own needs this evening, to leave Lissa wanting more.

But because she looked so sad and he was feeling generous, he moved behind her and undid the animal-print teddy, slipping it down past her waist so that he could enter her from behind. He took her hard, her supple body straining from his force, her wrists still bound above and her feet on the verge of slipping in the heels. His cock slid easily between her thighs, entering her, giving her just what she wanted.

Lissa's pussy was shaved, he'd done it himself that morning, and the bare skin felt delicious as he plunged his rod between the lips of her sex. He thought of the way she'd looked on the bathroom floor, spread out naked on the fluffy bath mat, while he'd dragged the razor over her most delicate skin. As he'd shaved her, she'd grown wetter and wetter, her own special moisture mixing with the shaving foam.

'You like that,' he'd said, 'you're all creamy,' and she'd simply sighed, unable to answer.

He had teased her with the shaving brush, tickling her nether lips with it, then parting her lips with two fingers and running the brush up and down over her clit until she'd climaxed from the sensation. Now, he was reaping the benefits of that early morning adventure. Her bare skin was so smooth that it was almost like rubbing his cock against a lustrous fabric, driving it into an envelope made of satin or silk.

While he fucked her, he lost himself in thoughts of what a decadent treat this was, having a model at his own disposal to dress up, to torment, to make love to as he desired. It was perfect that she got off on the same things. None of the others had been as precisely suited to him, to his needs, his fantasies. The dark, twisted thoughts that brought him to orgasm. This one, though. This girl was his match. Even if she didn't completely understand that yet.

And when he bought her the wig, when he turned her into a beauty of his own creation – oh, fuck, he couldn't even fantasise about how good that was going to be.

The motion of Colin's thrusts kept Lissa off balance, and he didn't move to help her. Instead, he let her feel as if she would fall until her wrists were stretched to the full limits of the chains. Her body strained and, as she made a whimpering sound of fear, he put one hand on her waist to steady her. Then he thrust in again, going in deep so that she could feel the full length of his cock inside her, pressing against all those divine places. He teased her endlessly, stroking in and out of her pussy, before giving her only the tip of his cock. Rocking it against the mouth of her cunt until she whimpered for more. He wanted to hear her beg him to take her, because as soon as she did, he would start to fuck her nonstop, slamming into her until she could feel his balls slap against her skin.

With just the head of his member inside her, she needed more, and he was gratified when her whimpers of fear turned into moans of pleasure.

He could be kind. In his own fashion, he could be kind.

Book Two:

The Accomplice

Art is the accomplice of love.
Take love away and there is no longer art.

– Remy de Gourmont

Chapter Nine

*T*he patron received the first of the pictures by airmail.
He knew what they were, had been waiting
impatiently for them to arrive, and yet he specifically
saved that package out of all his other mail to open last.
Staring at the brown envelope with the neatly handwrit-
ten address, he decided to take a drink first, a good
drink, before discovering the mysteries that lay within
the padded package.

He searched his drinks cabinet for something with a
bite. There was red wine, amaretto, campari. But none
of them interested him. He wanted a wash of numbness
to cover him, to take him away. There. He found a bottle
of eighteen-year-old whisky, a present from a pleased
client. That was what he needed. Knowing exactly what
to expect somehow made it even more difficult for him
to find the nerve to open the envelope. He'd have
thought that the opposite would have been true.

After his first drink, and then a second, after pacing
across his office until he could actually see the tread-
marks from his leather loafers in the thick, red carpet, he
picked up his letter opener. When he turned over the
package, he noticed that written in bold black marker on
the flap were the words, ART IS SIGHT. Without bother-

ing to contemplate what that might possibly mean, he finally tore open the seal and emptied the contents.

And there she was.

Beautiful, just as Colin had promised she would be. Stunning, in a little outfit that suited her body as if it had been created specifically for her. Her breasts, although small, were ripe and full, made fuller still because of the push-up bra. It was an ingenious contraption, with openings for her nipples. He instantly fantasised about sucking on them, drawing her close to him and placing his lips around her right nipple and then her left. Licking all around them slowly with the tip of his tongue before drawing them into his mouth and suckling. He would make them stand up firmly, like tiny jewels, would nip at them between his teeth and make her moan.

Even though the photo was in black and white, he imagined that he could see the pinkness of her flesh, and in the second picture, this one with her ass to the camera, he believed he could make out the crimson lines that striped her bottom and her thighs.

She'd been a bad girl, hadn't she? Just as Colin had said.

His penis stirred within the loose confines of his ebony silk boxers. He thought of relieving himself, spreading all of the photos face-up on his heavy oak desk and taking his cock in hand. He could easily visualise it – shooting his come over the glossy pictures, then setting them on fire with his antique silver lighter. But that's not what he truly wanted, was it? A solo party? No. That wasn't what he had in mind at all.

Instead, he set the photographs on his desk. There were several more in the envelope, along with a hand-written letter from Colin. The patron took note of this, but didn't make a move to pull out the rest of the pictures. Plenty of time for that later. For now, he needed another drink.

And he needed it quickly.

Chapter Ten

*I*t was a dream. It had to be. Lissa understood this but didn't fight it. She was secured to a bed, her wrists held together over her head, but not cuffed. Something startling and cold pressed against her flesh and she tilted her head down to see what it was, but found that her vision was blocked.

No, she realised, she was awake. She could smell Colin's aftershave, a spicy, exotic scent, and she could feel his eyes on her, watching her. Slowly, she turned her face towards the window, sensing the light as it came through the blindfold. This was no dream and yet she didn't know exactly what was going on.

'Time to wake up, Sleeping Beauty,' Colin said softly. His fingers released her wrists and wandered over her naked skin, along the sides of her ribs and then to her breasts. This was where she'd felt the cold – the sensation that had woken her. The blindfold was suddenly removed, and Lissa blinked rapidly as her eyes grew accustomed to the light. Colin sat on the edge of the bed, looking at her with an odd expression on his face. Lissa looked down to answer the mystery of the coldness, discovering that Colin had placed small silver clamps on her nipples. A delicate chain ran between the two clamps, and Colin had a hold of it between two fingers and was tugging gently.

'Do you like that?' he asked, still pulling on the chain.

How had she managed to sleep through him putting the clamps on her? She wondered that for only a second. The past few days had been a whirlwind of activity. Following the initial photo shoot, he had taken her, as promised, to a wig shop and purchased several different styles for her. This event had been followed by more intensely staged activities – each fuelled by his desire to mingle art with life. Although he hadn't brought another girl into their relationship, he had re-created several of the photos from the Bettie Page book. So she should have known by now not to be surprised by anything he did. But still –

'Do you, Lissa?'

She nodded, because even though she had never contemplated nipple clamps before, what they might feel like or whether she would enjoy wearing them, her body was responding as it usually did to his sexual overtures. Wetness pooled between her nether lips and, if Colin had lifted the polished cotton sheet and climbed between her legs, he would have been able to taste her flavour on her inner thighs.

Would he do that?

She arched her hips against the sheet, begging silently with her body for him to relieve her. Somehow, she knew from the look in his eyes that he wouldn't give her any release. This was simply the first step in another one of Colin's elaborate plans.

'I'm glad you do,' he said next, standing and beginning to get dressed. 'Because I expect you to wear those throughout the day.'

He can't be serious, Lissa thought, stunned. And then, just as quickly, she thought: Of course he's serious. Colin never joked about demands such as this. The clamps had a tightening device, like the type found on the old-fashioned screw-on earrings she'd used to play dressing-

59

up as a child. Colin had made them just firm enough to stay on, but not painfully tight. Yes, she *could* wear them. But how would she get any work done?

'I'll meet you at the museum,' he told her next. He knew her schedule, knew exactly where she'd be spending her day. Lissa watched him fasten the buttons on his neatly pressed blue shirt, observed him as he slipped on her favourite tie, a navy one with a subtle sheen to it, before searching through the small leather box on his dresser for a tie tack. She adored watching him dress. He had a subdued sense of style that never varied. Even when he dressed casually, there was something classy to his appearance that eluded most other men.

'Third floor, unisex bathroom, one o'clock.'

He fastened his black leather belt without looking at her, and she flushed as he stroked the silver buckle. It was an absentminded gesture on his part that managed to stir all sorts of emotions inside her. She knew the feeling of that oiled leather against her skin. He hadn't given her the belt often, but the few times had left their mark not only on her body, but on her mind.

'One o'clock *sharp*,' he repeated. 'And those had better be in place.'

She nodded as he left the room, and for a moment she stayed in bed, listening as he rummaged around in the office he kept in the adjoining bedroom. He was checking his e-mail. She could hear his modem humming to life and then the sound of his fingers working as he tapped in a response on the keyboard. Then, as Colin called out his goodbyes and closed and locked the front door of the apartment, she climbed out of bed and opened her lingerie drawer, preparing to start to dress herself. The weight of the nipple clamps made her think of little else and the sound that the tiny chain made was like a soft music to her ears.

How could she keep them on? She wouldn't. She'd slide them into her bag and then put them back on just before meeting him. Her hand went up to the clamps, ready to release them, but stopped. He'd know. Somehow, he would know what she'd done, she was sure of it. She sat on the edge of the bed, thinking. Again, her fingers wandered up to the clamps, but this time, they tightened the screws a little bit more.

Oh, God, that was good. It was all she needed. She lay back in the unmade bed, her fingers moving quickly to her pussy. Just a few well-placed strokes would bring her to climax. This was something she excelled at. She knew exactly how to touch herself to get off in the fastest manner possible. A hard circle, then a soft one, a flick of her thumb along the hood of her clit. Her fingertips fluttered quickly against her pussy lips –

But then she stopped again. He'd know that, too. He always sensed these things. And from the look he'd given her before leaving, she knew that he wouldn't be pleased with her. Did she want to tempt his wrath? No, not today. Lissa took a deep breath and then stood, walking again to her wardrobe and looking at her assortment of outfits. She would do as he asked, wear the clamps all day. And she wouldn't pleasure herself without his permission, but she also knew that she would get no work done.

There was no way to put a bra on over the clamps, she would have to go without one. Even though she wasn't large up top, she always wore a bra. Museums might house avant-garde art, but the people who worked in them tended towards the conservative side. Lissa always dressed in a refined manner. The thought of being naked beneath her blouse was new and somehow exciting.

After careful consideration of the items in her wardrobe, she chose a shirt that was loose enough not to reveal the clamps. Then she slid into the garters that Colin favoured, zipped up a short black skirt and slipped on a pair of heels. The nipple clamps made her feel sexier than she could have imagined and when she checked her appearance in the mirror prior to leaving the apartment, she saw the colour to her cheeks that usually only appeared after she'd made love.

Colin was on her mind all the way to the museum. One of the best things about him, one of the concepts she contemplated while riding the bus, was the fact that he talked to her. Really talked. Before their separation, Marcus never seemed to have time for conversations, as if five years of marriage had used up all of his need for discussions, drained his well of small talk. Or polite talk. Whatever it was people did over the breakfast table or dinner table. In the months before she'd left him, he had been unusually silent unless he had some fantastic new case he wanted to discuss.

But Colin seemed to enjoy talking to her. After spending hours tormenting her in some new way, he would release her, brush her hair away from her face, and kiss her. Even with her eyes closed behind a blindfold, she would sense that he was thinking about something. And that something generally surprised her. Just as she was ready for him to launch into a tirade about how she'd misbehaved, about what a naughty, sinful little fuck she was, he would begin a conversation about a new art exhibit opening in SoHo, suggest that maybe they fly to New York to catch it.

With Colin, it was more like her relationship with her boyfriend Beau, the man she'd dated prior to Marcus. Beau had possessed a wild streak that reminded her of Colin's, a need to test boundaries and to break them. But at the time, she simply hadn't been ready for him. Too young to enjoy the things that he suggested, to really let herself go. Now, she was ready.

How she liked to curl in bed with Colin, watching the rain outside, or watching the sun come up, chatting about the play they'd seen the night before – before he'd taken her back to the apartment and suspended her upside down in the doorway, used his belt to decorate her thighs and ass, her hair falling over her

62

face, brushing the floor, the weightlessness delightful in one sense, frightening in another. He always kept her in a position for longer than she thought she could stand it. He knew her limits and refused to accept them, which was exactly what she wanted from him.

Best of both worlds, she thought as she gathered her belongings and prepared to get off the bus at her stop. As she walked down the steps to the street, the chain between the clamps bumped against her skin, and all of a sudden she was wet again, certain that she wouldn't be able to stand it until one o'clock.

Chapter Eleven

Colin returned from his morning meeting a little before noon. Taking off his jacket, he went into the second, much smaller bedroom of the apartment, where he kept his home office. He turned on his computer, then loosened his tie while waiting for the machine to boot up. There was an e-mail from the patron that he wanted to re-read before meeting Lissa at the museum.

The screen hummed to life and Colin impatiently pressed a few keys to enter his password. Several new messages awaited him but he ignored them, opening a folder that contained 'old mail' instead. He read the latest from ARTLOVER, his expression showing a level of concentration that would have frightened Lissa if she'd been present to witness it.

The patron had liked the first round of pictures. The pictures of Lissa with her wrists chained to the ceiling of his apartment, re-creating images from the famous series of Bettie Page taken by Bunny Yeager. But now the man wanted something that showed they'd explored the outside world. Proof that Lissa was expanding her horizons. That they weren't restricted to playing solely in privacy.

This was part of Colin's mission – probe Lissa's plane of thoughts, fantasies, experiences. And when

ARTLOVER asked for something, Colin delivered. That was the deal, and for some reason Colin found that he enjoyed the assignments more than if he were in a normal relationship with Lissa. Or as 'normal' as any relationship Colin could have. (This thought made Colin wonder exactly what the word 'normal' meant. He couldn't be the only one who required dominance and submission games in order to achieve release, could he?) The addition of a third party added an intrigue that he appreciated. And the assignments made his mind – and his libido – work overtime.

Today, Colin had decided to take Lissa into the very world where she was most comfortable. The art world. Yes, it was going above and beyond what the patron requested, but then Colin had always been an over-achiever, hadn't he?

Chapter Twelve

*L*issa stretched her arms over her head and looked at the large round clock on the library wall. It was nearly one. Her heart raced at the thought of what awaited her, but she forced herself to remain calm. For an extra few moments, just to prove that she was in control of herself, she studied the notes spread carelessly on the wooden table before her.

Who was she kidding?

After another glance at the clock, she began to collect the papers. She only had five minutes to gather her belongings and then hurry to the bathroom on the third floor. No sense in testing Colin's anger by making him wait.

The library was located on the bottom level of the museum, available only to museum workers or those like Lissa who had a special pass. A heavy book of Italian art lay open on the desk, and Lissa shut it and stacked it with several others she'd spent the morning trying to read. As anticipated, she had got very little work done, her thoughts consumed by Colin and his plans.

In London to research a new book, Lissa had taken a year's sabbatical from her job at ART (the Art Research

Technology institute). She was serious about the project – a resource based on up-and-coming young artists and their older inspirations. In general, she committed herself to a rigid, self-imposed schedule, spending part of her time browsing through galleries and the rest at the different libraries and museums. If she didn't plan her time wisely, the book would never get finished. There were too many other things in London to capture her attention.

Other things like Colin.

As she slid her notes into her black leather backpack, she chastised herself for letting the morning go to waste. Of course, it really was all Colin's fault that she had spent the past several hours fantasising about him instead of researching famed painters of the Renaissance. Most of the time, even with all of the playing they did together, her writing progressed smoothly. Perhaps this was because she found their romantic life so satisfying. She'd discovered that she could turn off the sexual segment of herself while at the library or museum. At least, she usually could. But today, her attempts to work had failed. Words blurred on the pages before her. Pictures she knew by heart had become impossible to decipher.

She patted her hair, smoothing a few blonde strands back into place, the movement making the clamps pull tighter on her nipples. She sighed at the sensation, unable to stop herself, then quickly grabbed her backpack. How had Colin known that she would like this new toy? Did she look like someone who would enjoy nipple clamps? Or, for that matter, handcuffs, or any of the tools they used together?

Pondering these thoughts, Lissa left the main room of the library and began to climb the stairs to the second floor. The artwork on display was a selection from local talents. Lissa had looked at it all during her first visit to the building and she passed by now without even noticing the paintings. Instead, she caught a glimpse of her reflection in a window and was grateful to see that she appeared composed, as always. No one would have guessed that her panties were already wet simply at the thought of what she and Colin were about to do.

But then, she didn't know exactly what they were going to do. The range of possibilities was what really made her excited. With Colin, she'd learnt that almost anything could happen. It was important never to try to second-guess him. He would always surprise her.

She trailed her fingers along the wooden banister as she started up the stairs to the third floor. A museum worker passed her and gave a quick nod, which Lissa returned, but her mind was still on Colin. Would he be there? Would he make her wait, pacing the tile floor and hoping that nobody else entered the small square room?

No. Pushing through the door, she found that he was there already and, without speaking, he locked the door behind her and bent her over the sink. Quickly, he slid her skirt up her thighs to her waist, and he grinned at her reflection in the mirror when he saw the wet spot on her panties. She had positively soaked herself during her morning away from him. Rather than take her under-pants down, he simply slid them aside, giving himself instant access to her pussy.

She thought he would fuck her right away, but he didn't. Instead, he went on his knees behind her, parting the cheeks of her ass and slipping his tongue between them, reaching forward to tickle her nether lips. Lissa moaned and gripped on to the cold porcelain edge of the sink, her fingers searching for purchase. Colin moved so that he had his face pressed against her now, and she could feel his warm breath, his tongue fluttering back and forth, dragging against her clit and then dis-appearing deep inside her. He was fucking her with his tongue and the sensations were overwhelming.

But somehow, she wanted more.

'Please, Colin –' she said, realising as she spoke the words that he rarely listened to her requests. He preferred to do things his way, at his own pace. But sometimes he would do as she asked, and right now, she simply couldn't keep silent. The nipple clamps were still in place, and the fact that they'd been on all morning had been enough foreplay for her. Now, she wanted desperately to feel his cock inside her. 'I need –'

He moved his mouth away from her long enough to ask, 'What do you need, baby? You tell me just what you need.'

It was so odd. He was the most refined of any lover she'd ever had, yet he could speak and instantly transform into a James Dean type, a tough young punk who was ready and willing to take care of her, in any manner she could visualise.

Hard. Raunchy. Dirty.

She stared into the mirror as she said it, almost unable to recognise the yearning on her face. 'I need you to fuck me.'

Standing, he had his cock out in a heartbeat, holding it loosely in one hand so that she could see how ready he was for her. He slipped it into her, lingering so that she could feel herself open around him, her nether lips parting like the petals of a flower. Then he began fucking her long and slow, giving it to her just as she'd desired. He stripped open her shirt and pulled on the delicate silver chain that ran between the clamps, whispering to her.

'You thought about me all morning, didn't you?'

She nodded. It was true. She had thought about nothing other than what he was going to do to her and how long she would have to wait until he did.

'Tell me,' Colin demanded, nuzzling the back of her neck, then kissing her beneath the heavy drapery of her hair.

'I couldn't sit still,' she said, looking at his reflection behind her own in the mirror. His sophisticated appearance was transformed with the glaze of lust in his eyes. He looked as hungry as she felt, and she found it in herself to tell him what most turned her on about this escape. 'It's such a sinful thing to fuck in the midst of such beautiful art.'

He liked that, she could tell, and he gave the chain between the clamps another pull, making her lean forward even further. From this position, her back arched in an s-curve, hips pressed against him, she could feel the full length of his cock slide into her. She yearned to be able to yell, to truly let loose, and that thought made Lissa wish she and Colin could have the museum all to themselves. Spread a blanket on the floor beneath her favourite pieces of art and go at it like animals, civilised animals, with the artwork on the walls around them.

'Talk to me,' Colin demanded. 'Tell me how it feels.'

Lissa felt his green eyes on her, and she lowered her gaze from their reflections in the mirror, staring at the taps, watching as drips of water fell into the white basin. Colin was always trying to get her to talk dirty, but she could never manage it. Even though she heard the words in her head, knew what they would sound like, she couldn't make her mouth move, couldn't force them through her lips. She would have loved to have told him exactly how it felt to have his cock pounding inside her. Deliriously powerful, the way his rod reached the most private parts of her body, stroking her languidly, then speeding up just when she needed the change of motion. How freeing it would have felt to tell him that his cock was her favourite toy of all – forget the clamps, the cuffs, the belt. All she needed was his flesh and blood, rocking deep inside her.

But she couldn't make herself talk the way he wanted her to. No matter how much he insisted, cajoled, or threatened. Finally, Colin did the talking for them.

'Not one of the pieces in this museum competes with you,' he told her just before he came.

Afterwards, Lissa wondered how Colin had known about the bathroom – both the location of it and the fact that nobody else seemed aware of its existence. She didn't trouble herself with the questions, just as she didn't trouble herself with the plum-coloured bruises that formed on her nipples, the fact that her breasts were sore for two days after their tryst.

Simply sliding into a bra brought back the experience and her raw nipples rubbing on the fabric caused an instant sensation in her panties. Colin would stare at her chest and grin, as if he knew and as if it pleased him.

Chapter Thirteen

*I*t was an audiotape. The patron realised this as his fingers wandered over the corners of the brown package. He slit open the padded envelope and the tape fell out, along with a small piece of white paper. On the paper was written: ART IS SOUND.

Colin was getting fancy. The patron closed his eyes, trying to imagine what he would hear when he slid the tape into his stereo. This time, he didn't linger long but grabbed the tape and hurried to the den. He had a full entertainment centre and he put the tape into the machine, reached for his headset, and pressed the 'play' button.

Standing in front of the stereo, he froze, understanding what he was hearing, but not having a visual picture to go with it.

There were moans, reverberations, as if Colin had fucked Lissa in an echo chamber. The patron closed his eyes, trying to imagine what he was hearing. Lissa sighed, and then started to say something but stopped herself. The patron pressed the 'rewind' button on the machine, not wanting to miss a word.

'Please –' she'd said. He rewound the tape and listened to her voice again, 'Please –' Christ, the sound of her begging made him instantly hard. He wished he'd been there, listening to her, wished – if he wanted to be honest with himself – that he had been the one fucking her instead of Colin. Because it was obvious now, as he let the tape continue, that this was what Colin was doing to her. Sliding his cock deep inside her and making her moan, making her beg when he gave her just the tip of it. She wanted the whole thing, greedy little girl, wanted to feel the length of his rod plunging inside her.

Colin was giving her instructions, telling her to talk dirty, but although the patron would have loved to hear this, Lissa hadn't obeyed. That was OK. She had time to learn, to expand her repertoire. Plenty of time.

The patron listened to the entire ten minutes of the tape before rewinding it to the beginning and listening to it again. For the encore performance, he took out his cock and worked himself to the sound of Lissa's voice.

To him, it was like a haunting melody, and he wondered, just before he came, when he would be invited to listen to the concert in person.

Chapter Fourteen

*S*ome afternoons, if she'd had a successful day writing, Lissa quit working early and spent the time lounging in Colin's apartment. She played his CDs, browsed through his books, and sampled the different brandies from his drinks cabinet. Sometimes, she walked slowly down his hallway, as if it was her first time in his apartment, admiring the photographs on the walls. Subtly erotic black-and-white pictures, they were more sexy for what they didn't reveal than for what they did. A nude woman draped with a semi-sheer cloth so that the viewer could not make out anything other than the indents of her body. Another shot of a woman's legs, the lens focused on the black seam running the length of her stockings.

Although Lissa had lived in Colin's place for several months, she still felt like a guest. It was actually a nice feeling. She had the use of his belongings, his expensive furniture, powerful stereo and library. It was close to the feeling she'd had when staying at a classy hotel. Because she hadn't purchased any of the items herself, they were all interesting to her.

Colin, upon convincing her to live with him after the Frankfurt Fair, had given her a key, cleaned out half of his cupboards for her clothes, and told her to relax. She could set up her laptop computer and her notes at the small writing table in his home office. The room also contained filing cabinets, an antique desk and more medical texts than Lissa would have believed existed. It was important, Colin explained, to be up to date on the latest in his field.

On the bottom shelf of the wardrobe, stood his erotic books, everything from the full collection of works by the Marquis de Sade to *The Story of O* to *Penthouse Letters*. Apparently, Colin felt that it was important to be up on these types of books as well. The resources were lined in alphabetical order in the small space. Colin told Lissa she was welcome to rifle through his erotic library, and he didn't even insist that she put the books back where she'd found them. He kept things in order for his own benefit, but wasn't a stickler about neatness when it came to her. The only important rule as far as his office was concerned revolved around his own computer.

'I'm sure that you appreciate privacy,' he'd told her as he showed her round on her first day in his place. Lissa had nodded, even though she didn't consider herself a very private person. The truth was that she'd never felt that she'd had secrets worth keeping, aside from her sexual fantasies. And she'd only written those in her electronic journal, which Marcus hadn't even known about. 'I appreciate it as well,' Colin had continued, as if Lissa had responded to his statement. 'My files would just bore you anyway, but I'd prefer it if you'd leave the machine alone.'

In answer to his request, Lissa had nodded. Why would she want to read any medical files? Besides, when would she have the time? She was busy with her own project.

But when her laptop died one afternoon at the library, and when it refused to respond after she'd plugged it into the power cord back at the apartment, she realised something serious was wrong with the machine.

'Shit.' It was all she needed. To have her expensive machine break down. Lissa checked the time. It was nearly five. Colin hadn't returned from work yet. Although he was on sabbatical from the hospital, he remained in contact with several other doctors, offering advice as they needed it. The note he'd left said he would be home by seven.

This was the perfect time for Lissa to work on her book, but without a computer, she wasn't capable. She looked at her box of discs, looked at her unusable machine, and then grabbed a disc, her longhand notes, and walked quickly into Colin's office.

This was a special circumstance, wasn't it? She had no interest in his private files. She would simply start her own folder and type in a few notes. Settling herself at Colin's desk, she prepared to get some work done.

She hit the 'on' button to start his computer. As she slid her disc into the drive and began mentally gearing up for the Chapter on antique marble, her eyes focused on an icon on Colin's screen. It represented his e-mail server and Lissa considered clicking it open to read his mail. Most likely, the messages were from his doctor pals. They would be mind-numbingly boring, nothing Lissa wanted to read.

Still –

She remembered finding a diary of her sister's in high school. She'd had the same feelings before she read it as she had now: shame that she even was considering reading Julianne's private thoughts, but excitement at the knowledge that she would learn someone's secrets. Julianne had found out and it had taken her months to get over the violation. Lissa should have learnt her lesson then.

But –

She might as well just read Colin's mail and get it over with, she decided. Now that she was aware of its existence, she knew she would read it eventually and she certainly wasn't going to get any work done until she gave into the desire. Excited, she tried to click on the e-mail icon but was foiled from the opening screen.

Of course. She should have known his e-mail would be protected by a password. That was just like him. And although Lissa tried several of the most obvious codes she could think of – BAD GIRL, SPANK, PADDLE – she could not gain access to his electronic world.

Now, her own book seemed less appealing. She no longer felt like working on it, or listening to CDs, or reading through Colin's stash of porn. Instead, she stared at the blinking icon for several minutes before finally shutting down the computer.

The apartment seemed smaller after she'd turned off his machine. No matter where she went in the place, her eyes were drawn to the door of his office. Finally, she slid on a sweater, grabbed her keys, and left. But on the landing, she realised she didn't have anywhere to go.

She was about to head back inside, when the stairwell to the roof caught her attention. She'd never been up there before. Quickly, she walked up the flight of stairs, then pushed open the door, ignoring the 'No Admittance' sign.

Outside, the fresh air revived her and she chided herself for being upset by Colin's coded mail. She walked the perimeter of the building, looking down to the street below, charmed when she came face to face with one of the stone gargoyles that made up the outlets for the drainage pipes.

She could just ask Colin what was in the e-mail. They didn't have any other secrets from each other. She was sure that his privacy policy was only that – a policy. If she really wanted to know what was on his machine, he would grant her access.

Wouldn't he?

Chapter Fifteen

*T*hat night, Lissa prepared herself to confront Colin about his e-mail. She had shared everything about her own life, shouldn't he do the same? She cleared her throat, about to speak, but as soon as they sat down to eat in his tiny dining room, Colin erased all of these thoughts with a single sentence.

'I've planned a short trip for us,' Colin told her.

Lissa stared at him, eyes wide.

'Nothing major. Three days, two nights.'

He was taking her away! Lissa's mind spun a quick fantasy at the statement. The happiness at the thought flooded through her and she fought to keep a silly grin off her face. She had to pay attention to what he was telling her, because there must be more to the situation than a simple getaway. With Colin, there was always more.

'I want to introduce you to the beauty of England,' Colin continued, sounding like the tour guide Lissa had read on the aeroplane to Europe from Los Angeles. 'You shouldn't think that London is all there is.' He paused and slowly buttered a slice of bread before asking, 'Would you like that?'

The thought of travelling with Colin definitely excited

her. They had spent the two months since their initial time together in Frankfurt entirely in London. But because Lissa was unhindered by a full-time job, she could go anywhere without having to check with a boss or clear the trip with family. 'I'd love to,' Lissa said. Maybe he would take her to a bed and breakfast. Although, honestly, she couldn't quite picture Colin in that sort of quaint setting. Perhaps a hunting lodge or even a spa. Maybe he would drive her to Bath. She'd read all about it, fascinated by the city's interesting history.

His eyes were on her and she quickly refocused her attention on him. She'd learnt to decipher several of his expressions and she recognised the one he was giving her now.

There was a price. Always.

'And of course,' Colin told her, 'I expect payment in advance.' Lissa swallowed hard over the lump that had formed in her throat. Was he going to punish her? She hadn't done anything wrong – at least, not that he knew about. He couldn't know that she'd nosed around on his computer, could he?

'How?' Lissa stammered, unable to remain silent.

For once, Colin didn't seem disturbed by her questioning of him. 'It's your turn to choose a place for us to play,' Colin said softly, and again, Lissa worked to keep the grin off her face. For the first time since they'd got together, she thought she wouldn't fail at this mission. Not like she had at the museum, with all the students and tourists bustling around and spoiling her plans.

'Are you ready?' Lissa asked.

Colin's face showed a rare expression for him: surprise. 'Now?' he asked.

She nodded and, without another word and with their dinner plates still on the table, she grabbed hold of one of Colin's hands, pulling him towards the doorway. Colin allowed himself to be led, asking no more questions, but raising his ginger-hued eyebrows in a quizzical expression. He obviously hadn't expected her to be quite so prepared for his request.

At the cupboard by the door, Colin paused, waiting to see if Lissa would grab her coat or an umbrella. She did neither and so he left his coat behind as well. Then, on the landing outside the apartment, Colin made a move to go down the stairs towards the street but Lissa shook her head. She found that being in charge felt extraordinary. Even if it was only for the moment.

Up the stairs to the roof in silence then Lissa pushed open the door into a light rain. She looked at Colin but he didn't hesitate, now understanding what she had in mind and quickly regaining control of the situation. The door hadn't fully shut behind them before he was undoing his slacks and motioning for her to undress.

'Take off your clothes,' he said, 'I want to see that amazing body of yours.'

Lissa had imagined that they might make love with their clothes at least halfway on but Colin shook his head, insisting that they get naked. Still, he seemed pleased with Lissa for finding the spot, and he smiled at her as she unbuttoned her dress and pulled it open.

'How long have you had this place in mind?' he asked, watching as she slid her panties down her thighs.

Lissa didn't answer. He wasn't the only one who could play at keeping the other off-guard. Except that he was much better at the game than Lissa, now making her wait before he came forward, motioning with his hand for her to strip off her bra, garters and hose as well.

Generally, Colin liked to make love while she still had on her stockings and heels. It was rare for her to be completely undressed during sex. Sometimes, he chose specific items for her to wear, and for him to destroy, while he fucked her. Slowly, she unfastened her stockings from the garter belt and slid them down her thighs. She could feel him watching her and she carefully unhooked the belt and set it on the ground at her feet.

Her bra was last and she held it in her hands for a moment, before dropping it, revealing her lovely breasts. Being totally nude had a different feeling, as if she'd bared not only her skin, but her soul, for him.

'You're beautiful,' Colin said, staring at her.

The cool rain sent chills through her body but Colin walked around her slowly, as if impervious to the temperature. He paused, observing her as if she were a statue, put there for his own personal delight. Then, after eyeing the rest of the roof and choosing a location, he positioned her with her hands flat on the brick railing that rimmed the rooftop, back arched, ass towards him.

He didn't warn Lissa before sliding his cock inside her. He simply parted her rear cheeks and drove forward, the rounded end of his cock slipping between her nether lips and probing, touching her deep inside. It felt so good – the mix of sensations like a dream. Cold concrete under her palms. Lights from the apartments around them creating a magical glow. Even the weather became part of the mood. The rain fell on her naked skin in an unbroken rhythm. And since her body had grown used to the cold, now the pattern of the rain was almost like background music to their lovemaking.

Colin pushed in hard and it seemed to Lissa that his cock was reaching uncharted places inside her. She felt the muscles in her pussy contracting on him, helplessly, as if trying to draw him in even deeper. Her body had a will of its own, and even though the storm grew harder, the warmth within her seemed to spread to the very tips of her fingers and toes. She arched her back so that Colin could slide his cock in even deeper. At this move, Colin made a noise in his throat, half a growl, half a moan. He always liked to take her from behind. It brought out an animal quality in him. Still, in general, he was fairly quiet when they made love. On the rooftop, as the rain grew harder, he grew louder.

Lissa's mind raced as Colin fucked her. There were people on the street five storeys below them. If they

81

looked up, they would see Lissa's bare breasts, her tousled hair loose and framing her face, her mouth parted with pleasure. But nobody looked up, and Lissa realised that shrouded beneath their umbrellas, none of the pedestrians had any reason to stare above their heads into a rainy night sky. The wind rose and lifted Colin's howls with it. Still nobody sought them out. This put Lissa more at ease and she felt her own inhibitions slowly sliding away.

Take me and become one with me, she thought. Drive in me. Through me.

The rain fell like teardrops on her face. The wind whipped her long hair upwards in a wild dance. And as Colin's body slammed against hers, Lissa responded, leaning her head back and screaming. It felt good to be loud. The release of it was something that she'd never previously experienced. As Colin came, he bit the ridge of her shoulder hard enough to leave deep marks. The pain mingled with the pleasure of his cock driving inside her and Lissa came with him, shuddering as the contractions pulsed through her body. She shut her eyes tight and Colin wrapped his arms around her, holding her to him.

The cold seeped into her consciousness quickly and Lissa rubbed her hands up and down her arms to warm them. Colin released her, grabbed her dress from under the ledge and helped her slide it on. The flimsy material stuck to her wet skin and didn't help to protect her body in the slightest. Without speaking, the two lovers hurried back to the apartment, dripping water on the stairs as they ran.

'Shower,' Colin said, just that one word, and Lissa followed him into the bathroom, getting into the tile shower with him and waiting, teeth chattering, for him to turn on the water.

They took turns standing directly under the hot spray, defrosting their bodies after the outdoor escapade. Lissa rotated under the showerhead with her eyes closed, letting the water wash over her long hair, then feeling Colin's hands around her waist, pulling her back against him.

His cock was hard again. Hard and demanding. Lissa wouldn't have thought she could make love again so soon, and her knees felt as if they might buckle as Colin started to fuck her, entering her from behind. Still, she was wet from their rooftop encounter, her pussy as relaxed and pliant as if it had been crafted from warm wax.

This time Colin worked slower, sliding against her soapy body, pressing her against the cool tiles of the shower. His hands sought out her breasts, strumming his fingers over her hard nipples, pinching them lightly between his fingertips until Lissa thought she would burst with pleasure.

'You like that,' Colin smiled, stating the obvious. 'Your body tells me exactly what you want.' He lathered her naked body all over with soap, running the bar along her ribs and then down her flat belly to her cunt. He used the hard bar of it directly against her clit as he continued to pound into her from behind. She was going to come from the feeling – she knew it – and found pleasure in the fact that she was getting clean while doing something that felt so dirty.

Colin dropped the soap and replaced it with his fingers, sliding his thumb and forefinger on either side of her clit and then pinching it. His fingers were slippery from the soap and water, slick from her own juices, but this worked to Lissa's advantage. As he searched for purchase, his fingertips pressed against her lips, nudged against her clit, causing miniature explosions of pleasure within her.

As he worked her with his fingers, he continued to fuck her with his cock, giving Lissa both of the sensations she craved. She was filled inside with his powerful rod and stroked outside by his probing fingers. Each time she thought she'd reached her limits, Colin backed off subtly, so that she coasted on the ridge of climax for what felt like hours.

Finally, Colin whispered, 'Now. Come for me now!'

Their moans reverberated against the tile walls, and as Lissa came, she started to cry. Her body felt as if it had been pulverised – pounded by the rain and cold outside on the roof, then heated to boiling beneath the driving shower and worked over again by the power of Colin's passion.

The two sessions were as different as Lissa could possibly imagine, and she had managed to climax both times. If she had tried to decide which way she'd liked better, she wouldn't have been able to choose.

Chapter Sixteen

*F*or the whole day following their rooftop encounter, Lissa walked around with a smile on her face. She could feel it, the feverish blush that returned to her cheeks whenever she remembered their outdoor adventure. And whenever she thought about what he'd told her at dinner. That he was planning a trip for them. So when Colin told her there was a change in plans, Lissa couldn't keep her disappointment to herself.

'But you promised,' Lissa said softly, her voice quavering with emotion. Her bottom lip was plumped forward, her eyes cast down at the floor. Even though she knew she must look like a displeased four-year-old, it was all she could do to keep from stamping her foot and throwing a genuine tantrum. She didn't think he realised how excited she'd been by the prospect of a getaway.

'Brat,' Colin said, laughing. 'Do you really think I'm going to give you a reward for pouting? If you do, then you haven't been paying attention to our lessons.'

Yes, she'd been paying attention. And of course, Lissa didn't think he would reward her but she couldn't help her expression. Now, she refused to raise her eyes to his, something that he never appreciated. When he spoke to her, he expected her to meet his gaze.

'It's a necessary change of plans,' he continued, refusing to offer her any further explanation. 'You ought to understand that.' He was referring to Lissa's own sense of responsibility. It sometimes thwarted their actions – she refused to cancel meetings in order to take a late lunch with him, would never disappoint someone when she'd given a promise. But that was the whole point, wasn't it? He'd promised *her*, and he was now disappointing her.

'We'll discuss it later,' he assured her, refusing to engage in the type of conversation she wished to have. Without another word, he returned to his computer, clicking open his mailbox to read incoming e-mail.

Lissa sighed heavily and then sat across from him at her own desk, trying to focus her mind on her work. She looked over the notes without seeing them. Finally, she shuffled through her papers, then slid them into the various colour-coded folders designating the Chapters of her book. She knew she wouldn't get any more work done tonight, not with the weight of disappointment hanging over her, and after several minutes she retreated down the hallway to their bedroom.

Lissa thought that Colin might follow her, but he didn't. After brushing her teeth, she undressed and slipped a cream-coloured silk nightgown over her head. Still no sounds from the other room. In their entire time together, she had never gone to sleep angry at him, and now she found herself desperately wishing he would join her in their bedroom. This was too much like the married life she remembered and the reasons why she had fled. Long silences. Angry looks.

She sighed heavily, and dramatically, hoping Colin could hear her down the hall and that he would hurry to their bedroom to talk. Getting no response, she climbed under the covers, turned off the light on the night table, and closed her eyes.

Although she wouldn't have believed it possible, sleep quickly approached. She hadn't realised how tired she

86

was until she felt the comfort of the down-filled pillow beneath her head. The polished cotton sheets wrapped her up in a gentle cocoon and anger slipped away from her as the dream world slowly approached. She slid one hand under the covers, touching herself lazily through her panties. Often, on the verge of sleep, she would play with herself. It seemed to help secure passage to a night of pleasant dreams.

She started, as usual, with a fantasy. This one was fuelled by Colin calling her a 'brat'. Despite what he'd said about not rewarding her for misbehaving, on the few times in the past when she had intentionally acted bratty, he had treated her like one. Punishing her for it in deliciously painful ways. In her fantasy this evening, she envisioned him telling her to put on his favourite of her skirts, a pleated red and black plaid micro-mini. She wore it with a pair of patent leather shoes, short white socks, and a pristine white blouse. After making her stand in the corner, Colin motioned for her to come forward, to touch her toes while he lifted the micro mini skirt at the back and lowered her plain white panties.

He would use a ruler on her. Although he'd never done this in real life, Lissa could imagine how it would feel. Her fingers rubbed over her clit, taking her closer and closer to climax. She squeezed her eyelids shut tightly, trying to make it last. She saw herself holding on to her ankles, trying to keep herself steady as Colin striped her bum with a wooden ruler. Because it was a fantasy, she could see angles usually hidden from her. She pictured Colin smacking the ruler against her flesh, visualised the stripes that the wooden ruler would make against her skin.

And then, as fantasy tears started to trickle down her cheeks, Colin unzipped his slacks and laid his cock against her smarting skin. As usual, he didn't warn her before putting it inside her. He simply used his hands to spread her thighs, then slipped the head of his tool into her pussy. She was wet, and he slid in deep, probing her inside while continuing to spank her – now, using the open flat of his palm against her bare bottom.

She was about to come. Her fingers made tighter revolutions up and over her clit. Then she let her middle finger slip down, dipping it into her dripping wet cunt. If only Colin weren't angry at her. She wished he were in bed so that she could confess this fantasy. She could hear him rustling papers in the other room and she thought about calling to him, asking him to come and join her.

No, she was a big girl. She could take care of herself. With a few more strokes, that grew harder as the urges built, she brought herself to the finish line. She bit down on her bottom lip as she came, but she continued to touch herself, more softly now, for a few seconds after she had climaxed. Caressing the sensitive area around her clit, teasing her inner lips before letting her fingers finally stop their motion.

Now, sleep was only seconds away. She could feel herself starting to drift off. Her last thoughts before her eyes shut were of Colin. She would make up with him in the morning. That's what she'd do. There was no reason to worry about it –

When a noise disturbed her, Lissa started in the bed, preparing to turn to see what it was, but finding herself unable move. This scared her more than the noise had and she tensed her body, testing her limbs to find that she was bound firmly into place and unable to move.

'Bad girl,' Colin said softly. 'Not to trust my intentions.'

Lissa opened her mouth, suddenly understanding what had happened and ready to explain. But she found that he had already placed a gag between her lips, obviously uninterested in what she might have to say for herself.

'I didn't tell you I was cancelling the trip. I told you there had been a change of plans. Do you understand the difference?'

Because she couldn't verbally respond, she simply nodded her head, her long hair tickling her cheeks. While staring at him, waiting for his next question, her mind raced to figure out what had happened. She realised that he had stripped off the top bed sheet and bound her to the mattress, her wrists above her head, her ankles spread apart. When she turned her head, she caught a glimpse of the clock. It was after 3 a.m. He had waited until she was deeply asleep before trying this. He was good at setting up scenarios while she slept, had proved that on the morning of their nipple-clamp adventure. But that event had seemed light-hearted. This time, Colin looked incredibly serious.

'We aren't going to spend the weekend at a country inn or a bed and breakfast. We are taking a special trip of my own planning and you will have to put your faith in me. I expect no more questions.' He paused for a moment before asking, 'Do you understand?'

Again, Lissa nodded. She wasn't surprised to see the black, braided riding crop in Colin's hand, but the sight of it sent a shiver of fear through her body. It also sent a wave of excitement that began in her pussy and radiated outwards to the very tips of her fingers. The conflicting sensations made it difficult for her to concentrate on what Colin was telling her, difficult even to remember to breathe. Still, she knew that she should be paying attention. Their games were all about rules.

Without trying, she managed to break two before he even started.

Chapter Seventeen

*L*issa slept until noon the following day, and when the alarm finally woke her, she saw Colin standing by the bed, already dressed. He tossed a worn leather suitcase on the bed. Lissa, lying limp and languid on the mattress after a night of multiple orgasms, waited to see if he would give her any additional information about their journey, but he didn't. He simply said, 'Pack for three days. Leave the rest to me.'

He refused to even tell her what type of clothes to bring before heading down the hall to the kitchen, although she could guess, from previous experience, what he would like. She could hear Colin making coffee. As the aroma filled the apartment, Lissa packed slowly, running her fingers over her newest outfits, the items purchased either in Colin's presence or with him in mind.

'You've got such a beautiful body,' he would tell her, 'why not set it off properly?'

Her fingertips brushed over the array of satin garter belts, the shimmering stockings she'd bought in three different hues. Undergarments were now as important to her as her outerwear. Because Marcus had no appreciation for frilly items, she had always settled for plain white cotton bras and panties. Now she hesitated over the rainbow of lingerie spread out before her. A cherry-coloured strapless bra that she would have dismissed as frivolous in her old life. A black velvet merry widow that she didn't even really understand how to wear; it had simply seemed like something she should own. And then there were the shoes. For someone who had lived in comfortable footwear for years, wearing high heels was a brand-new experience, slightly decadent and very sexy.

Colin entered the bedroom with a cup of coffee for Lissa, then sat on the edge of the bed with a newspaper in his hands, surreptitiously watching her pack. She felt his eyes on her and she looked up, giving him a smile.

When he smiled back at her, she felt herself relax. Wherever they went, it would be fine. Whatever they did, it would be perfect. She was with him; that was all that mattered.

Chapter Eighteen

*L*issa had no idea where they were going until they
arrived at Heathrow. From there, they took a plane
to Hamburg, but Colin refused to tell her anything in
the air, simply letting her drink her champagne, lots of
champagne, and wonder. This was his favourite way of
doing things. Keep her ever-guessing, never let her catch
up with him. It wasn't that difficult. This world was
brand-new to Lissa, while he'd had so much time to
grow accustomed to it.

He felt Lissa reach over and touch him, her fingertips
gentle on his skin. He took her hand in his and
squeezed it but didn't open his eyes. He guessed what
she was thinking. Would he fuck her on the plane? No.
Sometimes he let her go several days without coming,
keeping her on the very pinnacle before pushing her
over the ridge. Following these periods of denial, her
climaxes became unbelievably potent. Her body would
shake in such a way that he couldn't control himself –
he always ended up coming with her, whether he was
prepared to or not. He wondered what Lissa did to
bring out these new sides of himself. Whatever it was,
he liked it.

* * *

After the flight, they picked up a reserved rental car and Colin drove them directly to the Reeperbahn, not even stopping first to register at the hotel. The Reeperbahn was Hamburg's world famous – and infamous – red light district, but Lissa had never heard of it.

'Don't you ever watch travel documentaries?' Colin asked as she stared, eyes wide, at the sights around her. She shook her head. When she did watch television, which was rare, she generally chose historical art programmes or features on artists. No real surprise there.

While searching for parking, Colin explained that this region was a more complete version of the Sunset Strip in Hollywood. On Sunset, you could find a hooker if you looked. Here, the hookers actually found you, which was infinitely more civilised in Colin's opinion. There was even a street walled off from women. Only men were allowed to walk down it.

'But what's behind the wall?' Lissa wanted to know.

'Women.'

Lissa didn't understand. 'They *keep* women there?'

'Prostitutes sit in windows looking out on the street. Men walk up and down, staring in the windows, deciding which girl they want to spend some time with.'

'But why can't other women look?' The concept struck Lissa as sinister – a place forbidden to women.

'The prostitutes don't want the competition,' Colin explained. 'How would you feel if you were trying to sell yourself and someone else was giving it away for free?'

'What happens if a woman tries to go behind the wall?'

'The prostitutes throw things at her. Water or garbage.'

'Have you been down the street yourself?' Lissa asked, but Colin acted as if he hadn't heard her, exclaiming over their luck at finding a parking space and nosing the car into it. Lissa considered repeating her question, but didn't. If he said he had, she wouldn't be happy, and if he said he hadn't, she probably wouldn't believe him.

She watched as Colin locked their suitcases in the boot, all except one leather duffel bag of his, and then pulled out the umbrella he had packed. Under its shelter, Colin led Lissa towards the main thoroughfare.

'There's the gated street,' Colin told her, pointing. 'Really, all it does is add intrigue to the women behind the wall,' he continued, 'because there are prostitutes all over this part of the city. You don't have to look hard to find them.'

In a moment, Lissa realised that Colin was preparing her for what waited round the corner. Along one side of the street stood a row of prostitutes. As Lissa and Colin approached them, he remarked that they were always in that line despite the time of day or the weather. Lissa noticed that the women were dressed remarkably alike, stepping forward to talk to Colin as the two strode by. It was odd, Lissa thought, the way they approached men. Wouldn't it be more reasonable to let the men approach them? It was almost as if they hoped a man might not realise he was interested until they gave him their pitch, as if he might say, 'Oh, yes, that's what I'm in the mood for. A quick lay.'

The girls, down to the last one on the corner, all wore shiny skin-tight black pants and short jackets in a range of bright colours. Red. Violet. Fuchsia. Their jackets contained the hues of a field of wildflowers, adding a splash of brightness to the drab concrete wall that stood behind them. The majority of the women were blonde, with long straight or curly hair falling past their shoulderblades. From a few paces away, they looked identical. At closer view, one could see the differences in the shapes of their faces and the colours of their eyes. Maybe it was the expressions – ready, willing – that made them all look alike from afar. Some had amazing attitude, stepping out to get their faces close to Colin's regardless of the fact that he already had a pretty girl in tow.

Lissa pulled back in shock, unable to process it all, wondering whether Colin was going to purchase a lover for them to share. She knew it was something he might do. He'd revealed this fantasy to her several times. 'A girl,' he'd whisper, 'some untamed, wilful slut with her hot little tongue right here, against your clit, exactly where you most want it.'

She'd shake her head frantically, but sigh as he put his own tongue there, lapping at her for a moment before continuing to describe the fantasy. She had never been with a woman, hadn't even done the under-the-sheets exploring in her college years that Colin told her most women her age had tried at least once. Not Lissa, she'd never even come close.

'But you'd like to –' he'd prompted, still probing between her legs, again with his fingers and then with his tongue, making it difficult for her to concentrate on his questions. When he went down on her, she couldn't think straight. It felt so good as his tongue played tickling games inside her.

'I don't know,' she'd tell him, hesitant, slipping into a moan as he teased her ever onward. But once he'd suggested it, she caught herself staring at women in a new way. Wondering. Colin said that he loved this about her – the fact that she was ultimately suggestible. Anything he said became an instant possibility. Simply showing her the picture of Bettie Page being spanked by a nubile blonde beauty had made her instantly wet. The body didn't lie. Colin had found out for himself how aroused the photo had made her, sliding his pointer between the lips of her sex, then smearing her juices on her own lips and kissing them clean.

In front of a brightly lit stripclub, a barker called out to them in German, beckoning with one hand for them to come inside.

'What's he saying?' Lissa whispered, motioning to the heavy-set man standing in the doorway of the club.

Colin paused, listening, then quickly translated. 'He

says that the girls are all very young looking. They're shaved, so that even though they're eighteen, they look younger.'

Lissa, appalled by this, turned her head to glare at the barker as Colin pulled her past. The man just smiled at Lissa, winked, and continued with his spiel. It seemed to be working. As Lissa watched, several well-dressed young men entered the club, apparently less concerned with political correctness than she was.

'Maybe I'll shave *you* tonight,' Colin added, and Lissa suddenly lost interest in what was or wasn't correct, instantly excited at Colin's words. He had shaved her before, leaving a thin drag strip of her blonde peach fuzz down the centre of her lips. What would it feel like to be completely bare? Colin looked over at her and smiled, seeming to understand exactly what she was thinking. But didn't he always? She wondered if she could ask him where they were going. He seemed to be in such good spirits that he might not mind her questions. But why challenge him now? She managed to keep her queries to herself, and within moments the answer had revealed itself.

When they reached the main drag, Colin put two fingers under Lissa's chin to tilt her head up. She could see the red neon sign from where they were standing. The large letters spelled out: Hamburg's Erotic Art Museum, and when Lissa saw the sign, she sighed with relief.

Chapter Nineteen

*I*t was obvious that Lissa believed he was taking her to the museum as an art historian. She had visibly relaxed at the sight of the museum, letting Colin know her thoughts by her body's actions. He wanted to remind her not to underestimate him, but he kept silent. There was no need to reveal his entire hand. Not yet. Let her think whatever she wanted to.

Around them, the Reeperbahn throbbed with excitement. A street fair on one of the smaller avenues spilt revellers on to the main drag. People well beyond their drinking limit were becoming raucous, shouting to each other even when standing face to face. That's what always happened late in the evening. The drinking had been going on for hours, no doubt. It was almost midnight.

Lissa moved closer to Colin and he put one arm around her, protecting her. How odd. He was the one who punished her, tormented her, and yet she moved to him for safety whenever she felt unsure of herself. Now, walking amongst the partygoers and the prostitutes, Lissa slipped her gloved hand into his bare one. There was a sweetness in the gesture that pulled at him inside and made him ache. It would be so difficult to let her go. He shook his head, as if the action could clear his thoughts. She was his for six months. He didn't have to think about goodbyes right now. And here, they had arrived at the museum.

'Is it closed?' Lissa asked, sounding concerned. The lights were out. Niles had done him that favour, shutting the place up early at his request. Colin reached into his pocket and pulled out a key.

'Not for us,' he said, ushering her up the stairs in front of him and then moving forward to unlock the front door. There was a note taped to the handle and Colin scanned it quickly. Lissa tried to read the letter over his shoulder, but the words were in German and she could only make out what looked like a picture of a fish or lizard stamped next to the signature. Before she could ask any questions, Colin motioned for her to enter the museum and slipped the note into his back pocket.

The front room of the museum contained the gift shop, erotic posters, books, manuals and other sexual souvenirs. Colin hurried Lissa through it without stopping, pointing to the wrought-iron staircase curling along the far wall and nodding that he wanted her to go up.

'It's dark,' she said, still sounding unsure of the situation. Colin flicked on another switch and the staircase filled with light.

'Don't worry so much,' he told her, lowering his voice to add in a stern tone, 'and don't question me. Trust that I know what I'm doing.'

Lissa hung her head, instantly chastised. All Colin had to do was use a particular tone and she would behave this way, showing him with her body language that she was ready and waiting to be disciplined. To be punished. And punishing her was so much fun. She was a quick study in the world of erotic dominance and submission, but he wasn't going to give in yet, even though it was in his mind to whip out his handcuffs and chain her to the iron railing, to slide his belt free from the loops of his pants and tan her hide for doubting him.

His cock stiffened at the thought and he knew that if he simply brushed his fingertips against his metal belt buckle, Lissa would grow wet. Like Pavlov's dog, he'd trained her well. Still, he wouldn't give in. He wanted to follow his plan to the last detail. Ultimately, he knew it would be worth it.

Colin motioned again for her to climb the stairs, and Lissa turned and followed his silent command, walking up the steps to the next level, following the fanciful sperm-shaped silver arrows spray-painted on to the shiny black floor. From behind her, Colin observed the way her body moved beneath her clothes. He had bought this outfit for her himself, and the sleek black pants and black cashmere turtleneck sweater made her look like some fantastically attractive cat burglar. The added detail of her pointed-toe boots changed the look slightly, giving her a bit of a dominatrix aura. Just an aura, of course. Lissa was never in charge.

As soon as they'd reached the beginning of the exhibit, something in Lissa changed. Colin could sense it. In the museum, she was in her element, and she appeared to relax in one single motion, like a person inhaling deeply after being submerged under water. Surrounded by art, even erotic art which wasn't her field, she instantly found her balance. Lissa had tried to explain the feeling to Colin in the past and he had listened, but not fully understood until now. Art was like food for her. Or air. A necessity for survival. She breathed it in, walking from one wall to the next, observing each of the pictures, the tiny ivory carvings in cases in the centre of the room, the blown-up cartoons. Viewing each with rapt interest, she didn't even seem to remember that she was with Colin, appeared to forget entirely that he had planned this event for her, and most likely had other plans in store, as well.

Colin watched her. Rather than looking at the artwork, he watched *her*. He wanted to see when she would get it, when she'd understand the meaning of their visit.

Knowing Lissa, it shouldn't take her long. Although terribly naive, Lissa caught on quickly. She'd proved that to him repeatedly in their romantic life together, pleasing him with her ability to instantly accept almost any scenario, no matter how odd it might seem at first. Still, this evening, he enjoyed the wait. Anticipation was one of his favourite aphrodisiacs, and even though his cock strained against the fly of his slacks, he stood silently in one corner and observed.

Lissa studied the first few paintings in the exhibit. The curator had chosen to slowly expose the viewer to the power of erotic art. Rather than start with some wildly sexual pieces, the first room contained work that was more sweet than sexy. Lissa nodded to herself as she looked at the pictures as if thinking that this was the way that she would have set up a display herself, teasing the viewers at the start, then working slowly to the climax.

She turned towards Colin as if about to speak, but then her eyes caught sight of another picture. And suddenly, Lissa sucked in her breath. She'd found one of Colin's favourite pieces, a large portrait done in black and white. He had been at the museum for the initial showing of this artist, and he remembered his first experience with the picture. How the simple drawing, which showed a girl in garters, high heels and nothing else, had mesmerised him. It had been his first true encounter with the power of art, and the feeling that the picture gave him remained in his mind for weeks.

Apparently, it had the same effect on Lissa. She stared, open-mouthed, then her head jerked back as she looked over her shoulder at him. Understanding filled her eyes and a flush started along her jawline, creeping up to her cheeks.

She knew.

Colin smiled and began to unpack his bag.

Chapter Twenty

When the scene was set, Colin pulled out his camera and quickly slid the tripod together. It was an expensive piece of equipment, one that he had researched carefully before purchasing. He'd taken pictures all over the world and, even though he referred to this pastime as a hobby, he was more than an amateur photographer. Now, he focused on setting up, hardly glancing at Lissa. Yes, he caught the frightened expression she threw him, but as she didn't speak, he had no reason to reply. He wouldn't have anyway. This was one of those times when Colin preferred to let his actions speak instead of his words. If Lissa was worried, or frightened, then so be it. Within moments all would be explained, and he knew that she would relax as soon as she understood. Until then, he couldn't be bothered with coddling her. That didn't interest him in the slightest.

Of course, he wasn't going to explain everything this evening. Did not plan on sharing all that went through his mind with her. There were some things she wasn't meant to know right now. Some things that would have disturbed her. Those were best saved for a time in the future, several months away.

Right now, Colin worked with an intensity that he had rarely let Lissa see before. It was how he behaved in the operating room. Focused, precise. Although he was excited, he knew that Lissa wouldn't have been able to tell from his outward appearance. Contained, as always, he continued with his business, not looking at Lissa again until the preparations were complete.

Lissa stared, wide-eyed, as Colin set up the photographic equipment. She had thought he would simply dress her up to look like the picture, and then fuck her. That was all she had mentally prepared herself for. The camera meant that Colin was up to something else entirely. *Never underestimate me*, Colin had often told her, and here she had gone and done it again. It was the thrill of travelling with him that had set her back. If they'd been in his apartment, she was certain that she would have picked up the signs earlier.

'Trust me,' Colin said again, and Lissa closed her eyes tightly and worked to calm her fears. He'd taken pictures of her in his flat. This was no different. She tried to make herself believe this. But she was lying. It was absolutely and totally different. Here, they were in the middle of an art museum instead of bathed in the safety of their apartment. Thankfully, the museum was closed to the public, but that didn't stop her from worrying. What if someone caught them? Before she could visualise that experience, a new fear filled her mind, one which seemed infinitely more possible. What if Colin had invited others to join him?

Now that she was unsure of his motivations, her mind took her on a fantasy trip of countless other scenarios, each more disturbing than the other. She knew that Colin had a penchant for sex in public. Maybe he planned on inviting a live audience from the Reeperbahn to witness his own staged art show. Could Lissa handle that? She wasn't sure. She didn't ask him to calm her fears, however. He wouldn't tell her anything until he was ready. This she knew. So Lissa stood totally still, just as he'd demanded of her. She would not let him down.

My good girl, Colin thought. She tries so hard.

When he looked from Lissa to the painting, he could barely tell the difference. She wore black stockings, exactly like the model, and patent leather Mary Janes that looked innocent except for their squared four-inch heels. He had purchased the shoes from a mail-order catalogue, picturing exactly how Lissa would look while wearing them. Colin had even acted as her hairdresser and make-up artist, painting her face to match the one in the picture, sleeking her hair off her forehead and into a high, Barbie-style ponytail. It pleased him to be entirely in control of her appearance, from the way she was dressed to the racy look the cherry-red lipstick gave her mouth. He silently observed her for a moment.

The only obvious difference between Lissa and the model was the fact that she refused to meet his eyes. In the picture, the girl stared boldly out of the frame. Lissa's eyes were lowered as she studied the floor. Colin actually appreciated this attitude more than the model's direct expression, but in order to capture the image, he would need Lissa to look up at him.

'Nothing to be embarrassed about,' he told her. 'It's just you and me.'

Her eyes flickered upwards, towards the camera, and he understood.

'You, me and a Nikon,' he amended. 'Is that what's making you tremble?'

She didn't answer and he didn't press her. He could guess exactly what most troubled her. She had seen the array of toys he'd brought with him. They were packed in one of those containers that women use to hold jewellery while travelling, each pocket made of clear vinyl. He knew that Lissa could easily view the silver nipple clamps with their thin chains, the plastic butt plugs of various sizes, the handcuffs and leather blindfolds. Colin wondered if she'd noticed the room next to the one they were currently in. The S&M room, as he thought of it. This picture, for their first, was the easiest he'd planned for the evening. As they moved about the museum, he intended to take her on a steady progression. Upward, in his opinion, most likely down in hers.

As he readied the camera, he considered which piece of pornographic art they would next re-create. There was one of a pony girl from the fifties, dressed in a harness and heels, a tail protruding from her ripe ass. Colin envisioned himself on his knees behind Lissa, parting her beautiful round bottom cheeks, lubing up her hole with his tongue before sliding in the specially crafted dildo that featured a thick horse's tail on the end. They hadn't done much anal play, and Lissa could never ask him to take her there, even when he insisted that she vocalise the request. He wanted to hear the dirty words come out of her lips, but she hadn't been able to succeed yet. The good girl winning through once again.

Of course, he had known from the start that it would take longer than a few months to break her inhibitions. But that was all part of the fun, wasn't it?

Chapter Twenty-one

*A*s a pony girl, Lissa didn't even feel like herself any more. They were on photograph four, and Colin had been kind enough to hand over a small silver flask filled with very good whisky before attempting this picture. The liquor worked itself through Lissa, both warming her body and momentarily calming her fears. She thought she could actually feel it in her veins, pumping through her body to reach the tips of her fingers, the hard points of her erect nipples.

Alcohol made her feel slightly bold, which could cause her problems. If the liquor undid her tongue and she forgot her place, she might challenge Colin in some manner, bringing out his wrath. Luckily, she didn't get drunk from the few sips he allowed her. But she did relax as he bent her over and adjusted the horse-tailed dildo inside her.

'A perfect fit,' Colin said, as if he were talking to himself.

It felt so strange to have something in her there. What a wimp, she chastised herself. Even in her mind, she couldn't use the right words. Something in her ass.

That was better. She closed her eyes as the blush came over her again. She knew that her face was flaming, but she couldn't help it. Colin had bent her over a chair and parted the cheeks of her ass, and then she'd felt his warm tongue probing. Although she meant to tell him to stop, she had said nothing at all. The sensation was overwhelming. Slightly naughty, slightly dirty, but it made her pussy spasm. She wondered if he was going to fuck her . . . there.

She shook her head again and her long blonde hair whipped back and forth. Fuck her ass. Why couldn't she say it? They had tried the act several times back at his apartment and she had never got over the embarrassment enough to even begin to enjoy it. Gripping on to the armrests of the chair in the museum, she had thought she might actually like it if he slid his cock inside her – again, she forced herself to mentally say it – in her ass.

But he hadn't.

Instead, he had slid a clear, synthetic dildo into her, working it gently until she felt entirely filled, and then fastening it to the leather and metal harness around her slender waist. Now, she almost didn't recognise herself when she caught a glimpse of her reflection in the glass of one of the paintings. The sight of the long, shining horse's tail protruding from her bottom almost made her laugh. But when she looked over her shoulder at Colin and saw his expression, the giggle died in her throat. He was staring at her with an intense frown, then looking over at the painting and back at her, trying to figure out what was missing, what he had to do to her in order to make her match the vision in the picture.

The rear of the girl in the painting was striped by a switch. Lissa saw this at the exact moment as Colin saw it. The model had been pulling her master on a coach, and he had whipped her to make her move faster. That's what Lissa thought, anyway, what the painting said to her. Would Colin whip her to get the same look for his photo? She was certain he would, but apparently he wasn't ready to do so yet. And she wasn't about to ask him when.

She understood why he was waiting. If he whipped her, then he'd have to fuck her, and that would bring a momentary end to their play. He could definitely take her several times a night, but she knew that he always liked to postpone the initial climax. He would make them both wait as long as he could stand it. Nothing she could do or say would hurry him when he wasn't ready. She'd learnt that much in her lessons from him.

Silently, he fitted her with a different pair of shoes. Her lover had come prepared for this little journey. She wondered how many times he'd been to this museum to view the artwork, how long it had taken him to set up this event. Had he performed this same sort of odd foreplay with other women? She considered asking, and then stopped herself. It wasn't that she thought he wouldn't tell her, but that she didn't want to know the answer. Why not let herself think that she was the only one he had ever played with? That she was special to him.

Colin, as usual sensing her questions before they reached her lips, whispered, 'I've always wanted to do this, Lissa. What a perfect little model you are.' He gave her bare ass a hard, open-handed spank, and the horse-tail jiggled in the most becoming fashion.

Chapter Twenty-two

*A*fter photographing Lissa as a pony girl, Colin decided that their foreplay had reached a peak. He needed to fuck her. Now. Before they climbed the iron staircase to the next level of the museum, where things might truly get out of hand. Especially if he didn't allow himself at least one climax in order to calm down. He knew that Lissa couldn't tell how excited he was. Outwardly, he appeared the same as always, totally in control. Inside, he felt like a kid on the first day of the summer holidays, ready to let loose in an explosion of pent-up excitement.

Colin sensed that Lissa, just barely balancing in the tall heels, was waiting for his next command. Instead of giving her one, he took another picture. A close-up. For an instant, the bright white of the flash blinded her, as he had known it would. He went forward quickly while she was still blinking, pulled her over one bent and raised knee and spanked her bare bottom. He did not remove the horsetail first. He liked the way it bounced as he slapped her naked flesh.

The spanking was impromptu and had nothing to do with the picture he'd just re-created. He knew that the stripes in the drawing came from a switch, but he didn't want to get into a hardcore scene quite yet. Besides, switches were hard to come by. One had to find a proper type of tree, cut a thin branch, strip the shoots from the side . . . Paddles, crops or even his belt made much more sense. But he wasn't ready to get involved with any type of serious pain right now. What he wanted was to fuck Lissa's sweet ass, and he knew that she would have to be drippingly wet in order to truly appreciate it. He liked it best when she got off with him.

In this respect, he supposed that he wasn't a normal dominant. He knew of others, had spoken to them, who couldn't care less if their submissive partners reached orgasm. Ever. Colin felt that if his lover came with him, or at least close to when he did, it meant that all the twisted perversions he created worked as well for her as they did for him. And that's what he most wanted.

There was a high leather chair in the corner and he pulled Lissa over to it, half-carrying her because of the shoes, and settled himself more comfortably. Before continuing her spanking, he rocked the dildo inside her bottom. She moaned at the intrusion and he smiled to himself. She wanted him to fuck her here. He should have guessed that earlier. Now, they would get what they both wanted, but not before he had finished preparing her.

Lifting the thick, chestnut-hued tail, he punished the lower part of her bottom more seriously, giving her a series of stinging spanks that made her writhe over his lap. He liked it when she squirmed. The contact with his cock was delicious, and he continued the spanking for several moments just to enjoy the heady sensation of her hips rocking against his groin. He wondered if she could make him climax in this manner, if he could simply spank her until he shot his come against her flat stomach. For a moment, he considered trying, but then decided that it would be a waste. It wasn't what he really wanted at all.

He stopped when her skin had turned a deep, blushing

pink. He would work her harder, later, but for now he just wanted to give her a taste, an appetiser before they settled in for the main course. Roughly, he pushed her from his lap and issued his next command.

'Place your hands flat on the wall,' he said, indicating a blank spot between two large canvases. The pictures were perfectly suited for what he was about to do to Lissa. In the painting on the left, a scrumptious blonde had her rear to the camera and was holding on to her ankles, peering at the viewer from the side of one leg. On the right, another picture from the pony girl series depicted two stunningly beautiful women hitched to a cart, and a third being fitted by her master with a long horsetail. Colin would fuck Lissa between these two works of erotica.

'Bend at the waist and keep yourself steady,' he instructed. His voice was soft, but he knew she could hear him, and he watched as she hurried to obey. Lissa didn't question his command, simply tottered to the place he'd pointed to and did as she was told. He would make her wait while he got out the bottle of lube and a towel he'd brought from home to spread beneath them. This could get dirty, and although they had the run of the museum for the evening, he didn't intend to destroy the place.

Her ass looked so pretty now that he'd coloured it. And with the horsetail issuing from between her rear cheeks, she truly did seem like some mythical pony girl. This made him smile. More than anything they'd done in the past, this evening was his favourite. As he unzipped his slacks and pulled out his cock, he wondered why he enjoyed this event so much. And then, as he entered her, the feeling of her soft warmth enveloping him, he understood.

He had changed her. Transformed her into a vision he had created himself.

Chapter Twenty-three

'*T*ell me that you want it,' Colin said, his naked body pressed firmly against Lissa's. Her skin was slick and wet, and when he tried to grip on to her arms, his fingers slid against her.

Catching her breath, she tried to obey him, but found that she couldn't. It was too difficult.

'Tell me, Lissa,' Colin demanded, his voice more serious. She wondered what he could possibly do to her that he hadn't done already. Every part of her body felt used, distorted, as if it belonged to someone else. She couldn't believe they were actually fucking again. And yet her body responded as always, desperate for his touch, yearning to reach that magical finishing line alongside him. Crest together to a place that previously she had only imagined could exist.

'I want it,' she said finally, feeling his cock probing inside her, driving inside her where she was so wet and ready for him.

'What do you want?'

She had an idea, but even as she heard the words form in her mind, she couldn't believe that she was going to say them aloud. Colin wanted her to tell him what he already knew. But why should she? She should have some power, some semblance of a say in the matter. Despite what he might think, she had the ability to play at his game.

His cock was stroking in and out of her in deep, long thrusts. He'd made love to her twice at the museum after fucking her ass, after taking pictures of her in every style she could think of. Then, in complete disarray, with their clothes dishevelled and their hair mussed, they'd checked into their hotel, showered, and got into bed before he'd mounted her again. Now, it was her turn to surprise him.

'I want to taste myself on you,' she said softly. It stopped him. He was in mid-stroke, and he stopped.

'What do you mean?'

'I want to suck my juices off your cock.'

'Oh, you slut,' Colin groaned. 'You fucking wilful little slut.'

It was obvious that she'd shocked him, and she knew that it didn't matter what she was saying. It was only the fact that she was talking dirty. He'd never heard her say dirty words because she hadn't been able to get them out. Even though he'd insisted for months that she try to fulfil this command, she had been unable to comply. But this evening had changed her. He had put her in positions that she hadn't even heard of before, used her to re-create images that she'd seen only in the gallery of her mind. Why should she continue to play a shy waif of a girl? She could have a filthy mouth if she tried.

Still, her cheeks were flaming as Colin pulled out and spun her around. He pushed hard on her shoulders and she bent her knees and sank to the floor, mouth open, ready.

'I knew you had it in you,' Colin murmured, feeling her tongue flick out and lick at his balls. 'I knew you did.'

Book Three:

But Is It Art?

The Devil whispered behind the leaves,
'It's pretty, but is it Art?'

– Rudyard Kipling

Chapter Twenty-four

*B*ack in London, after three days of such intense fucking that it was difficult for her to walk much less think straight, Lissa felt as if she had just woken from a strange dream. Like a pornographic version of *Alice in Wonderland*, she had fallen down the rabbit hole and visited a place that changed her entire outlook on life. Not that her months prior with Colin hadn't already changed her. They most definitely had.

Yet something amazing had happened to her in Germany and now when she looked at Colin, she saw a different person. Not only a lover who matched her untamed, unnameable desires, but an intellectual who thought about art the way she did. One who actually had taught her to look at art in a new way, which was the most exciting ability for an art historian to possess.

She recalled the photographs displayed on the walls of Colin's apartment. They had appealed to her from the start, subtle erotic black and white pictures that told more in what they didn't show than in what they did. Understanding now that Colin was the photographer, she had a new respect for him, and with it came a new thirst for their romantic endeavours.

On the return flight from Hamburg, he had explained

his mission to her – to re-create the works of art that most affected to him. Pictures that pleased him. Sculptures that aroused him. Since he'd told her this, she had begun to think of suggesting works of art that she, herself, found erotic. There were pictures by Mapplethorpe that had always stirred her, and several by Man Ray that, while not actually pornographic, held an intense appeal. She could visualise herself naked, back to the camera, in the Man Ray picture of the woman turned into a musical instrument. The curves of her body, the arc of her back –

But even as these images flickered through her mind, she knew she wouldn't bring them up. Aside from the specific assignments he gave her, she couldn't always tell how actively Colin wanted her to participate in planning their dalliances.

No, she would wait until he asked for her feedback. Right now, it was a treat to put herself entirely in his hands, to see what he might come up with. One of the best things about him was his lack of fear when it came to the art world. Some people, especially when around Lissa and knowing that she had a PhD in art history, couldn't speak intelligently about art. They simply froze up.

In the past, her former self might have made a distinction when it came to erotica, wondering whether it really counted as art at all. Although she'd enjoyed pictures by Olivia, and the Varga girls of the 40s, she would definitely have placed the works into a category that was somehow less worthy than the pieces found in the museums she favoured. She'd had a change of heart, however. Colin had opened her mind to how truly remarkable the sexual arts could be. And if a picture was able to move one person, she had always said, then it was art.

The patron, seated with the photos of Lissa spread out on his satin bed sheet, definitely felt moved. He didn't wonder for one moment whether the photos were art or not. It just didn't matter to him. What was important was how the photos made him feel. And they made him feel amazing. His cock stirred, demanding attention, but he took his time. There was no need to rush, to hurry on to the next phase. As he looked over the pictures, he wished Lissa was with him, re-creating the poses in person.

He would have her start with the pony girl trilogy, just because the thought had never occurred to him before: a girl dressed in bridle and bit, ready to pull a carriage. Then, he would move on to the picture showing her as a dominatrix. Of course, he knew that it was only an illusion, the girl was a submissive. Still, he imagined coming on her shiny, patent leather gear, watching his jism slide down the slick material, gliding across it. He would like a picture of her in a catsuit cut from that same fabric and he made a mental note to let Colin know this request. Colin had claimed he would do whatever was asked of him. If this were truly so, the patron realised, he ought to take advantage of it.

At the bottom of the package, tucked into the hand-written note, were a pair of Lissa's panties. The note said: ART IS SCENT. The patron ran his fingers over the underpants before looking through the photos, matching them to the picture of Lissa in the schoolgirl outfit. White cotton panties beneath a pleated plaid skirt.

Lifting the soft panties to his face, he inhaled deeply. She was divine. It was easy for him to imagine pressing his face to the split of her body and licking her, slowly, getting his tongue in between her nether lips and finding her clit. Sucking on it until she was as excited by him as he was by her.

He considered getting the audiotape Colin had made for him, of listening to her, watching her, drinking in her heady fragrance, all at once. With the panties clutched in one hand, he rifled through the photos to find his favourite – one of Lissa looking directly into the camera.

He stopped himself. Before giving over to a solo night of pleasure, he reached for his laptop computer, typing Colin a quick e-mail that listed the next assignment. The patron smiled as he began to enter the short message, certain that Colin would appreciate his creativity. He was actually surprised by his own fantasies. Now that he knew they had potential for coming true, he found that his imagination spiralled almost out of control. One fantasy gave way to another, more twisted vision, which beget one that would top even that.

He checked the clock by his bed. It was almost 3 a.m. in London. Colin and Lissa were probably fast asleep, curled around each other, their bodies warmed by one another, skin pressed to skin.

No, don't think about that right now, he told himself. Concentrate on what to tell Colin. The mental picture of the lovers entwined nagged at him, but he glanced over at the photos and instantly smiled again. Yes, he knew just what to tell Colin; how nice to know that the e-mail would be waiting for Colin when he awoke. The freedom of electronic messaging was almost addictive.

Finally, after flicking off his modem and shutting down the machine, the patron took hold of his cock and both literally and figuratively got down to the business at hand.

Chapter Twenty-five

Colin was checking his e-mail in the office while Lissa was in the room with him. This was something he rarely did, but he was certain that she couldn't read his screen from where she sat. Still, he felt her eyes on him from over the top of a book on modern French painters that she was pretending to read.

He willed himself to act normally. He did not want to give away his emotions with his body language, but he knew that the tense way he held himself was out of the ordinary. With his shoulders back, he must look like someone sizing up a potential fighting partner.

Relax, he told himself, act normal in front of Lissa. He could feel her eyes on him as she stared at the back of his head, and he inhaled deeply, then reread the e-mail.

ARTLOVER appreciated the panties, the photos, the tape. But he wanted something more. Although Colin had expected this and had planned for it, that didn't change the flash of fury that burnt through him. They had made a deal and he felt that ARTLOVER was rushing him. The man should have trusted Colin to do what was right, to make the correct decisions at the proper times.

He felt like putting his fist through the wall, like

sweeping his computer off his desk with one out-stretched arm, watching the machine slam into the floor and disintegrate into a mess of sparking electronic rubble. But he did nothing except lean back in his chair and stare at the computer screen. He couldn't show his emotions, not with Lissa in the room, pretending to work on her book. She was watching him, he sensed it, and he quickly turned off his e-mail server, then shut off the computer entirely. He needed to make a call. In private. Unable to do so with Lissa in the apartment, he created a story about having a morning meeting. He would use his cell phone to call Jackie. From the lobby, he could set the plan into motion without her eavesdropping, questioning him about what was going on.

As he bent to kiss Lissa's forehead, the words 'I love you' came to his lips. He stopped himself from saying them. It had been a thoughtless statement, almost automatic, but he'd never said it to Lissa before, didn't even know if it was true. Didn't know what she would do if he said it.

His brow was furrowed as he walked out of the apartment. What was happening to him?

Only moments after Colin had left the apartment, Lissa crossed the room to his computer. It was almost as if the machine had a magnetic pull on her, drawing her forward against her will. As she pressed the 'on' button, her mind played out a variety of scenarios. Aside from wondering what she might find, she also thought about what Colin would do to her if he caught her. How would he punish her? Were there ways he hadn't tried yet? She'd had a taste of his belt, riding crop, paddle. He had used the removal of senses, keeping her in the dark, and in silence, refusing to let her speak. What else was there? These thoughts excited her, didn't deter her at all from trying to gain access to his computer.

Sitting on the edge of his seat, she tried tapping in different codes in the hope that she would crack his e-mail password. It was crazy, really. Who did she think she was? One of the players on *Mission Impossible*? Or Miss Marple, now a star in some pornographic thriller that would make Agatha Christie roll over in her grave?

But it didn't matter who she thought she was. The simple fact was that she couldn't stop herself. There was no way to focus on her work when she found herself alone in the apartment.

Bad girl, she thought to herself. But that's what he called her anyway. Wasn't she simply living up to his expectations? Thinking this, she spent over an hour typing in different passwords in an attempt to log on to his e-mail server. She entered code after code, but nothing worked. Not his birthday. Not his favourite number. Not the words that most suited their relationship: P-A-I-N. S-P-A-N-K. O-B-E-Y. B-E-H-A-V-E.

She was *mis*behaving, now, she knew it. But it gave her such a thrill that she couldn't stop herself.

Jackie wasn't in when he called and Colin had to wait until Lissa left for the museum before he tried to reach his friend again. He sat at his desk, staring at the wall as he mentally formulated his request. He wanted to explain it just right. Jackie, as part of the inner circle, would understand – but he wasn't too bright. Colin wanted to make things simple.

As he placed the international call, he thumbed through the portfolio of photos from Hamburg that lay in an open manila folder. Lissa, at her most submissive, stared at him from his favourite picture. She was delightful, every part of her, every nuance. He set the handset back in the cradle before Jackie answered the line.

He would do this his own way. ARTLOVER couldn't choreograph every segment of the relationship. It was time for Colin to take charge of the way things were going.

Chapter Twenty-six

*T*he breakthrough came unexpectedly. Colin had logged on to his computer to read his e-mail but he hadn't pressed the 'enter' button when the phone rang. He had chosen to take the call in the bedroom, and Lissa, walking by the office, saw that the computer was on. The code couldn't be read – it was an indecipherable list of small black dots – but she highlighted it and saved it with a few key strokes. Now she didn't need to know what it meant. She could simply insert it into the password space the next time he left the apartment, which, as it turned out, was directly after he got off the phone.

'I have to go out for an hour or so,' he said, striding past her to the office. She could hear him turning off his machine and then he reappeared in the living room, his heavy black trenchcoat over his suit. 'I expect you to be ready for me when I get back.'

She could only guess what that meant, but she wasn't surprised when he walked to the sofa and bent to kiss her. His mouth tasted of peppermint and he slipped the candy from his tongue to hers.

'There are more in the bedroom,' he said. 'Right by the bed. You keep one in your mouth until I get back.'

Sucking on the candy, her lips turned up in a smile.

He wanted her to give him a peppermint-flavoured blow job, something they had read about together in a sexy magazine. It was supposed to be a body-shaking experience, tingling in a delightful way, and she felt herself growing aroused in anticipation. As Colin winked at her and then turned to leave the apartment, she reconsidered her plan to snoop.

Why would she want to ruin what they had together?

She didn't. But only a few minutes after Colin had left, Lissa found herself at his desk, her heart racing. When had she last been this excited? She couldn't remember. The sex things she did with Colin made her feel amazing inside. Turned on and alive with desire. But this was totally different. She remembered the feeling and instantly categorised it – as a child, she had gone in search of her birthday presents in the weeks before her party, stealthily making her way to the attic, to the garage, looking under her parents' bed. And the feeling had been exactly the same. A sort of sick charge at the thought of what she might find, while a part of her hoped that she would find nothing.

She pressed the controls that brought the password from memory. Then hit the 'enter' key and closed her eyes. Would it work? Almost instantaneously, the computer accepted the password. Now was the moment of truth. She could shut the online modem down, pleased with herself for being able to crack the code. Or she could plunge into a whole new aspect of her relationship with Colin. By reading his private materials, she would be opening a darkness between them. She understood this.

After a moment, Lissa turned off the computer.

The rest of the afternoon passed in slow-motion. Lissa attempted to work, spreading her notes on the table in the dining room, stacking her books at her side. She couldn't remain in Colin's office now that she knew how to get online. Instead, she poured herself a glass of red wine and for almost an hour she pretended to read. But who did she think she was fooling? She stared at several of her favourite pictures, tracing her fingertip over the lines on the page, before finally closing the book and walking back down the hall.

Moving quickly, as if she might once again lose her nerve, she rebooted the computer and re-entered the password. This time, she didn't pause to consider what she was doing. She simply began to click open the different files of mail.

Nothing exciting at first. Most of the folders contained medical correspondence that were not only boring to her, but almost indecipherable. The words made no sense at all to her. She closed one after another, feeling partially disappointed that she hadn't discovered anything disturbing about her lover, and partially relieved.

Suddenly, an icon began to flash on the top of the screen indicating that Colin had new mail. She clicked on the icon and read the tagline. There was a message from someone called ARTLOVER.

She closed her eyes, wondering what to do. Should she read it? Would he be able to tell if she had? When she opened her eyes, the e-mail continued to flash repeatedly, like a neon light, beckoning to her. Just as she was about to click on it, the phone rang. It was Colin.

Did he know what she was doing? Could he have guessed? No. He was calling from his cell phone with instructions for the evening, a change of plans. Turning off the modem and the computer, she walked down the hall to the bedroom, to dress as Colin had requested. He was taking her out to dinner.

Chapter Twenty-seven

*L*issa's peppermint-scented breath made Colin smile. She always tried to please him. He slid one hand up along her spine to the back of her neck and pushed her down, so that her head was in his lap. It didn't matter to him what the cab driver thought. All that was important was how he felt, and how Lissa felt, and on some much lower level, how the patron felt.

But the patron had nothing to do with the blow job Colin was receiving in the back of the roomy black cab. And, really, this was what put the smile on Colin's face. Something was happening in his head. He was separating the events choreographed specifically for ARTLOVER, from those that were more to his personal taste. While he continued to send updates via e-mail, he carefully chose which stories to share. Tonight's would be his alone.

Lissa worked him like a pro, her red-glossed lips caressing him as she bobbed her head up and down on his shaft. He was proud of her. She hadn't struggled or blushed when he'd made her unzip his pants. Sometimes her embarrassment got the best of her, stopped her from immediately obeying him. Of course, that only gave him yet another reason to punish her, so he honestly didn't mind.

Her lips locked around his cock and her tongue flicked up and down, stroking him expertly. He had explained to her exactly how he liked it, and she had paid attention. Now, she used one hand to cradle his balls, and then her soft fingertips searched out the area beneath them, touching the tender skin and sending shivers through his body. She knew just how to drive him wild, and after enjoying the experience for several minutes, he wrapped one hand in her hair and pulled her off him. Immediately, she replaced her mouth with her hand, jerking him off in the manner he favoured. A quick stroke followed by a softer, slower move. What a good little student. She worked hard to treat him just how he liked it, and he looked down to watch her small hand stroke his rod. Her fingernails were painted a shiny, pearlescent white, and her wedding ring shone against her skin.

Seeing it made him grimace, and he instantly lost the desire to climax, taking Lissa's hand and removing it from his cock. Lissa gave him a questioning stare, but he simply kissed her on the cheek and put his arm around her, holding her to him. He didn't have to explain why he wanted her to stop. They were almost at The Marquis.

Although Lissa had never heard about this particular spot before, she'd read about restaurants like it. There were two in New York, where diners were able to choose from a broad range of sexual delights listed on the menu. They could be spanked by waiters, put over some handsome dominant's knee or the lap of an attractive dominatrix and paddled to tears in front of the rest of the crowd.

The restaurant Colin chose on the outskirts of London was of the same theme. With rich red walls and a dimly lit interior, the chic hot spot provided the perfect ambience for a sexually charged meal. Tall candles, truly sculptures of wax, created to look like naked women, burnt in gothic wall sconces. Smaller versions lit each table. Although the restaurant seated nearly a hundred, the tables were set far apart. As Lissa and Colin were led to their reserved spot, Lissa had a feeling of privacy despite the fact that other couples were already seated at tables and booths around the room.

Lissa looked around the restaurant, noticing that the waitresses were all clad in fantasy dominatrix attire, and the tall, handsome man standing behind the bar looked as if he could break someone in half with one hand. He seemed to size Lissa up as she and Colin were seated at their table, and Lissa mentally told herself to behave through the meal. She could tell that Colin was only barely restraining himself, although she didn't know why. Any little indiscretion she might make would give him reason to take her, to punish her.

But even with those thoughts, Lissa had a difficult time keeping her eyes only on Colin. From the handsome bartender to the bevy of waitresses, the staff at The Marquis were magnificent-looking. Their own waitress was an exotic-looking woman, with caramel-coloured skin and warm brown eyes. Her long, hard body was clad in a slick-looking catsuit that shone in the candlelight. When she took their order, she focused her almond-shaped eyes on Lissa and gave her a cool smile, baring small, animal teeth. Lissa instantly had an image of the woman astride her, bending to bite along the ridge of Lissa's collarbones, and then lower, leaving kitten-like bite marks all along her naked skin.

Why had she thought that? It was so unlike her. Lissa felt herself blush, and she looked at her hands as they wrapped themselves around each other, nervously.

'You're flirting,' Colin said, as he poured wine for each of them.

Lissa was shocked. 'No –' She shook her head. She hadn't been, had she?

Colin nodded his head towards the waitress, who was

now approaching a table across the room, one hand wrapped around the thick handle of a wooden paddle. The diner she spoke to pointed to an item on the menu, then indicated he wished to order it for his dinner partner, a brunette whose mussed hair signalled a recent bedroom romp. The waitress pulled out an armless wooden chair, yanked the customer over her lap, and began to spank the woman's upturned, panty-clad bottom. Lissa sucked in her breath, stunned. She understood that this was a normal occurrence for The Marquis, but she still hadn't prepared herself for it.

'You're up next,' Colin said softly.

Lissa tore her eyes off the spectacle and turned to look at him, frantic. 'No –'

'What did you say?'

She bit her bottom lip, understanding exactly what sort of a predicament she was in. If she told him 'no' again, then he'd have the perfect excuse to spank her. If she didn't, he would have the waitress spank her for fun. It was a win-win situation for Colin, and a no-win situation for her, but as she thought that, she realised that her panties were already wet.

'What did you say?' Colin asked again, his voice holding a more menacing tone than he'd used all evening.

Lissa swallowed hard and closed her eyes, making her decision to choose the lesser of the two evils. But which answer was the right one?

'I said "no".'

Colin didn't linger, didn't wait for the dominatrix to return to the table and take their sexual order. Instead, he had Lissa over his own lap in a second. Unlike the customer nearby, whose dominant partner had allowed her to keep her panties on, Colin stripped Lissa's down her thighs. Her white cotton underpants dangled from her ankles, her skirt was pushed up to her waist. Colin's hand came down hard on Lissa's ass and she moaned, but held herself still. She didn't kick or squirm, didn't try to get away from him, didn't beg him to stop. She was behaving as if she had been bad, as if she knew that she deserved the spanking.

Flirting. Yes, she'd been flirting with the waitress, but that's not why he was punishing her. There was a quality to her attitude, an oddness about her since he'd picked her up at the apartment, that let him know something was up. Sometimes, Lissa told him that she was ready to be punished simply by the way she held herself. A look she'd give him, a posture.

He didn't know what it was about this evening, but he knew how much she hated being punished in public, and he was pleased to start her with that. Humiliation was the true punishment to Lissa. Pain simply made her wet.

He watched her reddening ass cheeks quiver. He understood that she was hoping the pain would obliterate her guilt. It didn't matter to him what she felt guilty about. Honestly, he didn't really care why she wanted to be spanked. He adored spanking her and would do so simply for his own pleasure before attempting to find out what was wrong.

And, if he were to be totally honest with himself, he'd wanted to paddle the living daylights out of her ever since he'd seen her wedding ring glinting in the dim back seat of the cab. Yes, she'd worn the ring from the start, ever since he'd first set eyes on her in Frankfurt. But for some reason, this evening it had angered him. He'd use that anger in his punishment of her, channelling it all into the weight of his palm as it connected with the reddening cheeks of her naked ass.

Within his black suit pants, his cock grew hard as he spanked her again. He liked taking his time, getting her in the perfect position, smacking her hard all over her ass and the top of her thighs.

Oh, Christ, was she lovely. His anger melted as he looked down at her, but that didn't make him go any easier on her. The beauty of her nakedness, of the way she lay draped over his lap in perfect paddling position, simply made him want to spank her longer, and harder.

Lissa sucked in her breath as Colin continued the spanking. She realised that he was going to spank her until she cried. She had a high pain tolerance, often would cry from embarrassment long before she'd cry from hurt. But Colin had a way of combining the two feelings, making her bottom sore and letting her know what a naughty girl she was at the same time.

And she had been naughty, hadn't she? She'd snooped on his computer, trying to crack his code – and succeeding. He didn't know why she wanted to be spanked, but she composed herself and took it like a champion, giving herself over to the pain.

And in that way, giving herself over to the pleasure, as well.

Chapter Twenty-eight

'*T*ell me what it was like for you at home,' Colin probed. He still had on his white shirt and tie, black suit pants and polished shoes, but his black-and-grey checked dinner jacket was off, hanging on the back of the closest chair. Lissa, with her hands above her head, naked save for her wrists bound in thick expensive silver cuffs, stared at him and tried to work her face into a smile.

She felt as if she were on a shrink's couch, except that this shrink held a riding crop in one hand and was smacking the black, braided tip of it almost absentmindedly against the palm of the other.

'I don't know what you want me to say.' Her legs were spread apart beneath the white sheet and her ankles were bound with soft cloth to the lower two posts of the bed. While she watched, he nudged the sheet up a bit from the bottom, using the edge of the riding crop, bending low to peek under the tent of sheet the crop created. She felt exposed, watching him watch her, his head bent, an unreadable expression on his face. No, not unreadable. He looked like a little boy peeking into a girly show, getting his first glimpse of a bare-naked lady.

From his bent-over position, he said, 'I want you to

130

tell me about your life with your husband. I want you to tell me why you left him.'

She considered the request. She was captive, completely at his mercy, but he wasn't satisfied with that. He wanted to reduce her to something even less, mentally push her while physically keeping her on edge. Psychological warfare. It was potent. She wondered why she suddenly felt so alone.

'Things just didn't work out.'

He stood suddenly, pulled the sheet off the bed completely so that she was totally accessible to him, and said one word as he struck her with the crop.

'Liar.'

She heard Colin speak at the exact same moment that she felt the pain, looked down to see the angry red line appear in bold relief on her right thigh. She sucked in her breath. 'How would you know?' she asked, even though it wasn't the smartest move on her part. Why antagonise him when he was in this type of mood? Why push him when he was so intent on punishing her?

'I know because I know you,' he said. 'You plan things out over and over in your head. Obsess about them. There must have been a million reasons why you left him, and you can't even think of one to tell me? I don't believe it.'

Lissa closed her eyes. She hated to admit to failing. She'd chosen the wrong man to marry, it was as simple as that. What more did Colin want from her? What else could she say? Although she could understand his anger when he thought she'd flirted – and, honestly, she *had* flirted – with that woman in the restaurant, she couldn't fathom why he was so interested in something that had happened before he met her. How could he possibly be jealous of a husband she'd left before she'd even met him?

The crop nudged against her, and she opened her eyes to see Colin glaring down at her, his green eyes so dark that they looked as if they'd turned an inky black.

Why was he doing this? She asked him, just that word, to counter his statement that she was a liar. 'Why?' Her voice was soft, lost in her throat, her eyes still seeing past him. In the mirror across the room, she caught a glimpse of herself. She looked younger than thirty, much younger, her hair loose and falling past her shoulders. Her eyes still wide open from the sting of the crop. There was a flush to her cheeks that she thought made her look as if she'd been running. A healthy flush. She waited for Colin to respond, and then realised he was waiting for her to look up at him. When she did, he spoke.

'Because it's a way to make you hurt,' he said, just as softly, raising the crop again and daring her with his gaze to watch as he brought it down. She felt the blow, accepted it, her body growing warm all over from it. 'And,' he continued, still speaking softly, going to his knees on the floor by the bed and pressing his cheek to the hot line of pain he'd left with the crop, 'I adore seeing the look in your pretty grey eyes when you hurt.'

The pain was immense. A blow from the crop hurt infinitely more than anything he could do with his hands, or a paddle, or a belt. And yet there was something inside her, a fine hot wire burning within, that had accepted her need for pain. Accepted and welcomed it. She considered what he said, and almost smiled.

He was right. It summed up their relationship perfectly. Two puzzle pieces that fit together with the tears from her eyes and the heat that burnt from his. She leant her body as far back as it would go in the bed, moving away from him so that she could look down at him. He now stared at the line he'd inflicted on her skin, watching as the welt formed and grew a darker red, changing colour each second. Tomorrow, it would be a purplish hue, the colour of a ripe plum. Now, Colin's mouth left kisses that went up and down the line from the crop.

He loved her. She felt it in his kiss.

Chapter Twenty-nine

Colin wasn't sure what was happening to him. He had made a deal, but now he found himself dreading the e-mails from ARTLOVER. Everything about Lissa captivated him and he felt sick inside when he imagined having to let her go.

Did he love her?

Maybe that was it. He knew she didn't understand why he'd gone so hard on her the night of their dinner at The Marquis. Of course, it hadn't actually been about her at all. It had been about him, and the e-mail he had received, the latest request.

He shook his head to clear his thoughts, then looked over at Lissa, sleeping soundly at his side. She was lovely, but that's not why he was so captivated by her. There were plenty of other lovely women in the world. No, Lissa was special. She had awakened to the pleasures in his life with more intensity than he could have dreamt of before meeting her.

With Lissa so peacefully asleep, he moved carefully, not wishing to wake her. Silently, he climbed out of bed and reached for his black silk dressing gown from the back of the chair. He put it on as he walked down the hallway to his office, preparing to respond to ARTLOVER.

Of course, Colin would do as he asked. That was the deal. He would do as he'd agreed and he would enjoy each moment of it. He knew that.

But he couldn't help but wallow in the pain that threatened to pull him down. What would happen when he received the final assignment? What would happen when he had to let her go?

Chapter Thirty

*T*his trip took more work for Colin to plan than the previous one. While Hamburg's museum adventure had only required a single phone call to an old friend, this trip was more intricate. It didn't bother Colin. He relished each stage of the preparations and he grew sexually aroused simply by thinking of his plans. In the days before their journey, he could take Lissa passionately several times in a night and still not be fulfilled.

Lissa, on the other hand, was pulverised by the multiple orgasms. She would gaze at Colin with her eyes half closed, a look of total abandonment on her face. Her expression would let him know that she was ready to sleep, while Colin's cock would grow hard again, and he would be forced to roll her over, to press against her, to slide in one more time and shoot deep inside her, groaning like a creature possessed as once again he came.

Of course, Lissa never complained. She wasn't silly enough to do that. But she did look at him quizzically when she rolled back over, as if wondering what thoughts were making him so terribly excited. She stared at him even more quizzically the night before their next trip – but this time it was because Colin *didn't* fuck her.

'Get some sleep,' he said softly, 'we have a busy day ahead of us.'

He knew this didn't turn off his libido but he had plans and he would stick to them. Although she threw him a few bedroom glances after she'd finished packing, Colin stayed true to his schedule and didn't make love to Lissa. He wanted to. God, she looked amazing in the new black nightie he'd bought her, the lacy material barely skimming the tops of her slender thighs.

She wore matching panties that had a tiny ruffle along the bottom edges, a look of faux innocence that nearly demanded that he rip them off her. Shred them and fuck her through the tatters. He knew what the fabric would feel like as it tore between his fingers. Still, he wanted her to be aching for it by the time they arrived at his planned destination, and it wouldn't hurt him to be a bit desperate, either. After turning out the lights in the room, he simply kissed her on the lips and then took her into his arms until she fell asleep.

He remained awake for hours after, planning and replanning the trip in his mind.

Chapter Thirty-one

*T*he journey to Paris was far more eventful than the one to Hamburg. Even the final preparations before they left the apartment were exciting. Colin watched from the bed as Lissa dressed in the morning, sliding on a pair of black satin panties and a matching bra, and then slipping into a sleek red dress and her favourite broken-in leather jacket. Lissa could feel his eyes on her, and she turned and struck a model's pose, one hip cocked towards him, asking, 'Do you like what you see?'

Unlike most men, who would have immediately said 'yes', Colin regarded Lissa carefully. Then he smiled, and said, 'Of course,' before adding, 'all except for one small detail.'

Lissa looked into the mirror to see if she could guess where she'd gone wrong. Was her hair uncombed? Did the outline of her bra show through the thin material? Colin stopped her. 'You'd have to have X-ray vision to know the part I dislike.'

He didn't want her to wear panties. She guessed this from his comment and quickly slid them back down, kicking them off and striking the pose again. The dress's silky lining brushed against the shaved skin of her sex, making her extremely aware of her nakedness. Colin gave her a pleased nod as he climbed out of bed. She was learning. He hadn't been forced to voice his request, she had guessed it simply from the expression on his face.

As usual, Colin dressed much more quickly than Lissa, and in minutes they were ready to leave. But where were they going? Colin still hadn't told her where he was taking her and Lissa knew better than to ask. He'd tell her when he was ready. Lissa let the excitement of the unexpected wash over her. The one clue she had was that Colin had told her to bring her passport. This meant that they were definitely going out of the country, might be headed anywhere in the world.

When Colin hailed the cab with the instructions to go to Waterloo Station, Lissa turned to look at him, surprised. She'd been certain he would take her to the airport. Now, she was more confused than ever. What part of England required her to show a passport? Had he only said that to fool her?

'Don't worry about anything,' Colin said, nuzzling his lips against her neck, 'except behaving yourself.'

Lissa blushed, even though she knew she hadn't done anything wrong – at least, not yet – and attempted to compose herself. Reservedly, she laced her fingers together and placed her hands in her lap, but this act only served to remind her that she had no panties on. She spent the rest of this part of the journey wondering whether Colin would turn the trip into a re-creation of the famous scene from the movie *No Way Out*. She'd loved watching Kevin Costner and Sean Young making love in the back seat of a limo. Doing it in the back of one of London's famous big, black taxis would be almost as sweet. And if he wasn't planning on fucking her, would he at least touch her during the cab ride? Slide his fingers under the hem of her dress and probe upwards to stroke her naked skin?

No. He simply wrapped one arm around her and stared out the window at the passing sights. When they arrived at the station, he picked up both of their suit-cases and Lissa had to hurry after him. She couldn't keep the smile off her face when she saw where he was headed. The EuroStar. He was going to take her on the Chunnel to Paris. Lissa had always wanted to travel on it, ever since the opening, and she felt a new burst of excitement course through her.

The excitement was coupled with another erotic thought as she and Colin boarded the train and moved to the first class cabin: would he have sex with her in the Chunnel? If he did, they would join the Mile Low club, which she'd read about in a magazine. Mile High was doing it on an aeroplane. Yard Wide (a joke) was doing it in the back of a vintage VW Beetle. But the Mile Low club could only be achieved on the Chunnel or on a submarine – and the latter wasn't too likely to happen, even with Colin and all of his unique connections.

In their plush seats, Lissa again was aware of her lack of panties. She had on thigh-high stockings and polished leather boots and, each time she crossed her legs, she felt herself grow wetter. She considered whispering this to Colin, but he didn't look the least bit interested. Odd for how he'd been behaving during the past few weeks, as if he simply couldn't get enough of her body. Some mornings she'd had a difficult time walking, feeling pulverised from their nighttime activity.

Still, she chose not to mention her arousal to Colin. He seemed almost as if he were in another world, and after ordering them each a drink he began to read the *Herald*, not paying any attention to her. If he was aware of her distraction, he didn't let on in the slightest. Lissa sighed, loudly, but received no response. Resignedly, she attempted to amuse herself by staring out the window.

The first part of the trip, through London and then the British countryside, was beautiful. Lissa sipped her glass of white wine and watched the landscape whizzing by. The passing images made her think about a variety of artists, and how each might paint such a landscape differently. As usual, visions of art calmed her, and she momentarily forgot about her need, the urgent desire to come which had consumed her for the better part of the morning.

Colin didn't interact with her until the train had actually reached the Chunnel and the windows took on a cloudy darkness as they entered the underground tunnel. Then, as if awakening from a trance, he lowered his paper and faced her with a look she instantly recognised. It was all she needed to be turned-on all over again. That one, simple look from his dark-green eyes sent shivers through her body, and she pressed her legs together tightly, feeling the wetness start to seep between them.

'Meet me in the bathroom,' Colin said, standing and walking quickly towards the rear of the carriage. Lissa craned her neck to watch him go, staring at his well-dressed form from behind and visualising what he looked like naked. Wasn't that something that men did? Undressed women with their eyes? It showed her how hungry she was for him, and she hesitated only a moment before standing and following after Colin through the carriage. She didn't register the looks on any of the other passengers' faces. Her mind was totally consumed by thoughts of Colin and what activities he might have planned for her.

'I know you've been waiting for me to fuck you –' he said, after shutting and locking the door to the private bathroom behind them. It was a larger compartment than one found on an aeroplane, but not by much. Yes, they could manage, but it would be tight. That thought made Lissa smile. She had faith that she and Colin could contort themselves into any position required.

When he lifted her up on to the tiny counter, Lissa spread her legs wide and waited for Colin to enter her, but he didn't. He never did what she expected. She should at least have learnt this by now.

'– But I'm not going to.'

Instead, he pulled out a harness and a tiny vibrator that he'd concealed in his pocket, sliding the straps up her legs and fastening them quickly into place. The vibrator slid in easily – she was already very wet – and he secured it to the harness and then lowered her dress.

'I'm not going to fuck you,' he said, 'because I told you that I wanted you to wait for it until I was ready. But that doesn't mean you can't have a little pleasure in the meantime.' He touched the remote control device in his pocket and the tiny vibrator whirred into action.

Colin left Lissa alone in the bathroom to rearrange her outfit, waiting for her back at their velvety seats. She emerged seconds later, her face flushed, giving him an expression that he could only categorise as a 'please don't embarrass me in front of the pretty cabin steward' look.

She sat back in her seat at his side and slipped one hand into his. Her eyes shone with excitement, and he gently nudged the switch on the remote control to the lowest setting, watching as Lissa gave him a brave smile and closed her eyes. Although the vibrator was tiny and its motor was indiscernible, Colin was sure that it felt immensely powerful to Lissa. She swallowed hard and sat up even straighter in her seat as Colin played with the setting on the miniature device.

Watching Lissa fight for control within herself was one of Colin's favourite pastimes. He played with the switch until the train exited the tunnel and bright sunlight poured into the cabin. Lissa hadn't climaxed yet, and she gave an audible sigh of discontent as the vibrator was turned off inside her.

From 'don't embarrass me' to 'please let me come' in only ten minutes. Colin couldn't have expected more from himself. He kissed Lissa's cheek and leant towards her to whisper a line from his favourite Tom Petty song. 'The waiting is the hardest part.'

Chapter Thirty-two

When the train pulled into the Gare du Nord station at a little past noon, Colin still refused to tell Lissa his plans. Instead, he simply grabbed hold of their luggage and carried it to a counter at the station. Here, he gave instructions in French to the lovely Parisian woman behind the counter, asking for the suitcases to be brought to an address that Lissa didn't recognise. He hadn't given the name of a hotel, which surprised her. But rather than ask him what he was up to and give him a reason to spank her in public, she remained quiet.

She could easily visualise him thrusting her over one raised and bent knee, lifting her skirt to reveal her naked ass, covered only by the black band of the harness that still held the vibrator inside her. Although the thought was a turn-on, she played a quiet meek girl, standing at Colin's side without disturbing him.

From the train station, Colin indicated they would be taking the metro and hurried Lissa down a steep set of stairs to the landing. Lissa felt as if she were on a roller-coaster ride, the whole day one whirlwind of activity. As soon as the metro arrived and they'd found seats, Colin began to play with his new toy again, starting the vibrator on the lowest setting. Lissa could hear the motor, but no one turned to look at her. She supposed it was masked by the sound of the train's engine. Still, she felt extremely self-conscious as Colin teased her closer to climax again.

She did her best to concentrate on thoughts of non-sexy things. Baseball. The stock market. Pond scum. It was all mind over matter, right? She wouldn't come if she didn't want to. She could feel Colin watching her as she struggled for self-composure, and after several metro stops he finally turned off the vibrator.

'We're here,' he said, taking Lissa's hand.

But where was 'here'? Lissa looked out of the windows of the carriage to read the sign of their destination. Blanche. She'd never heard of it, knew that they hadn't arrived at any of the famous sightseeing spots. Wasn't it just like Colin to choose somewhere out of the way, somewhere unexpected?

Colin led her through the throng of exiting and entering passengers in what seemed to Lissa like a dance. Lissa noticed the lack of pushing as people got off and on the metro. Even in the game of musical chairs that the passengers played, setting their sights on the best seats and hurrying towards them, there was none of the brusqueness or subdued anger that she'd sensed when travelling in the New York subway system.

Letting Colin guide them without paying attention to their direction, Lissa took in the posters on the walls of the subterranean tunnels. There were several advertisements for art exhibits that she wouldn't have minded checking out. After all, they were in Paris! The concept struck her as amazing. In California, one had to drive for hours to reach another state. In Europe, it was a simple train ride to arrive in another country. And France was one of her favourites.

Still, she knew that Colin had plans for them and she didn't think to suggest an afternoon visit to the Louvre or the Picasso Museum. So when Colin told her they were going to a museum after all, she looked at him, surprised.

'The Musée de l'Erotisme,' he continued, and it all began to fall into place for her. First, he'd taken her on the trip to the erotic museum in Hamburg and now they were headed towards the one in Paris. Was Colin planning on making a pilgrimage to all of the erotic art locations in Europe? She tried to remember the names of any others. There was one in Berlin, she thought, and there must be one in Amsterdam. Of all the European cities, *that* was the place for it. And even though she considered the United States to be more prudish than Europe, she'd heard of a sex museum in New York City. Would he take her back to the States to visit that one? Again, she didn't raise the question. Instead, as they walked up the stairs and into the crisp, afternoon sunlight, she tried to get a bearing on her surroundings.

Paris's erotic art museum was located in the Pigalle section, an area that Lissa had never visited. On her previous journeys to the City of Lights, she had spent nearly all of her time in the world-famous museums or wandering through the neighbourhoods bordering the Seine and looking in the windows of the tiny art galleries. She should have known that Paris would have a red light district. Yet although the place felt dirty, when all of the rest of the city seemed to sparkle, Lissa found that she actually didn't mind the grimy quality. It simply piqued her interest as to what Colin's next surprise would be.

Walking next to Colin along the pavement she was at first reminded of the Sunset Strip. But then she realised that this neighbourhood was actually closer in style to the Reeperbahn in Hamburg. It was more open than Hollywood, where you could find just about anything you wanted, but you had to look a little first. Here, sex shops lined the streets, their doorways covered only with black slit curtains, like the strips of rubber that blanketed the opening of a car wash. Each time a patron entered or exited, Lissa would catch a glimpse of smut magazines lined up before the counters and various sexual devices stacked in boxes along the walls – dildos, vibrators, the occasional inflatable doll. She thought about asking Colin if he'd ever used one of those, but since she wasn't sure how she'd feel if he had, she kept her mouth shut.

'Would you like to go in?' Colin asked, apparently noticing the intensity with which Lissa stared at the stores.

'Not really,' she said, shaking her head. 'They're all pretty much the same, right?'

Colin's eyes glowed at Lissa's response. 'So you've been to one in the past?' he asked, his interest obviously piqued. As they walked, he quizzed Lissa about her experiences. And when Colin asked for more information, Lissa always complied.

Yes, she'd been in sex stores before: the Pleasure Chest on Santa Monica Boulevard and Drake's on Melrose. Her college boyfriend, Beau, had taken her to both locations, trying to get her to loosen up about sex. 'There's more to life than the missionary position,' he'd told her, pointing to an array of handcuffs, collars and leashes, vinyl dresses.

At the time, she'd been too shy to let herself go. That's why Marcus had been such a welcome change. He'd been the stable, solid type of man she had believed that she was supposed to marry. His conservative views on sex had seemed to match her own. Brush your teeth before you do it. Make sure you're powdered and sweet-smelling. When, after ten years, she'd found herself fantasising more and more about Beau, about the way he'd talked to her and the things he'd said, she was startled. It took a while before she'd understood that now she was ready for what had frightened her at the age of eighteen.

Of course, she didn't tell all of this to Colin, she only told him that she'd visited a few of the stores in

Hollywood, wondering what they had behind their blackened windows. And that she had been somewhat disappointed with what she found.

'I don't think you'll feel the same way about the place we're going today,' Colin told her as they finally approached the building. 'It used to be a cabaret, was only turned into a museum several years ago.'

Lissa could tell that he liked playing the role of tour guide. She listened with half of her attention, focusing with the rest on the large painting of a woman on the wall of the museum and the words Musée de l'Erotisme below the picture.

As Colin held the door open for her, Lissa hesitated, wondering what lay in store for her here. She knew that her lover must have planned something special, as he'd done in Hamburg, but she also knew that it wouldn't be the same thing. Her questioning glance towards Colin brought forth no explanation. He smiled blandly and led her by the hand through the door, paying their admission to the bored-looking girl behind the counter, then steering Lissa to the lifts.

Lissa looked over her shoulder at the cashier. Had a look passed between the girl and Colin? Was this another set-up that he'd planned with the owner? The girl didn't raise her eyes to meet Lissa's, focused instead on a magazine she was reading. If she did know Colin, she was doing a perfect job at pretending that she didn't care.

'There are seven floors,' Colin explained, pulling on Lissa's wrist to get her attention. 'We take the lift to the top and then walk down. That's the best way to see it all.'

Seven floors, Lissa thought, still trying to guess what Colin would do at this place to surprise her. He couldn't fuck her now, could he? He hadn't brought her here after-hours, as he'd done in Hamburg. She glanced at him. The weather was surprising for February in Paris – no snow or rain – and Colin had on a black cashmere sweater and black slacks. He didn't have a bag with him, so he couldn't be taking pictures of her, could he? Not unless he had one of those new mini-cameras, so small they could fit into a pocket without causing much of a bulge. She looked towards the crotch of his slacks and then flushed as he laughed at her.

'None of that now, Lissa,' he said, as if he knew exactly what she was thinking.

Despite his assurances, as they stepped into the lift, she wondered if he would make love to her in the tiny compartment. She could easily imagine it. Colin would press her against the mirror at the back of the lift, strip open her dress, pump into her hard and fast while the lift rose to the top of the building.

It didn't happen. The ride was far too quick. And, Lissa thought, the security camera, posted in one corner of the lift, must have given him pause as well. It was one thing to make your own videos, but something else entirely to be captured on tape by a stranger.

As they stepped on to the black-veined marble landing, Lissa stopped trying to second-guess Colin and let her senses take over. When looking at art, erotic or otherwise, she always tried to shut down the intellectual part of her brain and let the artwork speak to her. The difficult task was in trying to appreciate a work of art without bringing any baggage to it. Sometimes, as it was for her now, this proved to be an impossible task. The top floor of the museum featured three-dimensional paintings created on tampons and pantyliners.

Lissa grimaced, instantly disliking the display but trying not to listen to the voice in her head that said, 'This isn't art, and it isn't erotic.' It was art if it worked for somebody, even if that somebody was the artist who created it. Still, she was happy when Colin motioned for her to follow him to the next level. The menstrual-themed art hadn't seemed to do anything for him, either.

They walked in silence to the sixth floor, and Lissa enjoyed the pictures here much better. These were black and white photographs of belly buttons, and she found the work so lighthearted that she was smiling broadly by the time Colin steered her to the stairway that led to the fifth level. Who would have thought that belly buttons could look so different? She'd have liked to have read the review of this display, to have seen the photo that accompanied the text. How could you choose a specific belly button picture to represent the whole series?

On the fifth landing, Lissa's eyes grew wide. This floor featured sex in motion, statues that had actually been fitted with motors so that their parts moved. Listed as 'interactive sculptures' in the brochure, the first one which caught Lissa's attention was a bicycle being ridden by a pair of naked legs and a gorgeous bare ass. The legs peddled in endless rhythm, but the bicycle went nowhere, fixed firmly in place on a red pedestal. Lissa tried to dissect this work. Aside from the naked legs, she wouldn't necessarily characterise riding a bicycle as erotic. Although, if you stood behind the statue, staring at the ass, you could get into a sort of daze by watching the legs pump. Maybe it was something that worked more for men than for women. Before she could get lost in the piece, another item caught her attention.

This moving sculpture was definitely sexual. It depicted two lovers in bed, and the mechanics of the piece made the man move up and down on his prone bedmate. The woman wasn't motorised at all. Lissa got the feeling that the artist, a woman, didn't like sex very much. Or didn't like sex with men. If she had, wouldn't she have given the female part of her sculpture a little bit of action?

Lissa's mind was still focused on this work as Colin led her down the winding staircase to the fourth floor. Her boots made clicking sounds on the marble floor and she realised she'd heard no other footsteps since they had entered the museum. So far, they were the only patrons. Colin released her hand and walked ahead of her. She wondered if he were hurrying for a reason. Was something waiting for them on one of the floors yet to be discovered? He hadn't spoken to her at all since they'd arrived, but she felt his eyes on her as she observed the different works of art. Was he waiting for her to understand what he was planning? She had got the gist of it in Hamburg, but it had taken her a little bit of time. Now, her heart raced at the thought that she might have missed a clue on the floors above them. And if she had missed it, would he punish her for it? This made her legs tremble, and she gripped the cold, metal handrail for a moment, holding herself steady.

Colin, a few steps below her, turned to look up at her. 'Coming?' he asked, holding one hand out to her. She took it and walked on to the landing of the fourth floor.

Chapter Thirty-three

'*O*h, my God.' Lissa stood in the centre of the room, turning around slowly. She couldn't believe the art displayed on the walls. Even though she was staring at the pictures, a part of her brain wouldn't fully process what they were. Yes, she had known that Colin would surprise her with something. That was what their relationship was about. But she'd thought the surprise would be with sex, some trick he'd prepared for her, a swing hanging from the museum ceiling that he'd put her in, a pair of cuffs dangling from one of the sculptures that he'd use to capture her wrists. His goal was to turn her into a piece of art, but she hadn't thought that he would have actually put her on display.

'Do you like it?' he asked softly. Again, he was staring at her instead of the art, as if captivated by the expressions that travelled across her face – confusion, fear, disbelief.

Maybe she was hallucinating, Lissa thought. She shut her eyes and opened them again, confronted with her own image twenty times over, staring back at her. Not just staring, but pouting, primping, giving herself a come-hither glance. She took in the pony girl pictures, the ones in which she had been dressed as a dominatrix, the post-orgasm close-up in which her eyelids were half-shut and her mouth parted and hungry-looking. These were the photos that Colin had taken in Hamburg. All had been beautifully framed and were now hung on the walls of the main room. In stark black and white, they showed Lissa in all her stages, as a slut, as an innocent belle, as Bettie Page.

It was too much for Lissa to take in at once, and she felt her body starting to sag. Colin grabbed her, his fingers digging into her arms as he held her upright. Lissa allowed herself to be supported in his arms. She still hadn't spoken, hadn't asked him what the pictures were doing here, how they'd got here, or why he'd brought her to see them. Colin didn't offer any of the answers. Instead, he asked softly, 'Beautiful, aren't you?'

She didn't respond. Instead, she looked towards the beginning of the display, where the bio of the artist should have been posted. There was only a simple white plaque that read, 'Donated by an anonymous patron of the erotic arts'.

'When did these go up?' she asked.

Colin pulled the brochure from his back pocket and handed the folded piece of paper over to her. 'It's a brand-new exhibit,' he said, pointing to the shot the museum had chosen to represent the display. The photo was the one with Lissa on all fours in a black corset and heels, her chin tilted down, but her eyes looking up at the camera. No, not the camera, she thought. At Colin. She remembered the feeling of wanting to please him, of wanting to perfectly re-create the pictures he'd chosen. In the brochure, the curator had also included reproductions of several of the original pieces of art. No doubt, permission to reproduce them had been granted by the Hamburg museum. The curators at both must know each other. When she'd worked at the Getty, curators in other museums around the world had often done similar favours for her.

Colin brought Lissa's mind back to the pictures by

leading her to the largest one, the masterpiece of the exhibit. 'No one would ever guess it was you,' he said, wrapping one hand in her long hair and pulling her head back. Her body tensed as she waited to see what he would do next, completely on guard. 'That's the beauty of it, Lissa. You're infinitely malleable. You transform yourself for the camera,' he paused, 'and for me.'

Now, he motioned with his head to another security camera, this one keeping tabs on the couple from the far corner of the room. Lissa turned her head to see that there were cameras in each of the four corners.

'Are you ready?' he asked, helping her out of her leather jacket, then slowly unbuttoning her red dress and letting it fall open. His fingers were warm on her bare skin, tracing unreadable designs from her flat belly up to her breasts. She held her breath as his hands reached the clasp of her black bra and, as he opened it, she started to tremble.

'Ready?' she repeated, standing totally still. Her ears were perked for the sounds of footsteps coming from above, but she heard nothing. Had Colin, once again, set it up so that they wouldn't be disturbed? She thought that she understood now, but she wanted to hear him say it. Colin placed two fingers under her chin and tilted her head up, stepping forward and then bending to kiss the hollow of her throat. He lingered there a moment, his warm mouth against her skin, feeling her heart beat beneath her skin. When he moved back from her, Lissa's eyes looked dazed, but that didn't stop her from repeating her question. 'Ready?' she asked, wanting desperately to hear what he would say.

'Are you ready to transform yourself for me again?'

152

Chapter Thirty-four

Jackie Miller, in the security office located deep in the bowels of the museum, hit the button for an extreme close-up look. Then he focused the other three cameras and sat back to enjoy the show. This was part of the deal he'd struck with Colin, one small portion of the payment. Or, the way he preferred to think of it, a bonus.

The images from the cameras were displayed on four separate monitors. Screens on the walls around him showed activity on other floors in the building, but Jackie didn't glance their way. He was captivated, instead, by Colin and Lissa. Mostly, by Lissa.

What an ass the girl had. Colin hadn't lied when he said Lissa was a looker. Of course, Jackie knew the girl had to be pretty. He had been one of the first to see the 'Lissa exhibit'. But you never really knew how someone would look in person, without make-up or airbrushing. He remembered the *Playboy* spread he'd seen – or was it in *Penthouse*? – the one featuring Nancy Sinatra. He'd torn out the pages for his wall. The girl had always been a favourite of his when he was a teenager with her boots are made for walking song. Even now, he felt a yearning in his groin when a woman walked past him in knee-high boots, especially white ones. And look, he'd thought when he first saw the Sinatra spread, she was still bang-worthy at fifty. But then he'd seen her on some talk show, and man, what a rude fucking awakening.

Jackie returned to his sexual surveillance. Camera three was focused on Lissa's face. He'd angled the lens perfectly, over Colin's head, capturing her expressions. Her lips formed a word, and he wished he knew what she was saying. Still, even silent, this was better than any porno he'd ever seen, and he was quite the connoisseur of the X-rated video industry. It was better, because this was live action and it was private. There were shows in the district where you could see men and women going at it, but you were always in the middle of some crowd of horny men. Never alone. This was almost perfect. The only thing that could have succeeded it on a ranking scale was if he'd been able to choreograph the action himself. That would have been sweet, telling Lissa exactly what he wanted her to do, positioning and repositioning the lovers.

No, that wouldn't have been the best. In order to top this, he would have added a few more girls to the scene. And he'd definitely have replaced Colin with himself as the leading man. He lost himself in daydreams of this image, coming around again only when he noticed Lissa bending on her knees in front of one of her pictures, preparing to give Colin head. That made his own cock stand at attention, but he was a professional. He wouldn't give 'little Jackie' a reward until after the tape was finished.

He had promised Colin that he would edit the video before turning it in, choosing the best shots, and then bringing two copies by the apartment that evening. For the equivalent five thousand dollars, American, he had to admit that it was a pretty fantastic deal. And since he was planning on keeping a copy for himself, he would do an extra good job. He'd been messing around with video since dropping out of college. He knew exactly what he was doing. The fact that he'd had to block off

154

the fourth floor from the paying customers hadn't bothered him at all. He'd simply set up a detour as soon as he'd seen Colin and Lissa walk down the landing, and he'd only had to pay off the cashier up front and the other security guard. It had been easier than he'd expected.

Now, Jackie looked up at camera number two, the one focused on Lissa's rear. He tightened the shot with a push of a button and then smiled. This is where he would play if he were Colin. Get himself buried in deep back there, his arms around her waist, mouth pressed to the back of her neck, licking her. Biting her. He liked that position best, and he found that a lot of women appreciated it, as well. Even the French girls dug it, and he'd heard that they were more finicky than Americans. He'd never had a problem. But maybe it was that the type of girls he dated were less than particular. Since he'd snagged the job here, he'd discovered that the women he went out with from the neighbourhood were wilder than he was, always coming up with some concept that would never have occurred to him.

Of course, what Colin was up to now would never have occurred to him, either. So maybe he just lacked imagination. If that was it, then he should pay attention to Colin and Lissa. Maybe he'd learn something.

Chapter Thirty-five

*C*olin was definitely getting fancy. The movie travelled over the Internet to appear in the patron's email folder, with a tagline that read: ART IS MOTION. A movie projector-shaped icon indicated that all the viewer had to do was click once to watch.

It was before noon, but the patron poured himself a drink anyway. An important part of the ritual, right? Have a shot, then check to see what surprise awaited him. Of course, this wasn't totally going to be a surprise. He'd suggested the idea to Colin in the first place, hadn't he? But still excitement welled within him at the thought that all he had to do was type in a fantasy and Colin made it come true. It was as if Colin were some sort of sexual Santa Claus.

The patron settled on to the leather sofa and pressed the 'start' button on his laptop. At first, he wasn't sure what he was seeing. Then he realised that Colin had taken his request above and beyond the call of duty. All the patron had asked for was a video of Colin and Lissa fucking. But Colin didn't like to do things the normal way. The patron understood that, and yet he still couldn't quite figure out where the movie had been taken.

Was it in a museum? He paused the film to click open the file that had been attached to the movie. Here, Colin had forwarded him an electronic version of the brochure from the Musée de l'Erotisme. And now the patron understood. This movie had been filmed in the room where Lissa's photographs were displayed.

The security camera had been focused on a picture of Lissa dressed as Bettie Page. But the camera was motion sensitive, and as Lissa and Colin entered the room, it had turned its red eye towards them. The sweeping motion picked up several other pictures in the room, a blur of Lissa as a pony girl, as a dominatrix, all in leather with whip in hand. Then the camera caught the real Lissa, flesh and blood with her jacket on the floor and her dress falling open.

The patron had to smile. When Colin and Lissa had made the tape, it had been real to them. They'd fucked while surrounded by pictures of Lissa, fucked amidst a roomful of art. But by capturing their lovemaking on tape, their act had become yet another work of art, frozen forever in time but able to melt into action whenever the patron pressed a button.

His cock stirred as Colin slid off Lissa's bra and used it to bind her hands together behind her back. He wouldn't have thought of that. A bra had always been just a bra to him. Now, he leant forward and stared at the screen. He would have paid immensely for the pleasure of being able to hear what Colin was telling her.

But it wasn't that hard to figure out. No subtitles were necessary. Colin was going to fuck Lissa from behind, as simple as that. He bent Lissa forward so that her palms were splayed flat on the floor. She was limber, her body contorting easily to Colin's desired position. Then he parted her ass cheeks and looked down at her. The patron wished for a close-up, and suddenly, there it was. He shook his head, not understanding at first. Then he realised that the tape had been edited. There were several cameras in the room and all had been focused on the pair of lovemakers. Afterwards, Colin must have collected the tapes and had them spliced together. He was only surprised Colin hadn't added a soundtrack, filled with the bump-and-grind background music found on every porno flick he'd ever rented.

The patron took a sip of his whisky and leant forward, watching as Colin slipped the head of his cock into Lissa's pussy, seeming to just tease her with the tip. He must have had a friend working the camera, the patron decided. How else would he have been able to get such good shots? The pictures grew slightly grainy in close-up, were clearer to see when the camera pulled back. But they were still worth watching, and the patron actually placed one hand on the screen as if he might feel Lissa's skin through it.

He closed his eyes for a moment, imagining himself in Colin's place. When he opened his eyes, Lissa's face filled the screen in an extreme close-up, as if she were staring directly at him. As if she knew who he was and what he was up to. He had to shake his head to clear the image.

Then he watched, mesmerised, as the powerful rush of an orgasm flickered over Lissa's face. *This* is what he would watch, repeatedly, as he came. In a way, it would be like climaxing with her together.

Chapter Thirty-six

*P*aris, a little bit after dawn, reminded Lissa of a party before the guests had arrived. Shop-owners had begun to draw up the metal gratings in front of the windows, although no customers waited outside. Small round tables stood at attention on the pavements, but their chairs were empty, no patrons bent their heads together over cappuccinos or lattes or tiny espressos. The pavements were clean and still wet from the early morning washings, yet the only other pedestrians Lissa saw were several sleepy-looking Parisians out walking their minuscule dogs.

In response to the cool morning air, Lissa wore a crimson V-neck sweater of Colin's over her white T-shirt and faded jeans. Rather than rolling up the sleeves of the sweater, she let them dangle past her fingertips, keeping her hands warm. She liked the way the sweater smelled, the hint of Colin's cologne, and beneath that, the subtle scent of his skin. It was warm and comforting, and she brought one sleeve up to her face as she walked, inhaling deeply.

The previous day's activities had left her in a bit of a daze, and this morning she'd decided to take a walk while attempting to get her thoughts together. She'd left

Colin asleep in the apartment, leaving a short note to say that she'd gone out for an early coffee and would be back soon. She knew that he wouldn't mind. He understood that Lissa sometimes needed time alone. Even at their apartment in London, she often went out for early morning strolls by herself, in general after their most extreme nights.

'*Bonjour*,' she said, nodding to a shopkeeper who was rolling up the metal grating from in front of his windows. She could smell the scent of freshly baked baguettes and her stomach growled. She wouldn't buy one yet, she decided. She'd wait until she was on her way back to the apartment so that it would be warm and fresh when she brought it to Colin.

As she walked, she tried to remember exactly how she'd felt the afternoon before. Seeing the photographs of herself on display in the Paris erotic art museum had, momentarily, seemed more than she could handle. It had made her think that maybe she wasn't ready for Colin or his lifestyle. Still, this morning, in the grey light of day, she felt differently. The simple act of wearing Colin's sweater, of feeling at ease in his scent, let her know that she wouldn't end things. How could she? Not now, when he had issued her a challenge, daring her to find something more shocking than he had, asking her to come up with a scenario of her own.

Lissa strolled along the boulevard St Germain des Prés without seeing much of the surroundings. Part of her brain registered the sights she passed: café Flor, the old church, the Odéon metro stop. Then, as it had on the previous afternoon, her mind wandered back to Beau. The things that had bothered her in college now seemed somewhat endearing. The way he would show up in the middle of the night, unannounced, and try to get her to go down to the Santa Monica pier, to make love on a blanket spread beneath the worn, wooden boards. Had she ever done any of the things he'd wanted to? Some of his ideas had seemed shocking to her then, too, but they paled to the actions of her new life with Colin.

In the blur of memories, she located a specific instance, as if pulling it from a file drawer in her mind. The memory was from ten years before. She had just signed the lease on a new apartment, but her furniture hadn't arrived yet. Beau, on the pretence of checking out her new digs, had asked her to show him the place. When they'd taken the full tour, which only lasted several minutes because it was a tiny one-bedroom apartment, he'd spread her out on the thick carpet in front of the fireplace and made love to her. Then he had turned her, so that she could see their reflections in the mirrored panelling surrounding the fireplace. She had never watched herself during sex before, and that had seemed dangerously intense at first, but what he'd said was even more so.

'I want to fuck you every different way.'

The dirty words had turned her on, which was something that surprised her.

'I want to fuck you with you on top, on the bottom, on the side. I want to take you from behind.'

She'd moaned, looking into his dark-brown eyes in the reflection, wishing she could find words to respond, but not having the nerve to talk back. Not having any idea what she would say.

'I want to spank your beautiful ass,' he told her finally, and that image had made her come. It was the first time she'd ever climaxed during intercourse without the help of manual stimulation, and then that had made her cry.

A woman with a tiny, barking dog suddenly stepped on to the kerb in front of Lissa, and she caught herself just shy of crashing into her. The near collision woke her from her trance. She looked around, getting her bearings, then taking a left off the boulevard and turning down one small, crooked street to the art district. On a previous trip to Paris, she had been charmed by the tiny galleries that filled one of the lovely little neighbour-

161

hoods bordering the Seine. Art would clear her head this morning. It always did.

The hustle and bustle of an open-air market caught Lissa's attention. She passed by the stalls filled with a dazzling array of flowers, fresh produce, fish and fowl. She caught sight of a pair of webbed duck feet and realised that the owner of the stand had displayed the feet of each type of bird for sale. This was something that wouldn't have set well within the American market, she knew. But the French shoppers seemed less squeamish. Americans ate just as much meat, but they liked buying it in plastic wrapped packages, with no possible connection to the original animal.

Stepping around the edge of the last stall, Lissa entered the neighbourhood she'd been looking for. Here were the galleries she remembered, the small storefronts that sometimes held amazing secrets of the art world. The first one Lissa passed displayed several landscapes. They were competent, but they did nothing for her and she walked by without slowing. The next gallery was filled with African artefacts. Lissa paused to observe a carved wooden mask. She imagined wearing it while Colin fucked her, but the idea was more humorous than erotic. It made her smile, and as she did, several men entering a bank across from the gallery looked at her. One smiled back, and Lissa flushed and hurried on.

She was headed for one particular gallery. She had visited it the year before to see a show put on by a friend of a friend. The work was magnificent, sexual and startling, and she wondered what would be on display this time. She couldn't expect the same type of work, but she found herself hoping that she would like it. Art was what she truly needed this morning. More than coffee. More than a croissant. She needed good art to make her feel at peace. Then she could concentrate on the assignment she'd been given by Colin.

Chapter Thirty-seven

Colin read Lissa's note, which she'd left on her pillow by his head, and then climbed out of bed. He stood naked in front of the window for a moment, glancing down at the street below. Several children were on their way to school, walking with their fathers. The scene appealed to him, as it always did, although he had no desire to be a dad himself. This didn't detract from his enjoyment at watching, sneaking a peek into a world he would never personally understand.

After a few moments, he lost interest in the scene and glanced around the apartment. He wanted a coffee and he considered going downstairs to the café on the corner, but then changed his mind. He would make a pot here, so that it was ready for Lissa when she got back. She liked to drink American coffee, rather than the turbo brew that the Parisians favoured.

As the coffee percolated, he slid into his robe and walked out on to the balcony to observe the neighbourhood slowly waking up. This was one of his favourite times of day. Especially in Paris. The light in the sky was a pinkish gold and it glistened on the windows of the apartment buildings around his. It was going to be a warm day, perfect for sightseeing with Lissa. If it had rained, he would have taken her to the Catacombs. But that adventure could wait for another day.

He felt good this morning. The scenario at the museum had gone according to plan – better than planned, really. And afterwards, he had taken her to dinner near the Palais Royal, had bought them each brandies and helped her to calm herself. She had seemed shaken at seeing her pictures on the walls of the museum, but she had quickly recovered. What had truly surprised him was to hear himself issue her a challenge, asking her to plan a scene for him. That wasn't part of his scheme at all, but at the light in her eyes, he'd known it was a good idea.

He watched now as a painter set up an easel in an apartment across the way. An idea awoke in Colin's mind and he waved to the man. He had seen him on the street before, but they had never spoken more than bland words of 'hello' and 'good day'. There'd been no reason to interact before now. Yet the apartments were close enough that the two men could speak.

In perfect French, Colin called out to him, inviting the man to come over for coffee. He had a proposition for him.

Chapter Thirty-eight

Slowly, Lissa walked past a small art gallery window, hesitating in front to see which local artists had been chosen for display. She hoped that she wouldn't be disappointed but, at first, she was. Filling the front window were simple charcoal sketches of nude women. Sitting, reclining, sprawled out on the floor. They were well done, but they didn't give Lissa the spark she was looking for. She almost walked on, with the thought in her head that she couldn't expect magic every time.

Then she saw it.

In the back of the gallery was a statue of a woman that startled Lissa enough so that she leant forward, touching the cold glass with her forehead. For a moment, the artwork had fooled her, and she'd thought it was real – a naked woman bent in a yoga position on the floor of the gallery. Lissa squinted, realising that the statue wasn't breathing: a mannequin, not a human. The artwork was life-size, with long dark hair that fell over its shoulders. Its face was down, so that Lissa couldn't see the expression. Lissa guessed that the work had been done in wax.

Would Colin like it? Would he see the possibilities of having a waxwork created of herself? She looked up to read the number of the shop, then glanced around the street to get her bearings. Sometimes she had trouble with directions in Paris, but as long as she knew where the Seine was, she could get back to the apartment. She felt herself growing aroused at the thought of bringing Colin back to the gallery once it had opened, of showing off her discovery.

No, she realised, she wouldn't show him after all. If he was interested in a true challenge, wanting to be as surprised by her as she had been by him, then she would not tell him about her discovery just yet. Instead, she would contact the artist herself.

The hours were posted on the door of the gallery. As Lissa was making note of them, she caught sight of a woman in the back of the gallery, not a model, but a living person. Lissa waved, hoping to get the woman's attention. The pixie-like redhead gave Lissa a sleepy look, but started towards the glass door.

While she was waiting, Lissa smiled as her plan slowly began to take form in her mind. The assignment to find a piece of artwork to re-create had been difficult, but now that she knew what she wanted, she felt both at ease and excited about what the future would bring.

Lissa didn't generally use her fame to her benefit. However, being the writer of a best-selling art book did have its privileges. When she told the gallery owner who she was, the woman beamed and pointed to a copy of Lissa's latest book, high on a shelf behind her desk.

'So you're Lissa Daniels,' the woman said.

Lissa nodded, and then carefully, in halting French, began to describe what she wanted. The flame-haired shopkeeper immediately interrupted her.

'In English,' she said, 'I think my English is better than your French.'

Lissa blushed and started again, aware that this wasn't going to be easy to explain in any language.

The woman held up her hand, then asked, 'What was your name before you were married?'

Lissa gave her a confused look before answering, 'Aronson.'

The gallery owner's eyes opened wide. 'I thought it was you. I am Gizelle Merlhou.' When Lissa didn't immediately respond, the woman continued, 'You visited my house once, during a year you spent in France.'

And slowly it came back to Lissa. She had spent her junior year abroad in Paris, studying at the American University. Gizelle had been a teacher's aide.

The woman touched her hair now. 'This was black before. I like a change.' Lissa nodded, then focused on the gallery owner's dark-blue eyes, which were outlined with a shimmering silver pencil. She remembered Gizelle's eyes, and the way she had hesitantly spoken English with the students. And she remembered her visit to the woman's apartment on the final day of school for a party, all of the artists and students gathering around and smoking, drinking champagne, toasting each other's work.

Gizelle explained that she had recently taken over the gallery from a friend, and that was why Lissa hadn't seen her the year before when she'd come to a show. But now that Lissa realised she knew the woman, how was she ever going to confess her desire?

Gizelle prompted her with fingers, beckoning. 'You were asking me –'

Lissa closed her eyes for a second, trying to find the confidence to state her request. When she opened her eyes, she focused on Gizelle's red lips, plump and full, partly open. From the look on the woman's face, Lissa thought she didn't understand what she was asking. But the shopkeeper caught on more quickly than Lissa expected.

'We will have to ask the artist, Roberto,' she said, 'but immediately.' She was already lifting the telephone. 'But

I think he will love the idea. It is just the type of concept that would tickle his fanny.'

'Fancy,' Lissa corrected, before she could stop herself.

The woman smiled at her and nodded, unconcerned by the correction. She was dialling now and then, in rapid-fire French, repeating the request to Roberto. As she waited, listening, she gave Lissa a quick nod. He would do it.

When she hung up the phone, the woman explained how it would work. 'Roberto will meet you tomorrow afternoon to make the casts. It will take two months before the statues are ready. That gives me the time to set up the exhibition. You can come back in several hours?'

Lissa nodded.

'And you will be in Europe when the statues are complete?'

Again, Lissa nodded. Then, after considering how it might sound, she explained the rest of her request. Gizelle, eyes bright, listened eagerly and began taking notes.

Chapter Thirty-nine

Colin left the curtains wide open. Lissa wouldn't question why. She liked to bring plenty of light into the apartment. And most likely she wouldn't see that the curtains were open in the apartment across the way, as well. Why should she notice? And if she did, why would she care?

He looked out the window again and saw that the painter, André, had moved his easel into a new location. The man nodded his head at Colin and pointed to the telephone, which rested on a stool next to the easel. Colin would dial André's number and the painter would hurry to his work station, ready to capture their love-making on canvas.

This wasn't something that Colin was going to give ARTLOVER. Not everything was part of the master plan. Some of Colin's actions were for him alone – and he couldn't wait to hang the picture of Lissa in his office, to be able to stare at her lovely face whenever he wanted to.

Even after she was gone.

Lissa arrived back at the apartment only moments later. She hurried in, kissing Colin and then handing over the baguette and brioche she had bought on the way back from the gallery. There was something furtive in the way she moved, and Colin thought to quiz her about it, but reconsidered. Yes, she was most definitely up to something, but he would let her get away with the feeling of pulling something over on him. At least for the moment. Right now, he was ready to put his latest plan into action, and that required concentration. He needed to position Lissa just so, in front of the window, needed to focus on distracting her enough so that she didn't notice what was going on in the apartment across the tiny street from them.

'I missed you,' Colin said, setting down the pastries and taking Lissa into his arms. He had only a blue flannel bathrobe on, was naked beneath it, and his cock pressed against Lissa through the soft material. She smiled and set her hand on it, stroking him firmly through the robe. Her hand worked him steadily for several moments, and the sensation was enough to make Colin want to come on the spot, but he had control of himself.

'The city is beautiful in the morning,' he said, leading her to the balcony. 'I'd like you to watch it while I make love to you.'

Make love. He sounded like a school kid. Still, that's how he was feeling this morning, warm and still slightly sleepy, excited by the prospect of capturing their actions on canvas. Lissa stepped into the bedroom to set down her purse and Colin used this moment to press 'redial' on the phone, letting it ring in André's apartment one time before setting the receiver back in the cradle.

Everything was perfect.

From across the way, the painter watched Colin and Lissa. At first, the couple stood together, talking. The woman, svelte and light-skinned with white-blonde hair that made her look Norwegian, appeared to be telling the man a story. She moved in an animated fashion, and

170

for a moment the painter wished he could hear what she was saying. Then he suddenly stopped caring because the woman was taking off her clothes, and this was even more captivating.

She moved slowly, as if she were doing a strip-tease, and André watched, drawing quick sketches of her movements, hardly bothering to look down at the paper at all. He worked with a charcoal pencil, stealing quick glances at his sketches before smudging lines with the ball of his thumb to capture the action, the swirl of her hair, the graceful arc of her arm. She was gesturing to the man to come to her, and the painter watched as Colin moved forward. Would he strip, as well, and take her on the balcony, as he'd planned?

Not right away. Instead, he grabbed the naked woman by the wrist and pulled her over to the sofa. The painter moved closer to the window to watch, certain that he wouldn't be caught by the woman. She had enough to deal with as Colin pulled her over his lap, and caught her wrists in one hand.

Colin hadn't mentioned anything like this, and André watched, mesmerised. The woman struggled, for just a moment, before catching herself. Then she held herself perfectly composed as the man spanked her naked ass. The painter stopped sketching, shocked enough to drop his charcoal pencil. He could hear the sound of the man's hand connecting with the woman's bare bottom, and it excited him in a way that he wouldn't have expected.

After several good, hard spanks, the man let the woman go and then quickly stripped out of his robe before taking the lovely blonde in his arms. André retrieved his pencil and sketched the embrace. The couple were entwined, like one of the ancient statues of lovers displayed at the Louvre or the Musée d'Orsay. It was a timeless pose, and André flipped another page in his sketchbook to a fresh sheet of paper. He wished that he could tell the models to hold their position. He

171

needed a few more minutes to truly capture their bodies, their emotions, with his pencil. But he'd only got half-way through the sketch when Colin made his move.

He set the scene just as he'd promised André earlier, positioning Lissa against the balcony, face forward. André's curtains were half-closed and his apartment was dark. He didn't think she could see him. Yet it was surreal to have her faced towards him, separated only by the smallest distance, as she and her lover rocked against one another.

He wished that he could see her from the backside, would have liked to have witnessed the way her freshly spanked ass looked. But her face was what Colin had asked for, and the painter reached for a freshly sharp-ened pencil and continued to sketch quickly. He wanted to own it all. Colin had requested something very specific: the look on Lissa's face as she came. But in order to capture this one emotion, André needed to familiarise himself with her features, the way her eyelids fluttered as she grew more excited, the flush to her cheeks that indicated a heat he wished he could feel with the palm of his hand.

Lissa made a noise like a dove as she started to come, a cooing sound that stirred André deep within himself. He would have liked to have set the sketchbook down and undo his slacks. It would only take a few strokes for him to climax, and he could visualise it, standing behind the gossamer light curtain, shooting his come against the sheer fabric as it pressed against him in the morning breeze.

But this was a job. He had to concentrate. Later, he could spread his drawings around him on the floor, spiralling to look at each sketch as he worked himself with the same determination as he moved his pencil on the pad. That would be his reward for keeping his head together now. Still, he couldn't help but stroke himself once, through his faded, paint-stained khakis as Lissa made that sweet sound again, the soft coo that seemed uncontainable, as if she didn't know the moaning cry had come from her.

André sensed when they were close to finishing – it was obviously just a quickie – and he sketched even faster, then finally stopped and moved even closer to the window, still hidden behind the sheer curtains.

There. The look on her face as she came was sublime. Raw and yearning, filled with a desperation and then, as the climax flooded through her, a glow of total satisfaction. He didn't have to draw it. The look would be etched in his mind for ever.

Book Four:
Cheat

When you get to the point where you cheat for the sake of beauty, you're an artist.

– Max Jacob

Chapter Forty

Colin had decided to cheat. ARTLOVER wouldn't know it. Not by his e-mails or the gifts he sent via overnight delivery or through channels on the Internet. But still, Colin no longer felt bound by the rules of their agreement. Raised up on one elbow, he watched Lissa sleeping at his side.

'Plans change,' Colin said aloud – not realising he'd spoken the words until Lissa stirred in her sleep, raising her sweet face towards his at the sound of his voice. After making love on the balcony, they had collapsed on the sofa together, curled around each other in the warm morning sunlight. Now, Colin stroked Lissa's hair gently and she fell back asleep.

Oh, she was lovely. But that's not why Colin wanted to keep her. There was something deeper going on inside him. A turmoil he hadn't experienced for years. Usually, he was able to contain his emotions as cleanly as if they didn't exist. Now, he realised that he had been living a lie. He had been robotically sterile in his relationships. If he didn't let anyone get close to him, then he wouldn't get hurt.

Lissa had managed to break through his walls, his defences, and he couldn't believe he was losing control.

Not him. He'd always had the ability to remain calm when crises arose. This skill contributed to his expertise as a good doctor. So how could he explain his lack of control now? He couldn't.

The thing of it was that it felt good. Wanting her. Needing her. It felt amazing. He knew there would be a price to pay for it. There always was. But he had to trust his own emotions, and they were screaming at him not to let her go. So even though he had received an e-mailed request from the patron, he ignored it in favour of his own plans.

What Lissa didn't realise – and, of course, she realised very little about the truth behind their relationship – was that his scheme of re-creating works of art was just that. A scheme. Something that he thought would appeal to her artistic sensibilities. He was turned on by their actions. Definitely. Who wouldn't be? But there were other things that brought him more pleasure, other fantasies aside from those he'd explored with her. Today, he would share several to see how she responded.

He wondered what she would say if she knew the pleasures that awaited her. And he smiled and then gently woke her with a kiss.

Lissa was surprised when Colin suggested a day of sightseeing. She had never pictured him in the role of a tourist – and besides, she knew that he had spent months at a time in France. He owned an apartment here, for God's sake. Why would he want to visit the clichéd places with her? Still, she didn't argue. Their morning on the balcony had left her feeling satisfied and ready for anything.

But since this was Colin, the tour was unique. No guide book route for him. No normal tourist attire, either. Before leaving the apartment, he slipped the nipple clamps on Lissa and tightened the tiny screws, letting her know that a day of decadence awaited her.

It was only two blocks to the nearest metro stop. They walked past a florist's shop, past a café where men in blue work jumpers were drinking espressos on their mid-morning break. Lissa adored the environment, could understand why Colin chose to keep a place here. This wasn't a fancy neighbourhood, but the residential feel was somehow nicer than similar areas of southern California.

During their metro ride, they changed lines twice, but Lissa kept her mouth closed and didn't ask where he was taking her. The surprises kept her guessing, and she enjoyed the feeling of being off-guard. Would he choose a museum such as The Musée d'Orsay to bring her to? Perhaps, he would take her to the Eiffel Tower, fondling her in the lift as they rode to the top floor. She could visualise that easily, could even imagine him fucking her on the top platform of the famous tourist site. Impossible, she knew, even for someone like Colin. But wouldn't it be breathtaking, feeling him enter her while she was able to view the entire panorama of the Parisian landscape spread out before her.

As they stepped from the metro into the crisp sunlight, she reminded herself of the one fact that she always seemed to forget: with Colin, things were never what they appeared to be. He might suggest that they visit the sights marked on some touristy map, but there was no way they would behave as normal tourists. Because across the street from the metro stop was the entrance to a graveyard. *This* was where Colin was taking her.

Without a word, Colin led Lissa up the stone steps and through the cemetery. She took in the mausoleums, some several hundred years old. Many had cracked stained-glass windows and bars covering the doors. As they progressed through the graveyard, the sites grew older. Some were disturbed by trees, the roots knocking over the headstones and making odd ripples in the earth.

Lissa had never been to a cemetery in Paris before, and she stared, interested in the sights around her. Yet she was wary, wondering what Colin had in mind. There must be a reason for bringing her here. As Colin motioned to the area of the cemetery where they were headed, the sky above them, which had been clear all morning, now began to fill with clouds. Unlike the ones that had been strewn overhead the day before, these were heavy and grey, bulging with rain. Fat raindrops began to fall, and Lissa wished she'd brought an umbrella with her. She was surprised to see that Colin was without his. She'd thought that a Londoner would always have an umbrella. Maybe Colin would turn round, lead them back to the metro and choose another tourist spot to visit. Somewhere dry. Instead, as they passed other tourists who hurried towards the exit, some holding maps like umbrellas over their heads, Colin just smiled at Lissa and pulled her onward.

'This way,' Colin said, pointing.

It was an old grave. So old that the name was unreadable, and next to it stood a tiny building, a place in which relatives could mourn. She squinted to see if she could read the name on the grave, and then felt Colin's arms around her, pulling her against him so that she could feel his cock pressing at her through his slacks. Suddenly, Lissa realised that it didn't matter who was buried beneath this location. That wasn't the point of their visit. Colin was going to fuck her here. He had found a place that no one else would have ever considered, and he had managed to keep her in the dark yet again.

'Are you ready, Lissa?'

She should have guessed his plan. Instead, she'd been concentrating on the pull of the chain running between her nipples, on the way her ass felt beneath the tight slacks, still warm from the spanking Colin had given her earlier in the morning. He always seemed to know how to keep her guessing. But now that they'd arrived at the building, and she understood what Colin was up to, it made her stop, digging her heels against the cobbled road and pulling back on him with her hand.

'Shelter from the storm,' he said, raising his eyebrows at her.

'I don't want to go in there.'

'You're getting all wet,' he said next, as if waiting out a rainstorm in a cemetery was the most common thing to do. 'And I bet you're getting all wet,' he said again, with a different tone, making Lissa blush. Instantly, she was aware that he was right. She was wet between her legs, but why? Was it at the thought of fucking here? Or was it a learned response to the way Colin was touching her?

She didn't have long to contemplate. Colin simply pulled again on her hand, driving her forward and into the minuscule building. Instantly, his fingers were on the waistband of her slacks, pulling them down just far enough for comfort. And then his own slacks were open and he was taking her from behind. Lissa stared out into the cemetery, at the rain falling on the gravestones. At the greyness that surrounded them. A few painted concrete flowers were the only brightness that she saw, and even these had faded after years of exposure to the elements.

Colin slid his cock inside her, fucking her to the beat of the steady raindrops as they fell overhead. His hand slipped under her shirt to tug on the chain that ran between the clamps. Oh, Christ, that was good. The tug of it against her flesh made her pussy throb. A concept flashed through her mind – what would the clamps feel like on her nether lips? What would it feel like to have one on her clit? She knew that all she had to do was mention the thought to Colin and he would make it happen.

Still, she couldn't believe they were doing this here. And yet her body responded, as Colin must have known it would. She was wet, and excited, and she found herself moving against him, her eyes shut tight, head back, as he continued to pound into her.

She hoped that no one would catch them. She hoped that they would go unnoticed. And then, as Colin's cock sped up in its ride between her thighs, she simply hoped she would come. The magic of it, contracting around him to the rhythm of the rain pounding overhead, drove out any other thoughts of what was right. What was polite. All she wanted was release.

Colin gave it to her, his fingers wandering all over her body, up to her breasts to tug on the chain between them, then down to her clit, rubbing in rapid circles up and over, again and again. Lissa lost herself to the moment, letting the feeling of dreamy pleasure take her to a higher level.

'Oh, God,' she moaned softly, unable to keep quiet. 'Oh, that's so good.'

Colin didn't respond verbally, but his body pounded against hers, letting her know that she'd pleased him, that he was in tune with her. Physically. Mentally. Lissa leant back against him as she came, feeling his arms come up around her and hold her tightly to him.

Afterwards, as Colin led her from the building, her wet shirt clung to her skin and her hair was damp and matted. From the cemetery, Lissa was certain they would return to the apartment. At least, to get cleaned up. They didn't. Colin had other plans, and as usual he refused to tell Lissa what they were until it was absolutely necessary.

Chapter Forty-one

Who cared what people thought? That was Colin's motto. If it worked for him and Lissa, then it didn't matter what a stranger might say. He was trying to explain this to his lover, through actions rather than words. That was his plan. First, by making love at the cemetery, and now, as he led her back along the rain-streaked cobblestones, to the next stop on his twisted tour. He was pleased to note the flush of excitement in Lissa's eyes, their colour a darker grey than normal, rivalling the colour of the heavy clouds that remained above them.

The emotions within Colin continued to build. Over the past four months, he had tamed Lissa's need for questions, had moulded her to suit his own purposes. How could he be expected to let her go? She was his match. His perfect partner. He wondered when she'd realise that. He hoped it would be soon.

Still, rather than helping him to feel at ease, their fuck session in the cemetery left him on edge, yearning for sexual release all over again. It was as if each time they made love, he needed it more. That was fine. He could fuck her all day if he had to. He knew she would never complain.

His cock stirred in the confines of his faded Levis, and as he and Lissa made their way out of the Père Lachaise, he thought of pressing her against one of the walls of the cemetery, not caring if anyone caught them. But he changed his mind. That wasn't enough. He needed more.

But because it was him with these needs, he couldn't simply bring her back to the apartment and tease her with sweet sensations all afternoon. No. He had to scratch his itch in the oddest way possible. If they weren't going to incorporate a bit of pain with their lovemaking, then he had to add some other spice – the thrill of almost being caught, the danger of exposure, or in the case of this afternoon's plans, a bit of morbid curiosity.

He was taking her to another one of his favourite locations, and his skin prickled all over at the thought.

The grey concrete stairs to the Catacombs spiralled downwards. Lissa counted them in her head as they walked, knowing that they would have to walk up an equal amount in order to escape from the place. The walls had a dank, musty smell to them. It wasn't entirely unpleasant, more of a natural odour, like the scent from slowly decaying leaves, but Lissa took shallow breaths to avoid it anyway. Yet by the time they reached the bottom of the stairs, there was simply no more fresh air and she had to inhale deeply to catch her breath. She found herself wishing desperately that Colin had chosen a different sightseeing spot to take her to. Perhaps they could have visited the Arc de Triomphe. She had been there once, but it would have been different with Colin. Everything was different with him.

Colin put his hand on her shoulder, nodding to the tour group in front of them where a guide was explaining the history of the Catacombs. Lissa didn't understand French well enough to catch what the woman was saying, but it didn't really matter because she was too captivated with the first display of bones to pay much attention to the words. Colin leant forward to translate for her, giving her the choicest facts, the ones that would stick in her mind – some sounded like tall tales, meant to frighten the visitors, but he whispered them to Lissa anyway.

'A man got lost down here, once,' he told Lissa. 'He went down in his wine cellar and found a way into the tunnels. They discovered him seven years later, another pile of bones to join the rest.'

Lissa shuddered. Imagine walking around in the maze of tunnels, trying to find your way out. She felt suddenly claustrophobic as the guide took them around a sharp turn and the walls instantly narrowed. A child in front of Lissa grabbed her mother's hand and held on tight. Lissa did the same with Colin.

But why should she hold on to him for protection? He was her tormentor, torturer, always pushing her to the edge of her limits. And he did so now, holding on to her so that they were at the back of the crowd before nodding for her to step over a thin chain that separated one cavern from the main tour.

'I don't think we're supposed to go in there,' Lissa whispered. Colin gave her a look and then pulled her after him.

'I won't lose you,' he assured her, 'if you promise to behave.'

Lissa promised. Quickly. She didn't want to turn out like the man whose mummified remains were discovered seven years later after his disappearance. Of course, Colin would never lose her, she understood this, but she still said, 'I'll behave,' her voice quavering at the words.

Then, as Colin hurried her around a corner, she began to grow excited. She'd never have thought she would want to make love again so quickly after their time in the cemetery, but there she was, ready again. She always was ready for Colin.

He didn't speak to her as he led her down the dark tunnel. There were no bones in this area, and she could easily see how someone might get lost. All of the caverns looked the same, moulded from the earth, their ceilings so low in places that she had to duck to avoid hitting her head.

Lissa knew exactly why he wanted to take her here. There was a picture in one of his books about a concert held in the Catacombs. People had come down to this place to hold secret parties, and this was exactly what Colin wanted to do. Hold a private party in his own style, which meant that she was not surprised when he finally stopped, pushing her back against one of the clay walls and slowly unbuttoning her blouse.

She felt his warm mouth against her nipples, first one, then sliding over to the other. Her nipples encased in the clamps were instantly erect, and the feel of his tongue, and then teeth as he gently bit them, was enough to make her start to moan.

'Let yourself go,' Colin said at the first indication she was losing her inhibitions. 'Make a noise.'

'I can't.' She didn't want to draw attention to herself, could just imagine the horrified expressions of the tourists coming around the bend to find them. This was even stranger than their escapade at the cemetery. Who would have thought to choose a place like this? Only Colin.

'No one cares what you do,' Colin said, 'nobody but me. Everyone is concerned with their own selves, their own lives.'

'They'll hear us.'

He had a quick fix for this problem, placing the palm of his hand over her mouth. 'Yell into that. You'll still be able to scream, but the sounds will be muffled. If anyone hears you, they'll simply think the place is haunted.' He paused, looking at her, at the fear and desire in her eyes. 'And it probably is.'

She couldn't think about what he was telling her, because as soon as he finished talking, he went back to kissing her nipples, licking them, nipping fiercely at her skin before moving down to undo her pants and spread them open. He pressed his tongue against her panties, where she was still wet from their cemetery tryst, and she thought she would come just from the sensation. The urges built up inside her, and since Colin kept his hand over her mouth, she was able to let it out.

It started with a simple moan, low and hoarse, deep in the back of her throat.

'Louder,' Colin hissed, now rolling his tongue along the slit between her pussy lips, still shielded from his mouth by the thin skin of her panties. His tongue dug against the wet fabric, and the feeling of separation, of not having the contact of his mouth, brought her almost to the edge. If he would touch her, take her underpants down and press his face into her, then she would scream. Could she tell him this? Would he guess it for himself?

He did, using his free hand to slide her panties down her thighs, getting his face right up into her so that she felt his breath on her cunt a second before his mouth met her clit. It was too good. Finally feeling his lips there, his wet tongue meeting her own wet nether lips.

'I'm going to –' Lissa murmured, and Colin slid one finger inside her, then another, giving her something warm and satisfying to contract on.

Her knees gave way as she came, and Colin grabbed her in his arms, muffling her screams against his shoulder and holding her as those contractions ran through her body.

Chapter Forty-two

Colin felt pleased. He had given the patron what he wanted with the video, and he had played on his own terms with Lissa, as well. His new concept was this: at some point, she was going to be forced to choose between them. This is the way he would deal with the issue. He wanted her to understand which parts of the relationship had been orchestrated and which parts had been created by him alone.

The graveyard. The Catacombs. These were the types of ideas that best suited Colin. And he felt that Lissa warmed to them, even when she started out frightened or disconcerted at his suggestions.

On their trip back to London, Colin didn't try anything sexual. He let her sleep at his side, exhausted from the whirlwind of activity he had put her through. As she slept, however, he took her hand in his and gently, slowly, worked the platinum band off her ring finger.

It was time to let that go.

Chapter Forty-three

*B*ack into their normal schedule, Lissa caught herself often thinking about their trip to Paris. People were looking at pictures of herself. She couldn't decide how this made her feel. Excited, yes. And beautiful in a way she'd never felt before. While she worked, she would catch herself daydreaming, a text in front of her open, but unread. Then she would have to force herself back into it.

Sometimes, she and Colin worked in his office at the same time. One afternoon, while she tried to read, she heard him checking his mail. The modem roared to life, and Colin entered his password and began to read. From her desk across the room, Lissa couldn't make out who the mail was from. But Colin seemed disturbed by whatever it said. She saw him frown, and then shake his head, typing in a brief answer before sending it. Then he switched off the modem, stood and walked to Lissa's desk. She quickly lowered her eyes to her book, and he kissed the back of her neck, sending shivers throughout her body. Just one well-placed kiss could have her ready for anything he wanted to do. She wondered whether he would take her now, spread her out on her desk, knock the books on to the floor, lift her skirt and fuck her. Instead, he kissed along her neck to reach her right ear, telling her that he would be back later. He had something scheduled this afternoon.

The door to their apartment hadn't fully shut before Lissa was on Colin's computer. She'd kept his password memorised and hidden in a folder on the desktop. Now, she would finally use it to unlock whatever secrets Colin was keeping from her.

The first piece of e-mail was exactly what she'd expected. A doctor friend of Colin's requesting advice on a case. This obviously wasn't what had disturbed him. She went on to the next letter. This was slightly less mundane. A few lines from his agent regarding a reprint arrangement for one of Colin's medical books. Lissa went on to the third letter.

She didn't understand it right away. The letter was addressed to 'CAD' and was from the person named ARTLOVER who had written before. There were no pleasantries at the beginning, it simply launched into the body of the letter with the preciseness and lack of emotion of a telegram.

CAD,
    Most pleased. Good work so far. Would like to take things up a notch. Trust that you understand what this means.
    ARTLOVER

Lissa read the letter twice before deciding that she would snoop some more. She opened Colin's file of old letters and searched for an e-mail address that matched the sender's. There was one letter dated one week before, from when she and Colin had still been in Paris. She opened this letter and read:

CAD,
    A video e-mail. How clever. Much more thorough than I'd expected. Please continue with the plan.
    ARTLOVER

A video. And sent by e-mail over the Internet. Lissa had seen this device demonstrated at the Frankfurt book fair. Although she had no use for videos in her line of work, the concept of electronically sending a movie had been exciting. From what she'd seen at the show, she knew that this meant that there was probably a copy on Colin's computer somewhere. She hit a few keys to locate his outgoing mail, scanning the list for one with a video file attachment. It had been sent two days after their tryst in the Paris erotic art museum. She realised this as she hit the 'play' button, understanding what she was going to see in the seconds before it came on the screen.

There she was. Her back to the camera, long platinum hair over her leather jacket. And then there was Colin, slowly undressing her. How had he managed this, she wondered. And who was he sending it to? Surprisingly, she didn't feel anger, just shock combined with the desire to know what was going on. Was he bragging to a friend, a sort of e-mail version of guy's locker-room behaviour? No. It was apparently more than that. Based on the e-mail responses, it seemed as if Colin was acting as an agent for the man. Doing things that the man requested.

So where did Lissa fall into all this?

She closed the video file and looked back through the rest of ARTLOVER's e-mails. There were only two that she could find. One commented on the photographs, which she supposed must be the ones Colin had taken in Hamburg. The other mentioned Frankfurt, and Lissa realised from Colin's reply that he had known about her before their meeting. It hadn't been chance at all. Her heart pounded. Who was behind their set-up?

She considered confronting Colin, and she stood from the computer, pacing. But then, she realised, she'd have to explain how she knew. And he'd forbidden her early on to read his mail. Like Bluebeard, she suddenly thought, who had told his wives not to open the door to his cupboard – but one by one they had fallen for the trap and he had killed them. Colin wouldn't kill her, she knew this. But he might end their affair. Was it worth it to her?

It didn't take her more than a second to answer that question: no, she wanted to stay with him, to continue doing what they were doing.

But she also wanted to know what was going on.

Standing, her hands on her hips, she tried to figure out what to do next. If only she had a friend to discuss things with, someone she could talk with and discuss her situation. But there was no one she knew well enough in London. Perhaps Gizelle, the art gallery owner ... No. Even if she knew the woman better, the language barrier would be too difficult to broach.

Finally, she came to a decision. She would not mention the letters to Colin, but she would be more aware from this point on. She would play the detective and discover exactly who this mysterious patron of the arts really was, and why he'd connected with Colin to set up this remarkable love affair for her.

The key turned in the lock of the front door and Lissa quickly hurried back to her desk, bending over her art book. When Colin entered the room from the hall, Lissa sat in the leather chair, her reading glasses in place, her expression one of intense concentration.

'Enough work,' Colin told her, bending to kiss her forehead lightly, then lifting her glasses off and setting them next to her notepad on the desk. 'It's time to play.'

After one week, Lissa still didn't know who ARTLOVER was. Not to say she hadn't put her best sleuthing skills to the test. Each time Colin left her alone in the apartment she scanned his e-mails. She had gone through his files, both on the computer and in his drawers, searching for further clues. If Colin kept a journal, he had hidden it too well for her to discover. Aside from a few new sex toys, some still in their boxes, he hardly had anything of interest in his cabinets.

Before continuing her search, Lissa lingered over one

of the toys, an extremely large strap-on dildo. Why would Colin have bought this? It was obviously not for him to use on her – and she simply couldn't fathom him asking, or allowing, her to use it on him. That thought was ludicrous. She carefully put the item back in its bag before returning to her search.

And at the same time, she found herself looking for her ring. She had lost it on the last journey, and although Colin swore he hadn't seen it, said he hadn't noticed her without it, she felt suspicious of him.

After Colin did arrive home from work, she tried her best to listen in on his phone conversations, and made it her practice to get home before he did so that she would hear the messages on the answering machine.

Nothing.

So when Colin told her to pack her bags, that he was taking her on a trip to Amsterdam, she was instantly relieved. Here, she would learn more. She sensed it. This was the first time Colin had told her in advance where they were going, and she wondered why but didn't bother to ask him. If he didn't want to tell her, he wouldn't, no matter how many times she posed the question.

'Pack for a week,' he said, 'I'm not sure how long we'll stay, but it's always nice to be prepared.'

Yes, she thought. It is nice to be prepared. And she wasn't prepared in the least. She stared over at him, taking in his neatly combed hair, tortoiseshell spectacles firmly in place as they always were unless he was fucking her. His appearance hadn't changed at all since they'd met. He never let her see him in disarray.

While he went through his mail, she stared at him. He was secretive, self-contained, unbreakable. Yet it was now her one desire to find out what was behind his poised and careful appearance. Because even though she'd assured herself that it didn't matter, two questions consumed her waking hours.

Who was he working with? And why?

* * *

ART IS . . . LISSA the e-mail said. *Please come to witness her transformation. In person.*

ARTLOVER stared at the e-mail invitation from CAD. It was time, Colin said, to introduce him to the pleasures of the flesh, Lissa's flesh. The patron agreed with this, had been expecting it, but he found himself intensely nervous at the thought of being with her in person. What would happen? What would she do?

His worries didn't stop him from buying the plane ticket, from making the necessary preparations, from dreaming about her as he reclined in the first class seat. For months he had waited for this day, and now it was almost upon him.

Yet he felt a deep sense of trepidation. Colin wasn't letting him in on all the facts. He knew this, understood it, and could do nothing about it. He had to put his faith in Colin, but he promised himself to pay attention to what was going on.

Because Colin was definitely up to something.

Chapter Forty-four

'You don't want to stay in the heart of the city,' Colin explained as the cab wove its way gently through the traffic, parting the tangle of pedestrians and cyclists. 'Amsterdam can be a zoo.'

From the chaos around them, Lissa immediately agreed with this statement. She'd never seen such a motley assortment of people and vehicles. She was thankful to be safe in the taxi, safe with Colin's arm casually resting on her shoulder. Without turning away from the window, she asked him where they were staying. She knew that once they'd arrived in a city, he would often give her more information about his plans. He did so now.

'I've booked us reservations at the Princess. It's a hotel on the outskirts of town,' Colin told her, going on to reminisce about his previous visits to the hotel. He'd stayed there several times before, liking the quietness of the location, the subdued charm of the hotel itself.

Would ARTLOVER be there? Lissa wondered. The most recent e-mail to Colin indicated that he would be. Lissa felt her heart pounding at the thought. She had finally deciphered her feelings. There had never been anger at Colin for tricking her, only a desire to know who it was behind the affair. Someone, aside from herself and Colin, was enjoying the fruits of their lovemaking. This thought turned Lissa on more than any she'd ever had.

She wondered if she knew this mysterious patron. The only person she could think of who would be interested in her this way was Beau. And after choosing Marcus over him, he had simply faded out of her life. But recently, it was true that she had found herself thinking of him more and more often. How would she feel if the patron turned out to be him? She didn't know, wouldn't know until she saw him face to face.

Hoping Colin wouldn't read anything into her silence, Lissa busied herself by focusing on the chaos out the window. The streets were so narrow it was hard to believe how much activity was crammed into them. She stared in awe as the bicyclists manoeuvred gracefully around the obstacles of pedestrians, trolley tracks and bumps in the cobbled roads. Many of the bicycles were painted, and Lissa thought that some would have made a beautiful exhibit. Although she didn't see any tandems, the cycles often carried more than one rider: a mother and two children, or a boy with a girl clinging to the back. It all seemed very romantic to Lissa until, without warning, a slender trolley suddenly screamed its way past, and Lissa involuntarily flinched against Colin. No one else in the crowd seemed concerned by the proximity of the fast-moving vehicle. The walkers and bicyclists simply parted for the trolley and then closed in after it went past.

'The mess can look like fun,' Colin continued, 'but it's better to be able to escape in the evenings to a more private location.'

Lissa nodded and then went back to staring out the window. The sights thrilled her. She'd never been to Amsterdam, but from the stories she'd heard, she was sure she would adore the city. There was a famous Van Gogh museum that she wanted to visit, as well as several smaller galleries that were known to have extremely good selections. And then, of course, there were the stories of sex and sin that she knew Colin would introduce her to.

She looked out of the taxi, wondering where the girls in windows were. So far, she had only seen cafés, coffee houses (which she knew were really places to buy marijuana), tourist stores, bars and clubs. No prostitutes stood behind glass, beckoning to passers-by.

And then the cab pulled in front of a lovely brick building – they'd arrived. As Colin had promised, the hotel was small and intimate, with a tiny bar on the first floor and then five levels of rooms. Walking down the hall to their room on the top level, Lissa heard nothing from the other guests. The walls must be brilliantly soundproofed, she decided, and then wondered fleetingly if this was one of the reasons that Colin had chosen the place. Would he do things to her to make her scream? She turned to look at him, but his face held no answer.

'Don't bother,' Colin said as Lissa started to unpack. 'It's too pretty a day to waste any time. We can do that later.'

Lissa grabbed her faded denim jacket and followed Colin from the room. He took her hand as they waited for the lift, and once they'd entered it, he kissed her. Colin's kisses always transformed Lissa. Even now that she did not fully trust him, his lips on hers erased all other thoughts. She closed her eyes as he brought his hands up to cradle her face. It started out as a sweet kiss, just lips on lips, but before breaking away, he bit her bottom lip. Hard. Instinctively, Lissa sucked in the bruised lip, now opening her eyes wide to stare at him.

'Are you ready?' he asked.

Was he going to fuck her here? In the lift? No. They'd reached the bottom floor and Colin steered her out of the hotel and on to the street.

'Are you, Lissa?' he asked again, as they made their way along a winding street towards one of the canals.

She thought to ask 'ready for what?' but she was too smart for that. She knew what he wanted her to say, and she squeezed his hand and answered, 'Of course.'

'Ready for anything?' he asked next, pointing to what looked like a little café on the corner. Lissa smiled when she saw it. Little cafés in Amsterdam were generally 'coffee houses'. Yes, they sold coffee, and sometimes cakes or muffins, but they also sold marijuana. Colin was going to get her stoned. So this was what he meant by ready for *anything*. She felt relieved. They had never done this together before, but it seemed an appropriate activity in Amsterdam. Colin steered her towards the coffee house, and this was where their official Amsterdam tour began.

Inside the Greenery, a bar lined the side of one room. Across from the bar were wooden tables and benches. Low velvet couches and soft, colourful pillows filled the second room. The place had a sumptuous, Mediterranean feel to it, and the other customers appeared deeply relaxed as they reclined on the sofas or sprawled on the benches. It exactly fitted Lissa's mental image of a den of iniquity.

At the entrance to the coffee house, Colin bought two pre-rolled joints and two shots of espresso. 'The first to relax you, the second to rev you up.'

'Won't I end up the same place I started?' she asked. 'Each one nulling out the other?' She wasn't trying to be funny. She really wanted to know.

Colin looked her over carefully. 'You've never smoked it,' he said quietly, 'have you?' He moved her towards two empty spaces on one of the sofas.

'I have,' Lissa insisted as she sat down, 'in college.'

Colin gave her a disbelieving look.

'It just never did much for me,' she continued.

'You mean, you didn't inhale, right? Like your President Clinton.'

Lissa flushed. 'I *did*,' she insisted. What a funny discussion. Why was she trying to make Colin believe that she had done something that was illegal in her country? She didn't know, but it seemed important that he believe her and not categorise her as someone who'd had no experiences before she'd met him. Despite what he thought, she wasn't totally naive. She remembered sitting on the worn leather couch in her boyfriend's apartment, inhaling deeply from a bong and then saying, 'When is it going to work? I don't feel anything.' Beau, who was a major stoner when he wasn't studying for the bar, had told her to calm down and just let it happen. But it had never happened.

With Colin, it happened right away. Two hits from the first joint had her body feeling warm and malleable. She leant back against the sofa, staring at a colourful Moroccan-style mural painted on the opposite wall. She was so relaxed that she didn't even think to critique it. Her mind simply accepted the fact that this was a decoration, not a piece of art that needed to be identified and dissected.

'Are you still ready for anything?' Colin asked her.

Uh oh. She turned away from the painting to catch the look in his green eyes. He was telling her something, but she didn't know what. Suddenly, it occurred to her that he knew she'd been snooping. That he knew about her knowing about him. Her heart pounded and she thought of explaining that she hadn't meant to find the e-mails. That she hadn't meant to poke around on his computer. But wasn't he the one who should be explaining things to her? When she looked at Colin again, she realised that he didn't know. Maybe it was the pot, working through her, making her paranoid. She took another hit, let it out slowly, and kissed him, breathing the words into him as she exhaled.

'Of course, Colin. Anything you have to offer.'

Chapter Forty-five

Colin went to buy a second coffee, and while he was gone, Lissa stared at her reflection in a mirror on one of the walls of the café. She was wearing black jeans and a pale-grey turtleneck sweater beneath her denim jacket. Her long legs were crossed, showing a few inches of black leather boots. With her blonde hair up in a ponytail, she looked like a college kid, someone who was in Amsterdam for a quick adventure before returning to school. She had seen many of these girls along the winding avenues as she and Colin had driven into Amsterdam, could read the desire for excitement on their faces.

'You do feel it, don't you?' Colin asked as he returned.

Lissa nodded and closed her eyes. 'Mostly,' she said, her voice half a sigh, 'what I feel is relaxed.' Maybe that's why marijuana hadn't worked on her in college. She had never felt relaxed, totally focused on her work as a student and unable to kick back. She'd missed a part of the college experience, she thought now, as the drug loosened her.

When she opened her eyes, she took a sip of the espresso he'd bought her. He was already on his second, but she hadn't started her first. The caffeine hit her right away, but it wasn't what she'd expected. Her heart didn't race and her face didn't flush. Instead, she felt more energised, but it didn't affect her buzz. What she most wanted to do was walk, explore the city through her new-found awareness. Colin seemed to understand her desire. As soon as she was finished with the coffee, he stood and held out a hand to her, helping her towards the exit.

Outdoors, her senses continued to be heightened. She noticed the colours of the clothes on the cyclists, the way the clouds hung low in the sky above them. She felt almost as if she were inside of a painting, experiencing the colours with her skin, her eyes, her mouth. Was this how marijuana affected everyone? If so, she could see why some people were stoned all the time. Every sensation was intensified and she couldn't keep from looking all around her. She wanted to stare at the magazine kiosk covered with a graffiti mural. But when Colin turned her in a different direction, she was just as captivated by the lush blooms of the open-air flower market.

Lissa was glad to have Colin's hand in hers, guiding her through the crowds until they'd reached one of the circular streets that ran along a canal. Lissa stared at the houseboats below them, at the gathering of brown and white ducks paddling along in the water. A mother duck took her squawking yellow ducklings for a late afternoon swimming lesson. While Lissa watched, a fat calico cat leapt from the street to the bow of one of the boats, as if he also wanted a closer look at the ducks.

After glancing at his watch, Colin took Lissa's hand and pulled her onward. Suddenly, she wondered whether they were truly just walking, out to look at the city's sights, or whether he had a plan. Even through the slightly altered feeling of her mind, she decided that he knew exactly what they were doing, exactly where he was taking her.

Didn't he always have a plan?

Chapter Forty-six

*S*ex while under the influence was intense. It was one of the few times that Colin could get off without needing to exert his power. Now, back at the hotel for a mini-sightseeing break, he had Lissa on her back with her legs over his shoulders. Still feeling the high from Amsterdam's magic weed, Colin took his time. He lapped and licked at Lissa's pussy until he could feel her delicious, creamy liquid against his lips. He adored the way she tasted, and he told her so.

'You're so sweet,' he murmured, without moving his mouth from her sex. 'So fucking sweet.'

Lissa felt the vibrations of his words against her, and even though she couldn't fully make out what he was saying, the pleasure at the sound brought her almost to climax. If he continued to speak into her cunt, she would come from that sensation alone. Her thoughts were clouded, hazy, and yet that somehow added to the pleasure.

She could understand now why her college boyfriend, Beau, had always wanted to make love while stoned. She'd never indulged with him, hadn't understood why he said the pleasure of reaching orgasm under the influence was a whole different experience from normal sex.

Now, she got it.

'Tell me what you want,' Colin said suddenly, bringing her around to the experience at hand. 'Tell me what you're thinking about.'

This was his favourite way to torment her. It wasn't a painful torture, like receiving a spanking over his lap. But, even now, after several months together, it was still difficult for her to share her fantasies. She stammered and blushed, unable to speak at first with the climax so close that she could practically taste it.

'I'll stop,' he said, as always, holding the carrot out ahead of her. 'I'll let you writhe there, unable to reach the finish.'

No, she didn't want that. She would tell him, would drag some other fantasy from the depths of her mind to share. The thought occurred to her, however, even in her somewhat stoned state, that if she shared a fantasy, he would undoubtedly work to bring it to fruition. He had done so again and again, so she would have to be careful about what she asked for. Wasn't that a moral in a children's story?

Be careful what you wish for, because it may come true.

In Colin's opinion, it was a wonderful fantasy. Lissa wanted to come while others around her watched. She had got the idea from a famous 60s-era black-and-white photograph. Colin had seen it in a photography magazine, and it had affected him instantly.

The picture showed a woman in the centre of a large mat, ringed off by velvet ropes as if she were a museum display. The model in the picture was naked, and masturbating. She acted as if she were unaware of her surroundings, her appearance one of total, personal surrender. But she wasn't alone. Around her, the patrons of the exhibit watched. They were the main part of the photograph, the important part. The expressions on their faces were extremely telling. The men stared openly, lustfully. The women looked as if they thought it was uncool to feel insecure. So their main expressions were ones of obvious false acceptance.

'I've always loved that picture,' Lissa said, 'since I first saw it.'

'And you want to be the girl in the picture?' Colin asked.

'To have all those people gathered around –' Lissa let it hang there, wondering how far Colin would go to make this come true.

Because she'd done as he asked, confessing to him, Colin let her reach the finish line. Every sensation was heightened. The wash of delight as her climax finally flowed over her felt brighter. Her nerve endings seemed to vibrate with pleasure. It was as if her body was an instrument, and Colin played it with his tongue and fingers, strumming her. She wished for an audience to watch this sexual concerto. Would they applaud at the finale? Would they give her a standing o for her lying down o?

Chapter Forty-seven

*T*hat afternoon found them outside of the Erotic Museum – which, Colin patiently explained, was different from the Sex Museum located in the centre of the city. By the door stood a black and white marble fountain in the shape of a giant penis. Lissa watched, delighted, as the water shot out from the top of it, forming a great gushing spray high in the air above.

'Only in Amsterdam,' Colin said, smirking. He thought the fountain was gauche, but Lissa seemed to like it, especially in her mind-altered state. He knew that when she wasn't stoned, she would have enjoyed the statue less. After letting her stare for a few minutes, he herded her into the museum, giving a quick nod to the lovely brunette behind the counter as he paid their fare.

Lissa caught the look exchanged between the woman and Colin, but she didn't know what it meant. She stared hard at the woman for a moment, reading the name tag pinned to her breast: Gina. As the girl counted back Colin's change, Lissa continued to observe her appearance. She had long, chestnut-coloured hair that was pinned back from her face with a silver barrette. Her bangs were cut short, in a Bettie Page style.

Gina suddenly looked up, catching Lissa's stare and

responding with an easy, slow-spreading smile. Lissa flushed and raised her gaze, looking quickly at posters taped to the wall behind Gina. One was for the art exhibit in Paris' Musée de l'Erotisme, photos of Lissa staring directly back at her. Gina saw what Lissa was looking at, and her smile broadened.

She did know something, didn't she?

Lissa realised that she was probably trying to read more into each encounter with Colin than was actually there. Still, she could guess that Colin had set something up in the museum, something that might actually top what he had done in Hamburg and in Paris. What that could be, however, boggled her mind. She stopped trying to second-guess Colin as he led her up the stairs to the museum's first floor.

'You're supposed to go to the top and work your way down,' he told her, explaining why they weren't stopping at the first level. 'Just like in Paris, except there's no lift here.'

Lissa forgot about Gina as she started to take in her surroundings. This museum was very different from the other two they had visited. Housed in an extremely narrow building, it was both smaller and less cared-for than either the one in Paris or Hamburg. In fact, it appeared to be shoddy. The red-painted walls were peeling in some places. The stairs were dirty. The whole place had a smudged feel to it. But none of this detracted from Lissa's experience. Sex could be dirty, she knew, and the enjoyment of art could be enhanced by its surroundings. Perhaps the artwork they were going to see was of a dirtier variety than the exhibits they'd viewed in the other museums.

At the top floor, Lissa noticed to her surprise that there wasn't any art on the walls. Instead, mannequins dressed in leather and vinyl were positioned in various scenarios. There was a dominance/submission scene going on in one corner, with a vinyl-clad dominatrix towering over a cowering, nearly-nude male slave.

Against a far wall, a man appeared to be propositioning a prostitute who had her hand out, ready to collect her fee. In the centre of the small room stood a chair with bindings. It was empty, ready for some poor submissive to be bound into place. Lissa realised this just as Colin slid his arms around her waist and carried her over to it.

'Not here,' Lissa said, before she could stop herself. She had seen the line of people waiting to get in. This time, there was no way she and Colin would be uninterrupted. The thought of being caught in the museum made her stomach do a flip-flop. But then, they hadn't been caught in Paris – aside from the videotape, which had been planned by Colin, anyway. So maybe they wouldn't be caught here.

'Are you disobeying me?' Colin asked, interrupting her thoughts. His green eyes gleamed brightly as he began to undress her.

Lissa bit her lip. She didn't think she wanted to disobey him, yet she wasn't ready for a public scene yet, was she?

'Have I ever given you reason not to trust me?' Colin asked softly, his expression more serious.

He had, hadn't he? He was in cahoots with someone else and she knew it. Still, she shook her head.

'In all of the times we've been out together, have I put you in danger?' Colin asked.

Lissa shook her head again. As far as she knew, there had never been any actual danger to their adventures, all were so carefully choreographed by Colin that she had felt completely safe.

'Answer me,' Colin demanded. Now his voice had grown stern, reminding her with his tone that he always expected a verbal response to his questions.

'Never,' Lissa said, trembling as Colin continued to undress her. She could feel herself growing aroused, her nipples hardening as Colin flicked his fingertips against them. She felt the wetness start down below, and she wondered how long it would be before Colin fucked her. Generally, when he was acting out a planned scenario, he made her wait until she was nearly desperate. What would happen if she asked him to fuck her first, now, to get it out of the way. A good climax would relax her and help her to concentrate on behaving for him.

Before she could vocalise the request, Colin had pulled off her boots and was starting on the button-fly of her jeans. Was he really going to strip her bare in public? Yes, he was, she realised as he helped her step out of the jeans and then put his hands on the waistband of her grey silk panties. She closed her eyes as he slid the filmy underpants down her thighs, then allowed herself to be positioned in the chair. It was often easier for her with her eyes closed. She could pretend the entire scene was taking place in her mind, instead of in public.

She heard the metal of chains clink closed around her wrists, felt the leather straps around her waist and throat as Colin buckled them into place. Light entered the room from a skylight above her, and she had an odd sensation at being so vulnerable during the daylight hours.

When she felt the tip of Colin's cock brush against her lips, she immediately opened her mouth to take him inside. This was pure instinct. She didn't need him to command her to suck him off. She simply started, like a good girl, to work his cock. Still, her mind continued to ask questions. When was Colin going to explain what he wanted from her? Was he simply going to fuck her face while she was captured in the chair? That didn't seem up to his normal level of intensity. If he had brought her all the way to Amsterdam, he would have a more serious plan than that.

'Are you ready?'

Although this was Colin's question of the day, the words were spoken by a woman, her voice coming from the ladder that led into the room. Lissa squeezed her eyelids even tighter, not wanting to see the expression of shock on the next patron's face. Although maybe the visitor would think that they were part of the act, a piece of performance art commissioned by the museum. Then Colin stepped away from her, removing his cock from her mouth. She heard Colin address the woman, and she felt herself starting to relax. This might be an experience she had feared, but at least it wouldn't happen with a total stranger. Colin obviously knew this woman.

'Gina,' Colin said, 'so glad you agreed to join us.'

'How could I refuse such a request?' Gina asked, her voice tinged with an accent that Lissa didn't instantly recognise. The woman wasn't Dutch. Perhaps she was Italian. She definitely looked it. Lissa slit her eyelids so that she could observe the scene without committing herself. Gina was wearing leather pants and a ribbed white tank top revealing a colourful tattoo high up on one shoulder. Lissa opened her eyes wider to decipher what the tattoo was a picture of. It seemed to be a picture of a lizard, but Lissa couldn't see it well enough to be certain.

Gina, feeling Lissa's gaze, turned to smile at her. Lissa instantly flushed and wished she'd kept her eyes shut after all. But now that she had opened them, she resigned herself to working out Colin's plan.

An idea suddenly flashed through Lissa's mind, and her breath caught in her throat. Could *Gina* be the patron? Was that possible? There was no real reason for her to have assumed the person was a 'he', was there?

Lissa eyed Gina, as if she might be able to tell from simply looking at the woman. Gina met her gaze face-on, her expression revealing nothing. That didn't mean she wasn't the patron. ARTLOVER could just have easily been a woman as a man. Lissa had simply pictured the patron as a male, someone who would enjoy the photos of her, the videotape. But plenty of women would have enjoyed them as well, wouldn't they?

Lissa's thoughts got away from her, and she found herself unaware of what was going on as Colin began to slowly undress her new partner.

Chapter Forty-eight

*T*he first instalment of Colin's scene was more difficult for Lissa than anything they had done together so far. The afternoon at the Père Lachaise, at the Catacombs, at Hamburg's erotic museum, even the time she had worn the remote-powered vibrator – all paled in comparison to what Colin had planned for today. While Lissa was strapped into submission, Colin undid Gina's leather pants, slid them down her perfect, creamy thighs, and fucked her. Lissa knew that Colin's cock was still wet from its dance between her own lips and she couldn't believe that he had used her mouth as foreplay.

'Baby,' Colin said softly – and Lissa didn't know which one he was referring to. 'You're so beautiful.' And then after a beat, 'You're both so beautiful.'

Why was he making her watch? This was more than Lissa thought she could handle. She felt as if she were on the verge of tears, and she would have started to cry if Colin hadn't suddenly repositioned Gina so that the girl was face to face with Lissa, her hands on the armrests of the sturdy chair, her lips only a breath away from Lissa's own. Lissa wouldn't cry while this girl watched her. That would be even more mortifying than this was.

'Kiss her,' Colin demanded, and Gina, seeming to understand that Colin was speaking to her, instantly did, leaning forward and kissing the very surprised Lissa full on the mouth. Now all thoughts of tears or anger at Colin disappeared from Lissa's mind, replaced with an entirely new sensation. Lissa could feel Gina's smooth lips on hers, could smell the woman's floral perfume – sweet and light, like lavender.

'Kiss her back, Lissa,' Colin ordered, still fucking Gina from behind. His eyes were focused on Lissa to make sure that she obeyed and, after one halting moment, Lissa did, opening her mouth against Gina's and feeling the woman's tongue meet her own.

It was amazing. She had thought about doing this before. Of course she had. And with Colin suggesting it over and over, putting it into the front of her mind, she had even climaxed to it, rubbing her clit while imagining a situation very much like the one she was in now. Still, the reality of kissing a woman was unlike any of the fantasies that she had created in her mind. It was the difference between reading about a rich, no-flour chocolate cake and actually sinking your teeth into the first delicious bite.

Suddenly, she understood what the last elliptical e-mail from ARTLOVER had been about. He'd wanted her to experience lovemaking with a woman. How had he known that it would take her breath away? A different feeling about this mysterious patron flooded through her. He wanted her to be happy, to experience every-thing she had ever wanted. He was after her pleasure alone, and he was using Colin as a tool to give it to her.

But why?

Before she could spend any time wondering about ARTLOVER'S motivations, she felt Gina's fingertips brushing over her nipples. Gina's hands cradled her breasts, and Lissa could feel cool metal against her skin. She looked down, saw that Gina wore a multitude of rings, and that these pressed into her flesh as Gina stroked her, trailing lower, along her ribs, her fingers working their way closer to her sex.

If only she hadn't been captured to the stupid chair, she would have been able to touch Gina back. That's all she could think about, releasing her hands from the straps so that she could cradle Gina's face, kiss the girl's lips – bite her bottom lip – move her mouth down Gina's long neck and lick her there, in the hollow. She wondered what Gina's skin would taste like, what sounds Gina would make if she –

'Make her come,' Colin said, breaking through Lissa's thoughts. 'Use your fingers on her clit. She likes small fast circles that gradually slow down as she nears her peak.'

Yes, he knew her well, Lissa thought. Colin knew exactly what she liked. And Gina was a good student. She followed Colin's instructions precisely, rotating her soft fingers in circles up and over Lissa's clit until it felt as if it would burst with pleasure. Although the woman obeyed Colin, she employed her own method of touching Lissa. Seductively, she teased her, instinctively understanding when Lissa grew close to climax, and backing away to keep her on the edge. Lissa made a guttural begging noise deep in her throat and Gina grinned at her.

'Not yet,' Gina whispered. 'Let it happen slowly. OK?'

Lissa nodded. 'Yes,' she said, her voice hoarse, 'OK.'

A few minutes before, Lissa had thought only of how angry she was at Colin for putting her into this situation without any warning. Her anger had melted, her feelings changing from 'how dare he?' to 'when will I?' Because all Lissa could think about was how much she wanted to come. She had reached the stage where she couldn't help but beg, even though begging rarely did her any good when Colin was involved. Everything happened on his schedule. Still, Lissa tried.

'Please –' she said, not looking at Colin. Focused only on Gina's face.

211

'You like it?'

'Yes,' Lissa whispered, 'but please –'

'You'll come when I come,' Gina said, obviously enjoying the sense of power. Using one hand, Gina parted her own pussy lips and began to stroke her clit. She tugged on something, and whispered to Lissa, 'When I got my clit pierced, I came like a jackhammer.'

Shocked, Lissa felt her body stiffen. But at the same time, she longed to see what Gina's clit looked like. Did she have a ring through it or a stud? What kind of pleasure would it give Gina if Lissa pulled on the piece of jewellery with her teeth. Thoughts that she'd never had before exploded through her mind.

'Kiss me,' Gina whispered, and Lissa instantly obeyed, her heart racing as Colin sped up his actions behind Gina, slamming his cock into her at a rapid pace. And as he moved faster, Gina's fingers moved faster and Gina pressed her full lips to Lissa's, whispering the word 'Now' into Lissa's mouth.

The climax had a triple effect, working through each of the lovers and then combining to build their pleasure to an extreme. There was a heady silence in the room as all three partners came together in an instant of pure bliss.

Chapter Forty-nine

Colin and Lissa exited the museum to discover a light rain dripping down on Amsterdam. The moisture covered the city in glistening drops, made a percussion-like sound as the drops met the water in the canals.

'Do you want me to get a cab?' Colin asked. He had one arm over Lissa's shoulder, and the warmth of his body was soothing to her. She looked up at him, smiled, and shook her head. She liked to walk, especially when something nagged at her, as it did now. She was certain that the stroll back to their hotel would serve to clear her mind.

'We'll get soaked,' he told her, his voice mild. Even though the rain was light, they were nearly a mile from the hotel.

'Doesn't matter. You can get a cab if you want and I'll meet you.'

'Are you upset?' he asked next, sounding concerned.

Lissa shook her head. 'Not at all,' she told him, surprised that she actually meant it. She wasn't upset, and she wasn't even confused. She simply wanted to process what had just happened. But more importantly, she had the feeling that she was forgetting something important, something meaningful.

They made the walk in almost total silence. Lissa took in the architecture, observing the thin houses painted a brown the colour of gingerbread. The roads were narrow, and most had no pavements. Colin had to pull Lissa on to the edge of the canal several times to avoid cars. Lissa seemed dazed each time he saved her, giving him a bland smile before reverting her attention to the neighbourhoods as they passed through them.

Could she live here? she wondered. There was a magical feel to Amsterdam, that to her was unlike the feel of Venice – the other famed city of canals. It could be the marijuana, she thought, but she hadn't actually smoked that much. What she most liked, she realised, was the freedom. The freedom to get stoned, if you wanted to, to live on a boat in the canal, to have sex in a museum –

Colin grabbed her arm again, pulling her up on to an embankment as a tiny car whizzed past. In his embrace, she looked into his eyes, saw the worry there, and smiled. She was fine. Confused and turned-on, but fine.

She kissed him, feeling his arms come around her, the rain decorating her face and hair with tiny beads. He returned her kiss, parting her lips with his tongue, gently French-kissing her in a manner which made her remember Gina, and those soft lips against her own.

'We'll stay in tonight,' Colin proposed as they arrived at the hotel. 'Would you like that?'

Lissa nodded. She couldn't imagine getting dressed to go out somewhere, could not see herself trying to blend in with a normal crowd of tourists in some fine restaurant. Her world was still spinning from the events of the afternoon.

'Take a shower,' Colin suggested. 'I'll order us some food and have it brought to the room.' He still seemed to be treating her with kid gloves, as if she had just recovered from an illness or escaped a dangerous situation. Lissa understood that he was worried about how she felt about him fucking another woman. But this wasn't the image that consumed her. The only thing on her mind was the feeling of Gina's lips against hers, and the question: would it happen again?

Lissa retreated to the large, decadent bathroom to get clean. Her legs were shaking, and she leant against one wall while the water heated. How had Colin known exactly what she wanted? How did he know when not to go too far? Was she that easy a read? She didn't think so. If she was, then why hadn't any other lover been able to read her so well?

Perhaps it was all at the behest of the mysterious patron. But if that was so, then how did he (or *she*) know her so well?

Lissa ran one hand through her hair, surprised when it came back wet. She'd hardly noticed the rain during their walk back from the museum. But suddenly cold, she stripped off her damp clothes and hurried into the hot, steamy shower.

The water felt delicious, pounding down on her aching muscles, and she turned under the spray, letting it hit her all over. Who would have thought that an afternoon of lovemaking could be so strenuous? She knew she was sore because she'd been fighting the bindings. Maybe this was Colin's lesson of the day. Don't struggle so much. Simply let it happen. But she could never seem to do that. Everything required dissecting. She needed to challenge every new action, each unexpected sensation.

Her eyes were closed and she visualised the afternoon's activity while she lathered her body. It was difficult for her to believe that she had actually taken part in the decadence. But the memory flickered before her shut eyes like a movie on fast-forward. There was Gina bending down to kiss her. There was Colin, behind Gina, fucking her hard and fast, forcing Gina closer to Lissa's body with each stroke of his cock. Lissa had a tactile memory of what it felt like when Gina stroked her breasts for the first time –

Oh, she was getting wet again. A different kind of wet from the pounding spray of the shower. She considered taking care of that need herself, sliding her hand between her legs and making those rapid, hungry circles with her fingertips. The brush of her fingers against her sex let her know that it wouldn't take more than a few seconds in order to come. She gave into the pleasure for a moment, pinching her clit between her thumb and forefinger and moaning from the sensation. Remembering Gina's words about having her own clit pierced sent a shiver throughout her body. It was something she'd never considered before, wouldn't have thought the image would be the slightest bit erotic. But it was. She leant against the shower, feeling the cold tiles on her back, the hot shower on her front, cascading in a waterfall over her belly and down her thighs.

Where was she? In the museum with Gina, feeling the woman's hands on her body, running up and down. Next time, she wouldn't be tied down. She would tell Colin that she wanted to use her own hands, fingertips, palms to stroke the skin of her partner. Would he let her? Surely, he wouldn't deny her such a request.

Her fingertips brought her closer to climax when she opened her eyes and realised the shower was fitted with a massage device. She considered removing the nozzle from the base and giving herself a little bit of help. It was a hand-held type, with a massage rotation. But what would Colin say if he knew? He'd never told her not to masturbate. He probably wouldn't mind –

While Lissa showered, Colin brought in the meal and spread it out on a blanket in the centre of the floor. They would picnic in the hotel room – a romantic notion. He lit long ivory candles and dimmed the lights. The trip to Amsterdam was progressing exactly as he'd hoped. He was indoctrinating Lissa into new experiences, stretching her, testing her.

There was more to their trip than she could comprehend right now, but he had everything under control, which was exactly how he liked it. He listened to the sound of the water from the shower in the other room, and he quickly rummaged through Lissa's cosmetics bag, searching for a tube of her lipstick.

Red. Perfect.

He walked to the full-length mirror next to the bed and extended his arm over his head, writing a sentence at the very top of the mirror. The lipstick glided on the glass, and he smiled at his finished effort. Lissa might not even notice what he'd done.

But then, the message wasn't intended for her eyes.

Lissa took the handset and brought it between her thighs, manipulating the pressure until she found a rhythm that she liked. The water gushing against her felt amazing, and she played with the device, bringing the shower head closer to her clit, then moving it away. Teasing herself with the massaging spray until she heard Colin calling her name.

'Lissa!'

At the sound of his voice, she quickly set the shower head back in place, guiltily looking out through the steamed glass door to see if he had caught her. He hadn't. She hurried to turn off the water, then wrapped herself in a fluffy cherry-coloured towel and combed her hair away from her face.

Her cheeks were flushed, as they always were when she was on the verge of coming. But Colin wouldn't know that. He would think she was simply hot from the shower. She smiled at herself in the mirror and then walked into the bedroom to greet her man.

217

Chapter Fifty

'*L*ose the towel, Lissa,' Colin said, as Lissa entered the bedroom.

She let the crimson bath sheet drop away from her body, feeling suddenly glamorous, like a movie star from the 1940s or even the model in the famous painting by Botticelli. Venus stepping out of the ocean on an open shell, with her hair flowing around her, one hand positioned carefully to cover her nakedness. Art constantly crept into Lissa's mind, mingling with the scenes from her own life. Like the model's in the picture, Lissa's own skin seemed to glisten in the candlelight, and she stood a few paces away from Colin, letting him observe her before joining him on the floor.

'Come closer,' Colin said, looking up at her from the blanket.

As she walked forward, around the corner of the bed, she saw that he was naked as well. Once again, she realised how handsome he was, his body long and lean, strong and fine with muscles but not overly built. She had always liked men who had a slim, foxy look to their appearance, and Colin most definitely fitted the description.

The food was spread out for a feast, but Lissa

suddenly wasn't hungry any more. Not for the meal, anyway. She was hungry for Colin, for making love to him with her eyes open, for holding on to him without any hindrances. No blindfold. No bindings.

The candlelight drew their shadows on the wall behind them. Colin's lengthened as he came towards Lissa. She stepped into his arms and felt the comfort of being in his embrace. Rarely did they make love like 'normal' people. It was always about power and rules – *his* power and rules – and her submission to him. But standing, with his strong arms wrapped around her, she felt as if they were equal.

Colin motioned to the bed, but Lissa shook her head.

'I want to feel the air,' she whispered.

The windows of their hotel room opened up to a quiet street. Lissa moved out of Colin's embrace. She opened the heavy curtains and tied them back, then lifted the glass pane. The night was clear and she could see the stars outside. She offered Colin her body by bending forward at the waist, her upper torso against the window sill. Down below, on the street, she saw a man peddling a bicycle with a woman on the back, clutching him around the waist. She stared at the couple as they peddled off into the distance, and just as they turned a corner, Colin entered her, his cock parting her inner lips and finding the wetness between them.

Colin sighed at the sensation and Lissa bit her lip, stifling a moan. His hands roamed over her skin, giving her a light massage with his fingertips, tickling her gently at the back of her neck. She shivered, both at his touch and at the cool breeze coming in from the outdoors. When she shivered, her pussy contracted on his cock, and he moaned again.

It was like a dance, the two of them moving silently together, in perfect rhythm, perfect unison. They each knew what would please the other, and they acted on every bit of the knowledge. Lissa was glad that they were able to do this without the added spark of pain, the added complications of S&M. It was almost a relief to put aside the games of their relationship. She thought they would make it through this one time together without any additions.

At least, until Colin reached for a candle.

Several twisted ivory tapers stood on a low wooden table next to the window. Colin grasped the nearest one, which was tall and thin and made of twisted ropes of wax. Lissa could see his actions by turning her head to the left, and she watched as Colin extinguished the flame with a quick shake of his wrist. Before Lissa could speak, he brought the candle behind her back and let the wax drip slowly in a line along her spine. Mentally, she chided herself for the thoughts she'd had only moments before. Here, she had been proud of the fact that she and Colin were experiencing 'normal' sex. But now that he had changed the rules – again – a totally new set of feelings emerged within her.

Why had she wanted normal sex at all?

The pain of the wax was unlike any she had previously experienced at Colin's hand. Each flare of intense heat was instantly followed by Colin's breath, and then his tongue, to cool down her skin. With every drop, Lissa's cunt contracted fiercely on Colin's cock. This was her body's way of letting her know that pain was what she wanted. The added spark of something beyond average lovemaking. It brought her to a higher level, both mentally, as she prepared herself for the next, inevitable falling drop of wax, and physically, as her body neared climax much more quickly than it would have if Colin were simply stroking his cock between her legs.

'You like that, don't you, baby?'

Lissa made a guttural noise deep in her throat. She hoped Colin would take this as an assent.

'Tell me why you like it.'

He wasn't going to let her get away so easily. He wanted her to talk. Each event with Colin was like a test, and she constantly had to push herself in order to pass.

Colin's fingertips ran over the beads of wax that had already hardened on her skin. The trail ran all the way down to the base of her spine. Here, his fingers parted her cheeks, and Lissa sucked in her breath as Colin revealed the rosebud opening of her ass. Was he going to let the wax fall here?

'Tell me,' Colin demanded.

Lissa sucked in her breath. What should she say? What *could* she say? She didn't know why she liked the things they did. She only knew that her body didn't lie. It responded quickly and powerfully to every single one of Colin's games.

'Lissa –' Colin said, prompting her, waiting for her response. She saw in the full-length mirror to her right that Colin had taken the bottom of the candle into his mouth, was sucking on it, getting it nice and wet.

She knew what he was going to do a second before he did it. Still, the knowledge didn't prepare her for the intruding sensation of the candle's thick base as it plunged forward inside her bottom. Colin worked the candle slowly into her, his cock still in her pussy, and then he began to fuck her again, but now it was like being fucked with two cocks. He moved both rods simultaneously inside her, and the pleasure from this violation made Lissa want to scream into the night. Instead, she bit the insides of her cheeks to keep herself under control. In the back of her mind, she knew that Colin was still waiting for her to respond.

'I like it because –' she started, her voice hardly louder than a whisper.

'Yes?'

'Because I don't have to think any more.' Was that it? When she put herself into his hands, her responsibility went away. She had no choice in the matter. He took total control, and there was something immensely satisfying about that. Colin seemed to accept this answer. More than that, he seemed to expect it. When he spoke again, she thought she heard a smug tone in his voice, as if he'd known all along what she was going to say.

'Watch yourself,' Colin told her. For a moment, she thought he was telling her not to disobey him. Then she realised he wanted her to turn her head to the right, where she could actually see their reflections in the floor-to-ceiling mirror propped against the wall.

'What a vision you are,' Colin said next, his tone changing again, now sounding suddenly in awe of her.

Lissa stared at her reflection as Colin pushed the candlestick deeper inside her, massaging it in even when Lissa felt she was already filled to her limit. Her muscles contracted around the rod of the candle, holding tight, then releasing, as her body grew closer to climax. It wouldn't be much longer – the intruding feel of having a foreign object inside her, and the way that Colin was fucking her pussy, worked together to bring her to the ridge.

'I'm going to –' Lissa murmured, letting Colin know. 'Oh, God, Colin, I'm going to come.'

She gasped as Colin suddenly withdrew both his cock and the candle, and he grabbed Lissa around the waist and brought her to the mirror. He positioned her quickly, both of her palms pressed against the cool glass, her face forward, glistening grey eyes staring straight at her own reflection. Wolf's eyes. The words flickered through her mind as she came. Who had said that? Who had called them that? Then Colin entered her again, in both places, and began to fuck her at a more rapid pace, obliterating all thoughts of anything but what they were doing.

Forced to meet her own gaze, it wasn't easy for Lissa to keep her eyes open. Yet she knew this was exactly what Colin wanted. He'd given her the most difficult assignment and now he was obviously waiting to see if she would obey him. Lissa took a deep breath and focused on her face, on her parted lips, flushed cheeks. Her long hair, still damp from the shower, fell in loose curls past her shoulder blades. Colin wrapped one fist in it, pulling her head back so that her chin tilted up at an angle, giving her mirror image a defiant appearance. You looking at me? her mirrored self seemed to be saying. There isn't anyone else here. You must be looking at me.

Their reflections were made magical by the multitude of burning candles. The golden light seemed to melt around them, making Lissa feel as if she were staring at a picture obscured by water, thin and glittering. Her mirror image reminded her of a Pre-Raphaelite painting, a woman floating in a river, a halo of light around her. Every single stage of her life had a piece of art to equal it.

'Come for me,' Colin demanded. 'Come loud for me.'

She couldn't imagine behaving as he requested. Not in the hotel, where other people might hear her. Not with the window wide open to the street below. How could she? How could he expect her to?

'Now!' Colin insisted, and Lissa, even though she didn't think she could obey, felt her body responding as Colin requested, coming hard and fast and loud, her eyes shut tight, mouth parted, body trembling with mighty vibrations.

'There's the girl,' Colin whispered to her. 'That's my special girl.'

Chapter Fifty-one

Oh, she was a special girl. The patron agreed with Colin on this point. He stared, transfixed, at the vision before him. He was looking at Lissa, her hands sealed to the other side of the mirror, her breasts tumbling forward, perfect rosy nipples almost brushing the glass. He put his hand up, to trace the outline of her body, and as he did so he pretended he was touching her naked skin. Smooth and supple, he could easily imagine it. Then he placed his hands, palm to palm with Lissa's. Her hands were smaller than his, and his fingers stretched over hers.

On the mirror, Colin had written in lipstick: ART IS ANTICIPATION. The letters were in reverse, but the patron could easily read them. Just another one of Colin's clever touches. The words would mean nothing to Lissa, but everything to Colin and himself.

The patron returned his gaze to Lissa, focusing his full attention on her. She was almost ready to come. He could tell from her expression, and he wished that he could hear what she was saying to Colin. He fantasised that she was talking to him, and he wondered how he would respond. What a treat it would be to fuck her, to feel her skin against his. After seeing the pictures, the video, and now this actual live-action scenario, he was ready. In fact, his cock was *more* than ready. Now, all he had to do was wait until Colin gave him the go-ahead. That's why he was in Amsterdam. Colin had said that now was the time for his real-life experience with Lissa. The thought both pleased and frightened him.

The man stared forward into Lissa's eyes, and he felt his own breath catch at the moment that her climax flooded through her. It was obvious when it happened, her eyelids fluttered rapidly, and then closed. She bit her bottom lip fiercely enough to leave indents with her teeth. He wished he could bite her lip for her, and he took a step forward, as if he might be able to pierce the glass skin of the mirror and take her bottom lip between his teeth.

Colin didn't stop fucking Lissa just because she'd come. The patron knew this, although he couldn't actually see what Colin was doing to Lissa, since Colin was taking her from behind. But he had watched Colin fuck her against the window sill, so he had a strong idea where the candle was and what it was doing to Lissa.

How brilliant of Colin to choose this place to meet. The hotel was a former bordello, with specially created sound-proofed walls and two-way mirrors on the top floor. Colin knew the owners – not surprising since he seemed to have connections everywhere – and they had offered these rooms for Colin's private use.

Lissa was still pressed against the mirror, but now she seemed to have relaxed. The orgasm had washed through her, leaving her visibly drained and apparently sighing with relief. Colin was moving away. The patron realised he'd have to work fast if he wanted to bring his fantasy to reality. He'd been stroking his cock during the entire escapade, and now he took a step closer to the mirror. Lissa's eyes were open now, and she started to move.

'Don't go,' the patron muttered, 'not yet.'

He wanted to come on her body, watch his juices rain

down on her. He wished she were actually leaning against the mirror. Then he could shoot and see the snowy white liquid spread over Lissa's form. Instead, Lissa took a step away, and the patron had to content himself with watching Colin force Lissa to her knees, instructing her to open her mouth and clean his cock. Colin was already hard again, and Lissa seemed happy to comply, taking his throbbing rod between her lips and giving it a good, old-fashioned tongue bath.

This was better than any X-rated video the patron had ever seen. The action didn't seem scripted or forced, and the actors were so attractive. Sure, porn stars were attractive, too, but this couple seemed real. Their pleasure was most definitely genuine.

He didn't think he would be able to wait much longer before touching her. Colin had promised him. Soon. The patron reminded himself of this promise to calm himself. He wanted to make the moment last as long as possible.

But when Colin brushed Lissa's hair out of her eyes, the patron was able to stare into them, to see their depths, and this was what took him over the edge. That look of satisfaction, of desire mixed with lust. It was almost as good as if she were looking at him like that. He climaxed against the mirror and watched the designs as the thick liquid slowly trickled down.

Chapter Fifty-two

*A*msterdam woke far before Lissa and Colin. The clock on their bedside table read nearly noon by the time the couple were ready to face the day. Colin rose ahead of Lissa. She felt him moving in the bed, listened to him with her eyes closed as he called down to the kitchen and ordered a pot of coffee. When he headed for the shower, Lissa stretched, sat up in bed, and tried to jump-start her brain. Coffee was exactly what she needed, and when it arrived, she wrapped a thick, white robe around her naked body, gratefully poured herself a large cup, and went out on to the balcony to drink it.

A display of international flags decorated the front of the hotel. Lissa watched them dancing below her in the light breeze. The fabric of the flags made a flapping sound that was peaceful to listen to. As she leant against the balcony railing, she caught the sound of the door opening to the balcony on the next room. Although she turned to look, she couldn't see the occupant. A wooden trellis divided the two balconies and it was covered with a lush, floral creeping vine.

Knowing that someone else was sharing her view made Lissa feel slightly ill at ease, as if the person behind the vine might have known what she and Colin had done the previous evening, or even the afternoon before. She took her cup back inside the room and sat on the bed, waiting for Colin to emerge from the shower and tell her about today's plans. She knew that he was going to let her visit the Van Gogh museum. But he'd mentioned something else, something that sounded vaguely frightening, just before they'd dropped off to sleep.

She shut her eyes, trying to remember exactly what he'd said and how he'd said it. The memory came rushing back. He'd curled up around her and pressed his mouth to her ear, whispering, 'If you thought today was filled with surprises, wait until tomorrow arrives.'

Chapter Fifty-three

*T*he room was ready, exactly as Colin had requested. A small room with a window on to the alley. The bed stood a few paces back from the window and the curtains were open, letting in the grey afternoon light. A vase holding white and yellow jonquils decorated a small table by the bed. This was an extra touch. Colin had asked for the place to be clean and safe, but Gina couldn't help but add a bit of feminine refinement to the setting. She knew that Colin would approve.

A knock on the door startled her. She hadn't seen Colin or Lissa pass by the window. Had they come down the other side of the street? Although the room was fully prepared, her guest had not yet arrived. She checked the peephole, and then relaxed. Outside the door stood a tall, dark-haired man wearing a denim shirt and khaki pants. He looked like a model for a casual clothing catalogue. Although she'd never met him, she knew that this was Colin's partner, and she quickly opened the door.

The man didn't apologise for being late, didn't appear to Gina like the sort of person who would apologise for anything. Instead, he simply put out his hand and said, 'Gina. Charmed.' He had a nice voice, a deep American voice, and Gina offered her hand and smiled at him when he lifted it to his lips and kissed it. Charming.

He was handsome, she thought, his thick brown hair a little longer in the front than was fashionable. He had to shake it out of his eyes when he looked down at her, but somehow the gesture simply made her want to run her fingers through it. Soon enough. She must force herself to be patient.

'You know how this will work?' he asked, glancing around the room to take in the furnishings.

Gina nodded, releasing her fantasy of touching his hair and focusing on the answer to his question. 'Colin was very specific.' She removed her hand from his and then motioned to the black velvet curtains that hid a small wardrobe from the rest of the room. 'We'll wait together in there,' she said, 'until Colin gives us the word.'

Chapter Fifty-four

Colin steered Lissa down what had looked like a little alley between two buildings. After her first step she realised this wasn't just an alley, but a mall of women. She'd wondered when Colin was going to show her this part of Amsterdam. It was, of course, the most famous feature of the beautiful city. A place to view women on display, and then purchase one that best suited your needs. The concept of choosing a woman from behind glass was disturbing to her, as disturbing as the walled-off street at the Reeperbahn. But, in reality, now that she could see the girls under glass, she couldn't hide her interest. A series of full-length, floor-to-ceiling windows opened into little rooms. Next to each window was a door and inside each tiny room was a woman.

Even though she knew what to expect, the sight of the first prostitute startled Lissa. Coming upon the woman behind a glass window was more shocking to her than the line of whores outdoors in Hamburg. This sensation was completely different. Lissa met the first one eye to eye and then quickly lowered her head. Still, an image of the woman burnt in her mind, and she processed it. The hooker behind the window had been about forty, with a figure that was more pear-shaped than hourglass.

'You can look,' Colin said. 'They don't mind. That's what they're here for.' He sounded as if he were about to laugh.

'To be looked at?'

'To be bought. But they expect the looking. That's part of the business.'

It took an effort for Lissa to raise her eyes again. The woman in the second window was younger than the first, younger than Lissa, and was wearing cut-off jeans and a little black lace camisole.

The third room was larger than the first two. Here, two women reclined together on a red velvet couch. A man stood in front of the window, watching steadily. He didn't seem to notice Lissa or Colin, didn't have eyes for anything other than the women. Lissa hurried past him, her cheeks flushed, feeling Colin slowing her down with a pull to her wrist. She didn't want to stop, didn't feel comfortable looking with someone else, part of a crowd of gawkers as if the women in the windows were putting on a show.

She whispered this to Colin who explained, 'They *are* putting on a show. That's how they get people to buy. It's part of the deal.'

He let Lissa hurry through the rest of the alley, catching up to her at the end, where they were again on the edge of a canal, staring into the water. The clouds that had hung low all afternoon now threatened rain, and Colin led Lissa to another café, this one with a Bob Marley theme, and again ordered them two joints, coffees and, this time, a slice of lemon cake to share.

'How can they do it?' Lissa asked.

Colin didn't understand the question.

'I mean, I know that women are prostitutes, I understand that concept. But how can they stand to have people watch them?'

'Wouldn't you like someone to watch you?' Colin asked, his voice low so that only Lissa could hear him.

232

'If I remember correctly, you told me that being on display would turn you on.'

Yes, she *had* told him that. And it had only been the day before, transported by the dreamy designs that he traced with his tongue around her clit. Now, she stared at him, understanding slowly dawning. When she had taken a few hits from the joint, Colin asked her the question again. 'Haven't you always wanted to be on display?'

Lissa's whole body was relaxed and, at the same time, she found that her thoughts were coming to her more clearly. It was easier for her to think, as if a cloud had lifted in her brain. She didn't understand how a drug could make her think more easily. But maybe it was because she no longer felt inhibited. She didn't need to say the politically correct thing. Instead, she could say the honest thing, which was that yes, she had wanted to be watched, to have a whole crowd of people stare at her the way the man in the alley had stared at the two prostitutes.

Colin, gave her a broad smile. 'Are you ready to make that fantasy come true?'

And there it was. The real reason he'd brought her to Amsterdam. She looked at him to see if he really meant it. She took in his red hair, tousled from the weather, and his green eyes, shining brightly behind his spectacles. It was unusual for her to see him in disarray, and she found it oddly charming that he made no effort to smooth his hair back into place. Colin had a half-smile on his lips and, from his expression, she could tell that he did mean it. She guessed that if she said 'no,' he would leave it at that. He hadn't actually forced her to do something she didn't want to. And so far, everything he'd suggested had brought her intense pleasure.

Colin was waiting for her answer. She knew this, but she took her time formulating it in her mind. After another bite of cake, another sip of coffee, she said, 'Yes, Colin. I'm ready.'

Chapter Fifty-five

*A*nticipation was Colin's favourite game. He didn't act on their discussion immediately. Instead, he took her to one of the many sex stores that they had passed earlier in the day. The door was covered with black fabric cut into slits to let customers in and out. Colin didn't say a word to Lissa, simply grabbed her hand and pulled her in after him. It felt like entering a fun house, the fabric slits parting to let them through.

He didn't explain to Lissa why they were there. Instead, he let her wonder and worry what he might have planned for her. It was so much fun to watch her eyes widen, her lips part as if she might tell him 'no,' she didn't want to.

There were things he'd planned to do for the patron, things that they had agreed upon. And then there were plans he'd decided on specifically for his own pleasure. Someday, he would explain to Lissa which ideas had been born in his head and which had come from ARTLOVER. And at that point, she would choose between them. Maybe he was cheating, not playing by the rules they had originally set up. But plans changed, didn't they? And all was fair – and all that crap. For now, he walked to the front of the store, carefully watching Lissa from the corner of his eye.

Lissa felt her cheeks turn fuchsia at the display that immediately greeted her. It was a full-size, naked, inflatable doll that had been used to show off a variety of the items for sale. Someone had a sick sense of humour, because handcuffs kept the doll's wrists together, as if she could fight back. A black leather blindfold over the doll's eyes protected her from the prying glances of strangers, while one dildo rested between her lips and another fastened to a harness had been slipped into her rubbery pussy.

Lissa instantly averted her eyes, but the next sight did nothing to relieve her embarrassment. A wall of vibrators stood before her, each more intricate than the last. The first had a little beaver attached to the base, which moved in a rotating, 'clit-tickling' motion. Another, crafted to look like a bunny, had ears serving the same 'pussy-pleasing' massage techniques. Lissa noticed one that was ribbed with plastic bumps, another that had a cock-head on each end and seemed able to bend in a U-shape. Strange, Lissa thought. How would that work?

On a nearby table stood bottles of edible lubricants, strawberry-flavoured panties and chocolate body paints. Now, more curious than embarrassed, Lissa took her time studying the different items for sale. In a second room, she found a variety of sexy clothes – most made of vinyl, leather or PVC. She stroked the fabric of a shiny catsuit, feeling the plastic-like texture and immediately imagining what it would look like if Colin were to jack-off against it. Yes, it was tacky, but something about it made her pussy feel as if a tap had been turned on inside her.

She thought about trying on one of the plaid schoolgirl skirts on a rack on the wall, but then realised that she wasn't the one planning this outing. Colin might not appreciate it if she offered her own suggestions for how they might play.

But why had Colin taken her here? She looked around to see what he was up to, and caught sight of him making a purchase at the cash register by the front door. She was too late to see what he was buying. The clerk had already slipped whatever it was into a brown paper bag and was now eyeing Lissa with an interested expression.

'Can I help you, miss?' he queried, but Colin had her hand in his again and was leading her from the shop.

'What's in the bag?' Lissa asked as they headed back into the afternoon sunlight.

'That's the big question of the day,' Colin smiled at her, 'isn't it?'

Chapter Fifty-six

Colin brought Lissa back down the alley. This time, she looked at each of the women behind the glass windows. Some were older, some younger, but Lissa didn't lower her eyes when her inquisitive stare caught their attention. That's what they were there for, Colin had said, to be looked at. So she would look.

At an empty room in the centre of the alley, Colin stopped. They'd arrived. Lissa watched as he turned the knob on the door and opened it. He motioned for Lissa to enter and he followed after her, locking the door behind them. Lissa didn't say a word, but she understood that something huge was about to happen.

'This way,' Colin said, leading Lissa to the centre of the room. There really wasn't anywhere else to go. The room was small, set with a bed and a table with flowers. A partly opened door led to a tiny bathroom, and Lissa could see that it contained only a sink and a toilet.

Colin stepped forward and removed the first item from the bag. It was a blindfold. Of course, she should have guessed he would use this on her. Removing her sight was one of his favourite methods of keeping her off-balance. She shut her lids as he placed the black silk over her eyes and fastened it beneath her hair. She breathed in deeply, taking in his cologne, even smelling the flowers in the vase in the corner. The removal of one sense always seemed to heighten the awareness of others.

'Strip,' Colin said next. It was his first command and Lissa obeyed immediately, pulling her fisherman's sweater and T-shirt over her head and dropping them on the floor. Adding her boots, faded jeans and socks next to them. She stood before him in her bra and panties, waiting for the next instruction. He didn't issue one for a moment, letting her wait in silence. Finally he said, 'The rest of it. Take it all off.'

Her fingers trembled as she unfastened the clasp on her bra and let it fall. She slid her panties down her thighs and stepped out of them, then waited, hoping her expression was one of readiness and not defiance. She could not control the emotions that washed through her – fear, excitement, trepidation. How was one supposed to feel while preparing for a fantasy to come true?

She wondered if there were people already gathered outside, watching her, and she clenched her hands into fists at her sides to keep from bringing them up to hide her face. Even if there were no curious pedestrians passing by, she could feel Colin's eyes on her. What would he do next? She couldn't guess, but she wished he'd do something. Quickly.

'Do you trust me?' Colin asked softly. He was standing closer to her than she'd expected. She felt unbalanced, and when she suddenly reached her hand out, to steady herself, she felt herself instantly supported. But not by Colin.

Chapter Fifty-seven

*L*issa focused on the sensations. With her sense of sight removed by the blindfold, she relied on touch, smell and taste to guide her. But at first, she couldn't believe what her senses were telling her.

The man behind her wasn't Colin. How could that be? She knew this routine was a set-up by her lover, the entire concept of undressing her and putting her on display in a window. It was all part of his journey, his goal to re-create erotic art, and to re-create her.

Still, her senses told her that the man in the room with her wasn't Colin. The man didn't speak. That was another part of the trick, she realised. He simply moved her body on his, sliding her back and forth along the length of his cock. Sheathed in a latex condom and coated with a lubricant, his tool slipped easily into her cunt. It was an anonymous feeling. Colin never used a condom with her. Now, she squeezed this lover, tentatively at first, to see if she could cause a reaction. If he moaned, then she would know for sure whether this was or wasn't Colin.

His hands were on her back, his fingers running up and down along her spine. She shivered at his touch, which was gentle but powerful, like Colin's and yet unlike Colin's. This man was taller and thicker, his body more heavily muscled than her lover's. She breathed in deeply and caught a whiff of Colin's cologne, but that, she thought, was something else to keep her off-balance. It was simply a trick. But how could they possibly think she would be fooled into believing this was Colin?

And just as quickly, she thought: It's him. Those words rang in her mind before she understood what they meant. As the man slid into her, she simply knew. This wasn't Colin and it wasn't some stranger off the street – Colin wouldn't do that to her, wouldn't put her at that type of risk. No, this was the patron, the one who had spoken so eloquently about her photographs, about the video Colin had created. She had longed to meet him, and now she was. If you could call this a meeting. Yet, she couldn't confess to the man that she knew, could she? It would ruin it somehow if she confronted him. Besides, how could she be sure that Colin wasn't in the room as well. And how would he punish her if he knew that she had snooped through his belongings, locating his online code and reading his correspondence.

She was brought back to the action at hand when the man suddenly lifted her off her feet and carried her to the bed. She was docile, letting him raise her arms over her head without offering any resistance, feeling the cold bite of the steel handcuffs click into place around her wrists. Next, her ankles were bound with worn leather straps to the far corners of the bed. She was spread out, like some luscious dessert, and this made her think of her first time with Colin, in the hotel bed in Frankfurt. The way he had bound her to his bed and then treated her to such delicious rewards. Would the patron follow in his footsteps?

No. The answer came as quickly as her lips were forced apart by his cock. She tasted herself, tasted the latex of the condom and the sweet, cloying flavour of the edible lubricant. It was cherry – or something meant to be cherry. She licked over the condom, feeling the raised bumps – for her pleasure – and again smelling the scent of Colin's cologne. They were overdoing it, she thought, dousing this man in Colin's scent to confuse her. But then they confused her again, as she felt another cock, this one preparing to enter her down below. So Colin *was* still here, because this was unmistakably his penis, sliding bareback between her legs, where the patron had been only moments before.

She wondered why the men didn't talk. Now, when it was so obviously two people, what were they continuing to hide from her? She wondered if she should ask, but obviously she couldn't say a word with the patron's cock sliding in and out of her parted lips.

When she felt a third set of hands on her body, Lissa stopped trying to decipher the situation, and gave herself over to the pleasure of it. Hands stroked her, bodies moved against her, she could feel the sweat and lubrication mixing to create a gliding effect as she was rocked and rolled against the bed.

Oh, it was a woman. Those third set of hands belonged to a woman. Was it Colin's friend Gina? With her long, chestnut hair let loose to float and tickle Lissa's naked skin. Yes, it must be her, because Lissa felt Gina's ringed fingers tricking up and down her body. A silver ring on the middle finger of her left hand, two cloisonné rings on the second finger of her right hand. The fragrance of lavender flooded Lissa's senses as the woman pressed her body against Lissa's. Yes, it was most definitely Gina. She recognised that scent from the museum.

Lissa was brought back into the moment of the orgy adventure, as the patron's cock was replaced with Gina's pussy. Lissa hesitated a moment. She had never tasted another woman before, never been the one in charge of giving another woman pleasure. She was anxious and nervous. What if she did it wrong? What if she made a mistake?

But she didn't have any choice, as Gina's pussy was

pressed against her lips. Lissa simply started to do what she would have wanted someone to do to her. She used her tongue to delve between Gina's swollen lips, parting them to find the hood of Gina's clit.

Oh, yes, it was most definitely Gina. Again Lissa remembered Gina's startling remark. Something about coming like a jackhammer when she'd had her clitoris pierced. It had shocked Lissa at the time, but now Gina made a trilling noise of pleasure as Lissa found that silver ball and pulled gently on it. The metal was cool against her tongue, and Lissa played with the ball for several seconds just to hear Gina continue to make those sweet noises. Then she began to work in abandon, sliding her tongue deep inside Gina's pussy, doing the things to her new female bedmate that she most enjoyed having a lover do to her.

She found that she wasn't thinking about anything specific any longer. There were hands on her, tongues on her, fingertips running up and down her skin. And none of it concerned her. Pleasure was the main goal, her own pleasure, and she abandoned herself to this the way a surfer heads into the curl of a wave. The rush of excitement flooded through her, the out-of-control sensations washed over her, and she reached her peak and plunged.

Free-falling into a pleasure she had never known before.

Chapter Fifty-eight

*L*issa's body felt as if it were made of melted wax. Her long limbs were warm and malleable. Her hips, shimmying under the short, tight black dress, moved with a liquid ease. When Colin took her into his strong arms, holding her close, her body moulded itself to his and they moved as if they were one.

All around Lissa, women and men gyrated to the beat. To Lissa, in her relaxed, almost drugged state, the dancers seemed to move en masse, swelling up in a pulsating rhythm across the floor. Through half-closed lids, she took in her surroundings. The club was decorated to suit the mood. Mirrors along two walls reflected the scene into infinity. Half-naked waiters and waitresses brought drinks to those who preferred to watch, rather than join in. Silver cuffs attached to the non-mirrored walls were available for public use. Although several remained empty and waiting, most already captured subdued submissives for the enjoyment of their dominant masters.

Lissa looked at those moving on the floor around her. Black appeared to be the clothing colour of choice, with occasional red or metallic silver and gold thrown in like a seasoning to break the monotony. Lissa was wearing shiny black vinyl, an outfit Colin had purchased for her at the sex store, and the fabric glistened under the strobe lights.

'My pretty girl,' Colin whispered to her, his mouth close to her ear so that she could hear him over the throbbing beat of the music. 'How was all that?'

Lissa smiled at him, tilting her head back to look up at him in a coy manner. He knew exactly how it all was. He'd been there, participated, witnessed the change come over her.

'Did you like it?' he asked, and she was mildly amused to hear the slight sound of concern in his voice, just like the day before at the museum. Perhaps he was worried that he had somehow damaged her. That the events of the afternoon had been too much for her to process. Far from it, she could easily visualise herself spending many more afternoons in a similar fashion, basking in the pleasurable heat of so many different bodies. Who would have thought that people could fit together like that, creating a human jigsaw puzzle?

'Answer me, Lissa,' Colin suddenly demanded, and although his tone of voice remained the same, she could see in his green eyes that he meant it. She had a mental flash of what would happen to her if she didn't respond. He'd lift her dress, spank her here, in public. She wasn't wearing any panties or stockings, at Colin's insistence. The others in the crowd would have quite a show. But from the hedonistic goings-on around them, people dancing totally nude, girls in cages with their wrists chained above their heads, Lissa didn't think she and Colin would cause much of a stir.

Maybe he wouldn't spank her. Maybe he would take her over to the nearest set of handcuffs and chain her to the wall. He would unzip her dress and let it fall open, revealing her nakedness beneath it. Then he would offer her over to all the men – and women, too – for their pleasure. This thought appealed to Lissa and she lost herself further in it before being brought around again by Colin.

'Lissa,' he repeated, and she sensed the urgency in his voice.

'It was wonderful,' she told him, knowing that the words didn't suit what she felt. Wonderful was far too bland. Colin had made her secret fantasy come true. There simply were not words to explain what she was feeling. Instead, she danced with him, using her body to let him know. She felt completely altered, as if she still assumed the role of the prostitute she had played this afternoon. She was no longer Lissa Daniels, an expert art historian who was also an expert at hiding her emotions. She was now someone more evolved, a woman who could name what she wanted and go after it.

But what did she want now?

The DJ played music that could have been lifted from Lissa's personal soundtrack. First, there was Madonna, with a song from the Erotica album. Lissa's younger sister Julianne had given it to her for Christmas, and Lissa had been startled by the intensity of the lyrics, especially the chorus that mentioned pleasure with a little bit of pain. Now, she was no longer shocked at all. She rocked her body to the beat, feeling the words flow over her. Her hips shifted against Colin's as the music changed. She knew she shouldn't be surprised by the choices. They were in an S&M-themed dance club, after all, and the songs weren't aimed at her alone. But still, as Nine Inch Nails came on next, Trent Reznor crooning from the song 'Hurt', about violation and penetration, Lissa felt as if the song had been chosen just for her.

Colin pressed his lips to her ear and sang the most haunting single line along with Reznor: 'You let me do this to you.'

She had. What did that say about her? She had let him violate her . . . penetrate her . . . desecrate her. The white noise of the song washed over Lissa's body, and she moved away from Colin and danced by herself. Her long, blonde hair whipped around her face, and her body tingled all over when she thought of the different people who had touched it mere hours before.

She had let Colin transform her into someone who could not only speak her fantasies, but participate in them as they came to life. This was a good thing, wasn't it? The release of it felt marvellous, as if all of her negative energy had drained away. But maybe this was simply a reaction to the multiple orgasms she'd had. Who wouldn't feel relaxed after coming on a cock, tongue and fingers, within the space of a few hours?

The Red Hot Chili Peppers spewed out of the speakers with a blast of raucous sound. Lissa recognised the southern California band – everyone from LA was familiar with them – even though she didn't know their music very well. But now, it was as if Anthony, the tattooed lead singer, was speaking directly to her. In his deep, sexy voice, he sang about liking pleasure spiked with pain . . . That was *exactly* what she liked as well. In the past, if someone had suggested this to her, she most definitely would have denied it. She might even have acted disgusted at the thought. No longer. She would give herself to the sensations, give herself over to being re-created.

Yes, she liked pleasure spiked with pain. Liked it? Hell, she was learning to love it.

Book Five:
Jealousy

Nor jealousy
Was understood, the injured lover's hell.

– John Milton

Chapter Fifty-nine

*B*ack in Paris, the display was finally ready. Lissa told Colin where to meet her, explaining only that there was an exhibit she wanted him to see.

'But why aren't you going with me?' he asked. Unlike her questions, his demanded a response.

'Trust me,' Lissa said, waiting to see if he'd let her get away with it.

'I *do* trust you,' he told her, stroking her soft hair away from her face. She was wearing her hair down this evening, which was unusual for her. In general, she either pulled it back into a ponytail, or wore it in a French twist. With her hair loose over her shoulders, she looked younger and more vulnerable. He liked the look a lot. 'I do trust you,' he repeated, his voice lower, almost melodic, 'But are you certain that I will be pleased with the result?'

Lissa kissed him, leaning forward to do it. He smelled her hair and the minty fragrance of her toothpaste, and the real scent of herself. He wanted to fuck her, now, before they went to see this art show. His cock was hard and ready. All he'd have to do was grab her, throw her on to the bed, slide her skirt up and her panties down and take her. But Lissa pulled away before he could do

248

any of those things, before he could embrace her, before he could push her down on her knees and slide his cock into those pretty, red-glossed lips.

'Six o'clock,' she said, handing him a sheet of paper with the address of the gallery. 'Don't be late,' she added from the safety of the doorway, stepping through it and shutting the door before he could grab her and give her a spanking for sounding so uppity. She was giving him orders? Telling him where to be and when? He didn't know how to feel about that at all.

'Six o'clock,' he muttered to himself. He wouldn't obey. He'd show up when he was good and ready, not a moment before. Let her wait and worry and think about the tone of voice she'd used to issue her command.

During the few hours he had to himself in the apartment, Colin considered the structure of their relationship. ARTLOVER had come to Amsterdam. He had seen Lissa, had touched her, but hadn't taken Lissa away from him.

What did this mean? Was she his to keep? Had he won?

He thought about the foursome they'd shared. Truly, Colin had scheduled the orgy to see how Lissa would respond. And she had behaved as expected, obeying him to the very last detail. Didn't this prove that she loved him back? He wished he could talk to Lissa, considered explaining to her the plan in its entirety. If he spread it out for her to see, wouldn't she understand the motivations behind his actions?

But he hadn't been able to discuss it with her. He'd simply continued on with the farce, as if their experiences in Amsterdam had been just like those in Hamburg or Paris. As if they could fall back into their routine and never mention the changes that had occurred, the transformation they had shared.

Perhaps he would tell her tonight. Because he was certain that this evening things would come to a head.

After all, he knew more about Lissa's plans than she thought he did.

Still, he liked the sense of wonderment that washed over him as he poured a quick drink. An element of surprise was always rewarding. And, somehow, although he didn't know why he thought this, he was sure that Lissa wouldn't let him down. It's why he had issued her the challenge in the first place.

Of course, he had his own plans as well. But didn't he always?

Chapter Sixty

*L*issa's heart felt as if it were trying to escape from her breast. She had never been this nervous in all of her life. She knew that she'd taunted Colin, and that he wouldn't forget it, but that's not why she was feeling anxious. Colin, she understood. After six months of living with him, she could handle him. It wasn't his reaction she was worried about.

She had e-mailed the patron, inviting him to the opening as well, and she had no idea how all of this would turn out. It seemed to her that the whole relationship with Colin, the whole journey she'd been on for the previous six months was about to come to a climax. And this is what had her heart beating at triple-time.

Lissa had expected to be introduced to the patron before she and Colin had left Amsterdam. But Colin hadn't even mentioned the other members of their orgy, apart from asking if she'd liked 'the tools' he'd presented her with.

Still, Lissa hadn't been able to get the man out of her mind. When they'd returned to London, she had continually checked Colin's e-mail. Finally, she had written to the patron herself from an e-mail account at the museum. She found that she didn't care if Colin discovered she knew his secret. They were both guilty of hiding things from each other. But now, with her new-found confidence, most likely due to her sexual awakening that had taken place in Amsterdam, she couldn't keep from contacting the man herself.

Her tagline had simply read: Art is . . .?

When she saw the patron, the man who was collecting artwork based on her sexual pleasure, would she feel differently about him than she did now? When Colin saw him, how would he respond?

As she hurried to the gallery from the metro stop, she tried to push all of these questions from her mind. It was important to concentrate only on each individual moment as it occurred. There was no way to foresee the future, to guess the outcome of the evening, so why not enjoy the show as it unfolded?

She stepped through the front door of the gallery and into Gizelle's waiting embrace. Roberto stood a few paces away, and he smiled when he saw Lissa, then came forward to help with the final preparations for the show.

By the time Colin arrived at a quarter to eight, the small storefront gallery was filled, and people had spilled out on to the street, glasses of champagne and kir royales in their hands.

The crowd was buoyant, the atmosphere one of subdued partying. It was not unlike the feeling Colin had got in the New Orleans French Quarter when he'd travelled there one year for the Mardi Gras celebrations. People walking around with 'to go' cups of liquor, enjoying themselves as they wandered past voodoo shops and strip clubs. Of course, the French Quarter had a tackier feeling to it than this small Parisian neighbourhood, but the art appreciators here contained an element of that frivolity. They weren't drunk yet, but they were well on their way.

Looking around, Colin got the feeling that this crowd

was made up of artists. Their clothing was much brighter than the average French person's. In fact, they seemed to have decorated themselves, as if their bodies were works of art.

Flyers announcing the opening were papered to polls nearby and littered the streets themselves. Colin picked one up from the sidewalks, startled as he recognised the model.

He pushed through the crowd to get inside, and then hurried towards Lissa. He couldn't believe what he saw.

Lissa looked at the clock on the gallery wall. It was almost eight o'clock. So far, there had been no sign of Colin, and none of the patron. She wondered whether she had made a mistake in e-mailing this anonymous character. Each person who entered the gallery could be ARTLOVER, she reminded herself, although none matched the mental appearance she had created.

She took a deep breath as she saw Colin standing outside of the gallery. From the look on his face, he wasn't pleased. Well, so be it. He had issued her a challenge, and she had risen to it. If he couldn't accept the results, that was his problem. She worked hard to make her body relax, and she calmly turned and began a conversation with the few people standing around her. As always, talking about art made her more comfortable. She was in her element when discussing art work, and she did so now, working hard to ignore Colin as he stared into the gallery.

Chapter Sixty-one

*L*issa was stark naked, standing in the window.
   How dare she?
   Colin could hardly contain himself. His fists clenched at his sides, and he felt himself on the verge of losing control. With great effort, he took out a cigarette and lit it, inhaling the smoke deeply to calm himself. He only smoked when in Paris – it seemed like the thing to do – and he was grateful for the bitter taste of the Gauloise between his lips. His exhale of smoke was more of a sigh than anything else. He dropped the cigarette after two puffs and ground it into the pavement with his heel.
   If she wanted to play that type of game, he could top her at it in a second. Anger gave way to excitement that burnt through him as he moved forward, pushing his way through the crowd, jostling past people who refused to be offended by his brusqueness. It was in his mind to pull Lissa out of the window, thrust her over his lap, and truly spank the daylights out of her.
   'Bad girl,' he muttered under his breath as he entered the gallery. 'Naughty, sinful little fuck.' But when his hand connected with her wrist, he realised he'd been fooled. This wasn't Lissa at all, but a statue of her made in wax, perfect to look at, but only a piece of art. He

254

took a step back, observing the smoothness of the wax Lissa's skin, the expression on her face one of quiet calmness. For an instant, he caught himself smiling at the fact that he'd been tricked, and then he turned, to find the real Lissa.

She was everywhere.

It was instantly obvious to Colin that she'd got the idea from the exhibit in London. Although there, the bodies had been cast in iron, had been anonymous in their lack of faces and expressions. Only their tortured bodies showed pain, discomfort, unhappiness. Lissa's sculptures were more expressive. Here she was bent over, touching her toes, as if doing an early-morning exercise. From the rear of this vulnerable angle, one could see her beautiful ass and the space between her thighs, space which a friend of his had always referred to as 'factory error', girls whose thighs didn't touch at the tops.

Over in the corner, a Lissa sculpture sat cross-legged, reading a magazine. The magazine was real, although the Lissa was another waxwork, her long hair down over her shoulders, her lips parted, wax tongue peeking out.

Across the room, Colin saw a Lissa sleeping, her body sprawled on a day bed, knees apart, one arm thrown carelessly across her breast. He imagined himself, nude, climbing next to her in the bed, his head nestled against her neck, smelling her, kissing her, preparing to roll her over on to her side and enter her, spoon-style, for an early morning wake-up call. The thought of making love to a sculpture didn't bother him at all. He could easily visualise himself standing over her as he jerked off, ultimately coming on the waxy skin. The picture was clear in his mind – he'd enjoy watching the snowy drops of his semen as they beaded up and slid down the Lissa sculpture's arm, the flat of her belly, the magic place between her legs.

Through a throng of people, Colin could see yet

another Lissa. This one was positioned insolently, back propped against the wall, one leg up, smoking a cigarette. He couldn't figure out how the artist had done it. The cigarette actually appeared to be burning, the ash at the end growing longer. And then he realised that this Lissa was speaking to the people around her, that she wasn't a waxwork at all, but the real thing.

He was impressed. In the past, he had challenged her to find places to play, to set up situations for them to enjoy. Now, at the end of their six months together, she had actually managed to top him, managed to surprise him with something shocking, yet beautiful. Life and art entwined, overlapping one another in perfect synchronicity.

He moved closer, quietly, to hear what she was saying.

Chapter Sixty-two

*L*issa stopped speaking when she saw Colin. He was watching her intensely, and she suddenly forgot what she'd been talking about. The group around her waited patiently for her to continue, but then slowly they turned, as if one being, to see what had captured her attention.

'Don't let me interrupt,' Colin said. A slender, blonde Frenchwoman at his side quickly translated the words for her stockier acquaintance. The whole gallery had grown quiet, watching Colin and Lissa as if they were a tennis match, heads shifting back and forth from one lover to the other.

'Didn't know if you'd make it,' Lissa said, looking pointedly at the clock on the far wall of the gallery. He was two hours late.

'You know me and time,' Colin said. 'I have no real concept of it.'

Lissa smiled as the Frenchwoman translated again. Colin was being as bland as possible, giving her no hint of how he felt with his words, but telling her a whole different story with his eyes, with his expressions, and these were unable to be translated. He liked it, she knew that. He was impressed, and that was what she had hoped for. To show him that she could play his game as well, and that she could win at it if she tried hard enough.

Although, from the way he was staring at her now, she didn't know if 'win' was the correct word. Colin looked as if he had plans of his own, and she had never got better at second-guessing him. It was always to her benefit to stay quiet and to wait him out.

She thought of trying to talk to him, to explain how she had set up the exhibit, the intricacies of working with Gizelle, the gallery owner, and Roberto, the artist. But she didn't think Colin would be very interested. He made her so nervous with that dead-eyed look of his. She bent to rest her cigarette in an ashtray on a table at her side, and then stood up again, her back erect, acting more confident than she felt.

For the first time of the evening, she was truly aware of her own nakedness. Earlier, the excitement had fuelled her exhibitionist quality. Besides, she had felt as if she were part of an art show, not on display as a sexual object. But the way Colin stared at her made her feel confused – it was the look he gave her before punishing her, just that one simple expression on his face, and she didn't know what to do about it. She ran her hands along the tops of her thighs, and then up her ribs before crossing her arms in front of her breasts.

Suddenly, she wished she were alone with him. The main difficulty came from the crowd. They continued to watch the lovers size each other up. They seemed to sense that there would be some sort of show, something exciting to watch, more exciting even than the fact that this beautiful woman, the model for the show, had been walking around naked all evening.

The group parted as Colin stepped forward. One woman made a little, gasping sound, as if she thought Colin might strike Lissa. He didn't. He simply brought his face to her ear and whispered, 'I'm impressed.'

Lissa couldn't keep the smile off her face.

'And you know how much it takes to impress me.'

She nodded.

'But you also know that I can never be bested.'

Lissa's heart started to pound loudly in her ears. Her cheeks flushed as Colin reached out and drew a line down her breastbone to her navel, stopping at the top of her soft, blonde patch of hair between her legs.

The crowd, which had parted to let Colin through, now came closer around to circle Colin and Lissa. There was Gizelle, the owner of the gallery, and Roberto, the artist standing next to her. Both had mild smiles on their faces, as if they were accustomed to this sort of thing. Lissa, who hadn't known how Colin would take the exhibit, felt relieved that he liked it, but the way he was behaving sent a wash of fear through her. His lips had reached her pussy, and he wasn't standing up or moving away. He was opening her with his fingers as if she were a flower and her lips the delicate petals, and beginning to lick in a languid circle around her clit.

It would have been easier for Lissa to accept if he had been angry. If he had taken her by the hand to the back room and spanked her bottom for being so bold. But it didn't appear as if that were Colin's plan at all. He was going to make her come in public, fulfilling yet another of her fantasies, and she didn't know if she could handle it.

Colin moved his mouth away from Lissa's sex and motioned towards the owner of the gallery. The woman hurried to his side. In perfect French, Colin asked if she would remove the statue of Lissa from the front window. The woman nodded to two men in the crowd and they hurried to obey this request. Then, without a word to Lissa, Colin lifted her up and brought her to the front of the gallery. The people crushed outside the window gathered even closer to the glass, understanding that something momentous was about to happen.

Lissa shut her eyes as Colin positioned her, hands on the window, face towards the crowd. Colin wouldn't

259

have any of that, though, and he told Lissa in a dark voice to open her eyes. She obeyed at once, not wanting to test his mood any further.

'That's my girl,' Colin said softly. 'Now keep them open. No matter what.'

Lissa struggled to say, 'Yes, Colin,' as he got on his knees in front of her and went back to kissing her pussy lips, slowly and softly, making her wetter than she had been all evening. He pulled away from her once more, whispering something in French to the people standing behind Lissa, and then resumed his activity. Suddenly, Lissa felt hands on her, stroking her all over. At least ten of the guests were touching her body, and the sensation of all of those fingertips was electrifying. She struggled to keep her eyes open. The waves of pleasure moving through her made it difficult for her to obey this command.

She remembered a trick she'd learnt at a public speaking convention. Choose one person in the front row of the audience and one person towards the back to focus on. Make those two people your friends and speak solely to them. Lissa wondered if it would work in a situation like this one. She didn't have anything to lose, and she looked at the crowd, scanning the people furthest from the window. Her eyes fell on a familiar face. Gina stood across the tiny street, staring at her with a friendly, encouraging expression.

'Gina's here,' Lissa murmured, and Colin stopped for a moment and looked up at her.

'I told her about the opening. I hope you don't mind,' he whispered. His lips glistened with the juices of Lissa's pleasure, and she shook her head, fighting the urge to beg him to continue. She had been close to climax, but she knew that if she told him that, he would slow down further. He liked to draw every bit of pleasure out of her, making her work for it.

Taking a deep breath, Lissa looked back at the crowd. Gina's eyes were still on her, and Lissa swallowed hard, grateful to find someone she knew who wouldn't have any kind of problem with what she was doing now. But now the hard part. Locate someone towards the front of the crowd.

Her eyes flickered over the motley crew. A bald man with a scruffy beard stared at her with glazed eyes. No. Not him. At his side stood a tall, thin woman elegantly blowing smoke rings towards the night sky. Not her either. Finally, Lissa found the nerve to glance directly in front of her and when she did she sucked in her breath.

There was Marcus, looking at her inquisitively as if wondering just when she'd notice him. She recognised him instantly, but then questioned herself. He looked different. There was an unkempt quality to his appearance, as if he'd discovered his bohemian side during her absence. His dark hair was longer, falling almost to the top of his collar. His shirt was open and he wasn't wearing a tie.

As soon as her gaze locked on his, he smiled, and held up his champagne glass in a toast.

Chapter Sixty-three

'*I*t's Marcus,' Lissa managed to squeak out. Colin stopped what he was doing long enough to look up at her, and when she met his eyes she realised that there was something he knew that she didn't. Something he'd known all along, and that he was waiting for her to get it.

'My *husband*,' Lissa continued, not sure how to decipher the message in Colin's gaze.

'*Estranged* husband,' Colin corrected her. He appeared totally unconcerned, going on to spread her pussy lips and drive his tongue inside her cunt. The edge of his tongue flicked against her inner walls, and she groaned. It felt so good to have Colin kissing her like that, his actions not even the slightest bit gentle, a mimicking of how he took her with his cock. In and out and hard, reaching so far into her that his mouth was sealed against the nether lips of her pussy. He was going to make her come, simply by fucking her with his tongue. The feeling of being taken, powerfully taken, knocked everything else out of her mind. Colin's hands came around to cradle her ass, bringing her even closer to him. His fingers parted her rear cheeks, and oh, God – she had almost reached it –

But there was Marcus, staring fixedly at her. Her knees buckled and she struggled to regain her balance. Forcefully, she put one hand on Colin's shoulder and moved him back. Colin actually let her control him for a moment, which made Lissa feel even more uneasy. What was going on?

'How did he know to come here?' she managed to ask.

'You told him,' Colin answered matter-of-factly.

'I did what?'

'You told him,' Colin repeated. 'You sent him a detailed e-mail, inviting him to this gallery opening.'

Understanding rushed through Lissa, and she shuddered. Marcus had been the patron. All along, this whole time, her husband had been the one choreographing the amazing adventures. He had melted at the pictures of her from Hamburg, had commissioned the videotape from Paris, had been there, in the room with her and Colin and Gina in Amsterdam. She felt at once betrayed and relieved. It was Marcus – and somehow that changed everything.

Colin made a move forward, as if he was ready to continue pleasing her, but she took a step back. The audience of the gallery had closed in tightly. They seemed to think this was part of the drama put on for their amusement. Lissa sensed them, the heat of their bodies, but didn't seem to see them. She only had eyes for Colin, on his knees before her.

Thoughts spiralled through her mind. Colin had known that she'd cracked his e-mail code and had contacted Marcus behind his back. He had known, but apparently he hadn't cared.

Why hadn't she considered for a moment that it could be Marcus? She felt like an idiot, but then why *should* she have thought it was her husband? Marcus had never seemed interested in kinky sexual activities. And that was most definitely what she and Colin had been engaging in. The kinkiest possible activities, all at the behest of the mysterious patron.

Colin continued, undisturbed, as if his explanation – as if any explanation – might soothe her. 'He was interested. He wanted to see your transformation.'

'My transformation –' Lissa repeated, the words making as little sense to her as if they were in another language.

'From the shy little mouse of a girl that he married to someone who would actually let herself get fucked in front of hundreds of people.' Colin grinned at Lissa, casually stroking his fingertips along her inner thigh. 'It's what you wanted, isn't it? What you most wanted out of all of your other fantasies.'

Lissa was shaking all over. The hands which had been stroking her throughout suddenly pulled away, as if the audience sensed the change in the performance. Lissa wrapped her arms around her body, again feeling her nakedness. She wished she had a robe to slide into, a coat to slip on, a dark alley to vanish down.

'But how would he know?' she murmured. 'How would he know what I wanted? And how would you –?

'Your diary,' Colin said, smiling. Lissa suddenly wanted to slap him, slap that smug expression off his face. Instead, she turned quickly, pushing her way through the crowd. They didn't part as easily this time. Apparently, they believed this was also a segment of the act, something for them to witness and draw pleasure from. Lissa's path was hindered by people congratulating her on her openness as she tried to reach the small room at the back of the studio. But it meant that Colin couldn't get through to her easily, either. People kept stopping him to ask questions, to commend him for the honesty of his performance.

After what seemed like an hour, but was in actuality less than a minute, Lissa reached the back room. She hesitated, out of breath, in the tiny office, wondering what to do next. Gizelle, who had watched everything from the rear of the gallery, swept through the door after her and locked it behind them.

'I have to get out of here,' Lissa said.

Gizelle nodded. She seemed to understand, even though there was no real way she could. 'Go upstairs. To my apartment. I will get rid of everyone.'

'No,' Lissa shook her head. 'I need to leave.' She was pacing the office as if she were a caged animal, her long hair loose down her back like a golden mane.

'Please,' Gizelle said, motioning to the door that led to her apartment. 'Just walk through there and up the stairs. You can relax. Then decide where to go.'

Again Lissa shook her head. Her clothes were still in the centre of the gallery, where she'd stripped out of them earlier in the evening. It seemed like a different life. As she looked as if she were on the verge of running out of the office, naked, Gizelle quickly handed Lissa a long black coat that hung on the back of the door and kicked off her own expensive leather loafers.

'Come back,' Gizelle said, 'when you calm down.'

Lissa slipped into the shoes, and stumbled to explain what was going on, but Gizelle shook her head. 'Love triangle,' she said in her accented French. 'Sometimes one must be alone to discover where one's heart truly lies.'

This didn't exactly explain Lissa's emotional state. Honestly, she felt like an emotional punchbag, bruised on both sides by two different boxers. But rather than try to set Gizelle straight, she reached for her purse, which rested on Gizelle's desk, gave the woman a quick kiss on both cheeks, then pushed open the back door and hurried into the alley that ran behind the gallery.

Lissa could see the Seine from where she stood, and she ducked her head and walked towards it, knowing that as long as she knew where the river was, she could find her bearings in the city of lights.

Chapter Sixty-four

What a mess, Colin thought as he walked slowly back to the apartment. He could have taken the metro, but he wanted to tire himself out over the walk back to his neighbourhood. For once in his life, his plans had not served him in the manner in which he expected. Yes, he had known that Lissa had discovered the existence of a patron. She had tried to be sly and hide the fact from him, but she was such an easy read. Always. The expressions on her face, the look in her grey eyes, gave her away every time. Still, he had thought that once she had seen Marcus in person, she would instantly realise her love had faded for her husband. And that it had grown for himself.

Idiot, he chastised himself. Instead of winning her to him, he had managed to drive her away from both of them. If it hadn't been for the gallery owner's help, he would have been able to corner Lissa in the office, to explain everything from the beginning. But when he'd finally pushed through the crowd, the office had been empty except for Gizelle, who had given him a blank expression, as if she didn't speak English. The cunt.

He caught sight of his reflection in a closed shop window, the light from a street lamp behind him making

266

his image look ghostly and transparent. That's how he felt. It's how he was without her.

What if she wouldn't come back to him?

He paused in front of a bar, considering a lone drink. Scotch, perhaps. Straight up. He could definitely use it. But, no. He had to go back to the apartment. Maybe she would be waiting for him there. That thought made him quicken his step. Perhaps he would round the corner of rue d'Italie and see her sitting on the edge of the pavement. He could visualise the picture in his head, and it made the image seem real. Lissa, her hair loose over her shoulders, her expression a wash of confusion.

As he walked, he tried to reassure himself that even if she wasn't on his doorstep, he would find her. The problem was that he had no idea where she could have gone. Marcus, who might have had some concept as to where his wife would find shelter in Paris, had disappeared as well. Colin had lost extra minutes searching for him in the dispersing crowd, mobbed by young Frenchwomen who wanted their turn with him in the window.

With distaste, Colin had shaken them off. They did nothing for him. He wanted only Lissa, and when he found an empty front step at his apartment, he could have cried. He circled the block once, thinking she might have had the same thought as he had, that she might have gone to a nearby bar to numb herself. But she was not in any of the local hang-outs. Finally, he returned to the apartment building, walked slowly to the fourth floor, and let himself in. He poured a shot of whisky, and took it to the balcony, looking out at the night sky while he drank.

How had it all come to this? he wondered. The plan had been so simple, so easy to follow. But he had forgotten what happened when people's hearts got thrown into the mixture. Closing his eyes, he remembered the first time he'd seen Lissa, at the Frankfurt Book Fair, and all that their meeting had meant.

Chapter Sixty-five

She would not 'poor me' herself to death. Life could be worse than having been double-crossed by her husband and her lover. Many people had it tougher than she did. Still, as Lissa walked along the Seine, she felt miserable. And why shouldn't she? She'd been some pawn in a game between the two men she had most trusted in her life. Her husband, even though he was estranged, had never lied to her. And Colin – Colin – she'd put everything in his hands. Her soul. Her secret desires.

Her heart.

The water in the river shone silvery beneath the light of the full moon. Without the tour boats cruising along, it seemed larger, and older, as did the buildings on either side. Lissa approached Notre-Dame and stood silently for a moment, witnessing its majestic beauty. On a previous trip to France, she had entered the church, staring at the lovely windows, the famed altar. Now, she thought the outside was even more spectacular. In the moonlight, it seemed to command a sense of respect –

Her thoughts were interrupted by a rustling behind her and she turned, thinking that Colin might have followed her. What would she do if he had? She wouldn't go with him. And what if it was Marcus?

She didn't have to worry about confronting either her husband or Colin. She'd only disturbed two young lovers who were leaning against the concrete wall that lined the walkway. They turned to look at her and then returned to their business. As she continued along the river, Lissa could hear the woman moaning. Paris was a city for lovers.

So what was she doing here?

She would not wallow. She would simply make a plan. That was all she needed, a solid plan to get her world back together. She still had her book to write and a fine job to return to in California. Nothing dramatic had changed in her life. She'd simply spent six months in the midst of some sort of romantic farce.

But how could they? Just when she had felt at ease with herself, with her body and her desires, all of this had come crashing down around her.

At the next bench, Lissa sat down, wrapping Gizelle's warm coat around her body. She remembered suddenly that she was naked beneath it, and that made her feel more alone than she ever had before.

Chapter Sixty-six

Colin refilled his glass without noticing what he was doing. The whisky was one of the better brands, but he could have been drinking paint-thinner. All he wanted to do was obliterate the image of Lissa's face before she'd fled from him. That look of disgust and distrust. He didn't understand it. When she'd known about the patron, she had seemed even more turned on by the thought. Obviously, it was discovering the identity – that the patron was Marcus – that had made her feel betrayed.

Out on the balcony again, he remembered locating her booth in the huge maze of aisles at the Frankfurt fair. He closed his eyes and, once again, he was there.

She was faced towards him, but not looking at him. Behind her stood her book, a huge coffee-table book that featured some of America's newest art talents. She'd researched it for four years, Marcus had told him, and the thing was well-received, garnering her quite a bit of popularity at the show. She glowed, standing there in the three-cubicle booth, surrounded by other artsy-fartsy types. Colin put his hands in his pockets and took a few steps back, blending with the crowd so that he could better observe her. Marcus had given him a photograph, but it hadn't done her justice. The woman was radiant. Maybe the show did that to her, but Colin didn't think so. There was a light in her eyes he hadn't expected.

During a fraternity reunion, when Marcus had told him their sex life was nil, that the energy between them had all but vanished, the two men had come up with this scheme, this odd brainwave, based loosely on the Hitchcock movie, *Strangers on a Train.*

'I can't believe I'm asking you to do this,' Marcus had said over drinks in the hotel bar.

Colin, who'd subtly put the idea forward, in such a clever way that it made Marcus think he had come up with it himself, simply nodded. 'Sure, it sounds odd, but it might work. If I fuck your wife just right, it might actually save your marriage.'

This wasn't something a normal college buddy could suggest. But Colin and Marcus weren't college buddies. They were both part of a club – the Silver Dragons – a secret society that invited only twelve members a year to join. This was something that one dragon could suggest to another without fear.

The two had laughed in a manly way, pumping each other's hands when they'd parted. Colin had waited impatiently in his room that night, thinking that Marcus might change his mind, call and cancel the whole plot. He'd found himself pacing, from the bed to the sofa and back again, filled with nervous energy. But the phone hadn't rung, and Colin had got a ticket to Frankfurt and shown up here, waiting for the right time to walk into the booth and greet her.

Now. There weren't that many people nearby. No one to overhear what he planned to say to Lissa. Her back was to him, as she straightened several books on the shelves, and Colin strode forward, slid his arms around her slender waist, and pressed his lips against her ear.

She didn't scream. She didn't even tense up. In fact, in the few seconds he held her in his arms, she seemed to relax. Her body felt good in his embrace. Slender, yet lithe and firm like a ballerina's. Her body felt right, and when she thought to pull away, to turn around, he saw a hopeful look in her grey eyes. It made him more certain of himself than he'd been when walking forward. He always had a look of confidence to him, but often it was a bit of an act. With her waiting, her eyes now forming questions that he read with ease, he heard her say, 'I'm sorry.'

He couldn't believe it. This was all going to be so easy. Much easier than Colin had expected, than Marcus had prepared him for. Colin kept his emotions under control, responding gently, 'Of course, you would be. That's your nature.'

Marcus had been waiting for a report. Something to let him know about the progression of their plan. An e-mail message stating that all had gone as expected. 'Give her a bit of excitement. Wake her up a little,' Marcus had said at the reunion. 'I've seen the longing in her eyes. I don't know how to give her what she wants. So give her an affair to remember. We'll work it out from there.' A pause, his voice gone deep and husky, 'We have to be able to work it out. I don't think I could live without her.'

Marcus had thought the romance – if you could call it that – would be only for the duration of the fair. She'd come back to California, charged up, changed, and he could be changed, too. Show her how wild he was capable of being. Start over from scratch now that she'd melted and was ready for a new type of life. Marcus wanted to be sexy for her, to do the things he'd read about in her diary. Make love to her on the worn wooden bleachers of the amphitheatre at the Hollywood Bowl. Take her under the boardwalk at the Santa Monica pier. Join the Mile High Club with her in the new double beds on Virgin's trans-Atlantic flights.

Colin, however, had other plans. A week? He couldn't do anything properly in seven short days. And there was so much going on at the book fair. Signings she was required to attend. As guest of honour, she had to be there. Parties. Dinners. A special celebration in honour of her book. No, the real progress would happen after the fair, back in London. And he had just the connections to make it happen. Connections throughout Europe.

Maybe Marcus had got more than he bargained for. But then Marcus hadn't really known who he was bargaining with, had he? Colin had changed since medical school. Then he'd been a prankster, clever, the wit of the class. His stern good looks had hidden his true identity, always allowing him to get away with things that no one would expect of him. Now, he was more in control, more even-tempered. He had the same quick mind, but he used it for entirely different purposes.

With Lissa, his plan had been to win her for himself.

Now, looking out at midnight over Paris, he realised how mixed up his schemes had got. He was supposed to be the one in charge, the one who shook her up and made her relationship right again. But the power had shifted. When had she taken control and turned his world upside-down?

And how on earth could he take the power back?

Chapter Sixty-seven

*A*t three in the morning, Lissa knocked on the rear door of the gallery. She was drenched to the bone from the rain that had started over an hour before. Desperately, she hoped Gizelle would still be there. She'd left her clothes inside, but that was not why she'd returned. After walking along the Seine in the rain, trying to figure out what to do, she had realised that she had no other place to go. The types of people she'd passed along the river had convinced her to return to the gallery. Lovers pressed against the cold, stone pillars. Solitary pedestrians eyeing her carefully and with a frightening interest as she went by.

Gizelle found Lissa outside the gallery door, shivering and confused. Her blonde hair was tousled and wet, and her cheeks were flushed.

'Roberto said you would return,' Gizelle told Lissa, smiling warmly. 'He waited here to see if you needed help.' And now the gallery owner and the artist welcomed Lissa back inside, then hurried her to the apartment Gizelle kept up the stairs.

'You'll stay here,' Gizelle murmured, touching Lissa's damp hair, helping her out of the sopping coat. Roberto stood in the doorway, watching, his light eyes mesmerised by Lissa's form. He had seen Lissa naked, of course, when she'd posed for the sculptures. But there was something different in the way she looked now. As if she truly were one of those art pieces come to life. Gizelle had lit candles, and their light flickered over Lissa's shivering form. Lissa seemed to be stunned or in shock from the goings-on of the evening, didn't try to hide herself, didn't seem to know what to do with the large, white towel that Gizelle offered.

Roberto came forward and took the towel from the gallery owner, slowly approaching Lissa, as if afraid she might tell him to go away, then helping her to dry herself when she made no move to stop him. He worked from her shoulders down, slowly patting dry her arms and her hands, her back and her stomach, her thighs and her calves. Then he worked up her body, equally slowly, using the towel on the inside of her legs, reaching her sex and gently drying her there.

'Better, right?' he asked, his English halting, but his message clear.

Lissa looked down at him, her eyes wide. But she did nothing to stop him. She seemed as still inside as one of the wax sculptures he'd created of her. He wondered what it would take to make her melt. Roberto turned to look at the gallery owner, asking her with his eyes what he should do, whether he should continue.

Gizelle, her eyes also locked on Roberto, gave him a single nod, and he moved closer instantly, spreading Lissa's pussy lips with his fingers and then lapping at her cunt with the flat of his tongue. His dark whiskers tickled and Lissa jumped at the sensation, then put her hands on his shoulders, giving him the reassurance that she wanted this.

Gizelle moved closer to the twosome, standing behind Lissa and pressing her body against Lissa's. Gizelle's slender arms came around Lissa to begin touching and caressing the wet woman's breasts. Lissa sighed and leant back into the gallery owner as Roberto continued his work down below, sliding his tongue into Lissa's pussy and then bringing it back around to her clit again, making those desperately slow circles that had Lissa weak-kneed in moments. Gizelle, who was much stronger than she looked, supported Lissa's weight for several seconds, holding tightly as Lissa trembled all over from the magic Roberto was working with his tongue.

Lissa hadn't come from Colin's ministrations earlier in the evening. She was on the verge in only seconds from the way Roberto teased her.

'To the bed?' Roberto asked as he paused for breath. Lissa and Gizelle nodded in unison, and the trio moved to the bed located in the corner of the one-room studio. It was a king-sized bed, low to the floor, and covered with black satin sheets and a velvet comforter. Gizelle tossed the comforter to the floor and the three sprawled out on the shiny, slippery sheets. Lissa had never been in such a bed before. Everything about it was sumptuous. The mattress was firm below them, the sheets so smooth that when she moved her body, she slid against them. Velvety pillows provided support under her neck.

To one side of the bed, windows opened up on to a tiny balcony. Beyond it, Paris and the Seine lay shimmering beneath the moon. To the other side, a full-length mirror reflected the passion of the three lovers. It was to this side that Lissa faced. The pleasure of watching surpassed the orgy she'd experienced with Colin – when the blindfold had kept her from viewing those goings-on.

With Roberto on one side of her and Gizelle on the other, Lissa found that she no longer needed to think about what had happened this evening. She could let her worries slip away, paying attention only to what was occurring right now. Participating in the action, rather than being a passive player.

Roberto leant up on one arm and stared at Lissa, observing every dip and curve of her body. He knew her body so well from creating the waxwork of it, but now that he had the real thing to touch, he seemed almost in awe of her, unable to continue. Lissa leant forward and kissed him, on the lips, and this seemed to start his motor again, helped him to get back into the action.

'I like that,' Lissa said softly, stroking Roberto's chin, enjoying the tickling-scratchy sensation of his beard. 'It feels good on my skin.'

Roberto smiled at this and returned her kiss, rubbing his face gently against hers so that she could feel his whiskers, making Lissa laugh. Then he moved down her body, resuming his position between her legs. He had got a taste of her nectar, and now he wanted more. He told her this, in French, and Lissa lay back on the bed and sighed at the combination of the words and the actions. It was delicious, the smoothness of his lips and tongue, the roughness of his beard.

Lissa became the centre of attention. Gizelle bent to focus on her breasts, kissing one and then the other, making the nipples stand out firmly like tiny jewels. Roberto straddled one of Lissa's legs, so that she could feel his cock straining against her as he continued playing hide and seek with his tongue in her pussy.

There were few words during the lovemaking. Each partner took cues from the others' bodies. As Lissa sighed and raised her hips, Roberto swivelled around so that he could tap her clit with the head of his cock. This made Lissa moan, a sound that came from deep within her body, and Roberto took this to mean that she was ready for him to make love to her.

She was. Lissa spread her legs apart and Gizelle moved forward to hold Lissa's pussy lips open as Roberto slid the head of his cock inside her. There was something insanely decadent about having Gizelle as the helper. It was a role Lissa would have played herself, she realised, if Colin were present. She would have been the underling. Now, she was the central figure, and as she felt Gizelle's fingers slipping in her juices, she had to work not to come right on the spot.

It was important to her that she make this last.

Roberto's eyes were focused on her own, building a connection between them. Lissa kept her gaze on his, but she was aware of Gizelle moving, sliding down the bed, positioning herself at the edge. Suddenly, Lissa felt Gizelle's warm mouth on her toes. This was something she'd never experienced before, something she wouldn't have thought she would enjoy. And yet as Gizelle's tongue slipped up and around each one of Lissa's toes, the sensation was overwhelming. Lissa contracted hard on Roberto's cock every time Gizelle's tongue flicked out to connect with her skin. This made Roberto moan and thrust in harder, driving Lissa closer to the brink again.

When Gizelle started to move up Lissa's body, licking long strokes up the insides of her legs, Lissa could take it no longer.

'I'm going to come,' she murmured, reaching up to grip Roberto's arms.

'Wait,' he whispered. 'Come with me.'

Lissa struggled not to reach orgasm, but could wait no longer as Gizelle moved around her body, positioning her pussy over Lissa's open mouth. Lissa came into it, her lips locked on Gizelle's clit, her moans reverberating within the other woman's body. Gizelle came on the pulse of Lissa's climax, and Roberto, who had been staving it off as long as possible, groaned and shot his come deep into Lissa's pussy.

The three, still connected to each other, took several seconds to slip apart. But craving the heat and the safe feeling of being merged, they slept with arms entwined in the centre of Gizelle's large bed.

Chapter Sixty-eight

*U*nlike Colin, Marcus didn't even try to find his wife. When Lissa was upset, she always needed time on her own. There was no rushing her out of one mood and into another. Besides, even if he wanted to find her, how could he possibly track one woman in all of Paris? There were too many places for her to hide, too many artists she could call on to help her. Instead, he sat in front of his laptop computer and read through her diary one more time.

He believed that if he could climb inside Lissa's head, he would know what to do next. The whole experiment had been based solely on her fantasies. Yet now that reality had caught up with him, he was having trouble making decisions.

The doctor in him looked over his list. He had fulfilled almost every fantasy – through Colin, at least. She had made love in public, to be put on display, to dabble in the dangerously sexy world of S&M, to make love to a woman, to dress up in wild clothing. What was left? To connect with *him* on a deeper level. He shook his head. This was how he had failed her. How had he thought that giving her to Colin would work to make their own love a stronger bond? He tried to reassure himself. It had been a last-ditch effort. She'd already left him when he found the diary on a disc in her computer bag, tossed in the back of their wardrobe.

He pressed a button on his computer and watched as the movie of Lissa and Colin in the French erotic art museum began to play. The camera focused on her face, her parted lips, and he realised something he hadn't noticed before. When she came, she said his name. He saw her lips forming the word, and he heard the way it sounded in his head.

This was all he needed to know he could make it work. If he found her, he could make it all work out.

Now, all he had to do was find her.

Chapter Sixty-nine

Colin guessed, correctly, where Lissa was spending her days. He knew that she wouldn't be able to write. Not when she was upset. She needed a clear head to focus on her book. Yet she wouldn't remove herself from art completely, because art was the glue that held her together. And she had told him that the Louvre was her favourite museum in the world.

He waited for her at the café Marielle, sipping espresso after espresso and watching the tourists hurrying towards the glass pyramid that marked the opening of the museum. He wasn't sure how he felt about this particular work – whether it was truly art or simply a gimmick. The pyramid, a modern glass creation by I. M. Pei, looked odd in the centre of such a grandiose atrium. But at least it provided him with a specific place to watch for her. He knew that Lissa would use this entrance to approach the museum rather than take one of the escalators underground from the street. She actually liked the design.

On the third day of watching, Colin spotted Lissa in the courtyard. At first, he wasn't sure that it was her. Yes, she strode forward with her trademark walk, always moving with a purpose, but there was something different about her. He squinted as she approached the museum, then chastised himself. It was definitely Lissa, with dark sunglasses on and her hair swept off her face, revealing that neck he loved, the delicate collarbones he liked to trace with his fingertips. She had on a light-blue wrap-around dress, something he'd never seen before. Obviously, she had left without any clothes, without anything but the coat that woman had given her. She must have spent the last three days shopping, he decided. But there was something else different about her, something that went deeper than the new clothes.

As he stared at her, he realised that she'd changed other parts of her appearance as well. Her hair wasn't simply pulled back from her face. She'd had it crafted into a pixie cut. The look suited her, shaved years from her appearance. She looked like a young runway model, strutting forward in a pair of neutral-hued slingbacks, a matching bag over her arm and those dark sunglasses in place, as if she were trying to go incognito. Which, he realised, she must be.

He slipped several coins next to his saucer and stood, waiting for her to enter the museum before following her down the stairs. The Louvre, the largest museum in the world, had seven different departments. The painting section, with the 'Mona Lisa' at the heart of the exhibit, was the most popular. Colin stared at the maps above the ticket counter, trying to figure out which exhibit Lissa would have chosen.

He remembered one of their first weekends together, when he had wanted to learn everything about her. 'Tell me your favourite piece of art,' he'd demanded. It had taken Lissa a long time to choose. She preferred different types of art for different moods, and she'd tried to explain this to him. He recalled how she'd looked, tied to his bed, arms over her head, legs apart. That lesson had been on control, and he had brushed a feather duster over her body, just letting the brightly coloured feathers tickle her skin until the sensations were overwhelming. Making her talk while he tormented her was the fun part. And finally Lissa had given him an answer between bouts of laughter, managing to tell him, 'The Venus de Milo', because of its beauty and its age combined.

Colin paid for his ticket, then hurried through the exhibits. He saw none of the art as he walked through the corridors. The ancient Greek sculptures did nothing for him. He only had eyes for Lissa, searching out her pale-blue dress, listening for the sound of her footsteps. He looked in all of the rooms before finding her exactly where he'd expected, in front of the Venus.

It was obvious to Colin that Lissa didn't feel his eyes on her right away. She was mesmerised by the work, as always, and she stood before it as if she and the sculpture were the only things left on earth. To Colin, she had the look of a woman in a church, before an altar, making peace with herself and with her God. And because of the obvious sanctity of the moment, he felt loath to interrupt her, waiting, hardly breathing, for her to notice him.

Finally, the room was empty except for the two of them – three if you counted the sculpture of Venus – and Colin could stand it no longer. Stepping forward, he said her name softly. She heard his voice and turned to look at him.

The anger in her eyes startled Colin enough that he forgot what he had planned on saying. Although he'd worked out this scenario several times in his mind, for some reason he hadn't expected her to be angry. Confused, yes. Troubled by the whole arrangement, of course. But not angry. Could it be possible that after all this time, he was the one who was naive?

'Why are you here?' Lissa asked. Her voice was like a slap, and he had to work not to take a step back from her.

'To see you,' he said, surprised now at the tone of his own voice. He sounded cowed, as if he were the submissive one in the pair, the one who needed assurances, who required constant stroking. He forced himself to stand up straighter, was thankful that he had taken the time to dress carefully. His dark suit made him feel more powerful than if he'd simply put on Levis and a sweater.

'What do you want?' Lissa asked next. Her sunglasses were off now, and he could see the beauty in her face. She rivalled any of the artwork in the museum, he thought. He would be satisfied to simply stand where he was and look at her. Still, he wished she didn't sound so cold. All he wanted was to take her in his arms, to promise her that he would be hers for ever. To tell her that the plan, the experiment, had gone awry, and that instead of him sparking her libido, she had won his heart.

'What do you want, Colin?' Lissa asked again, and he was reminded of all the times he had questioned her repeatedly to get the answer he desired. Was she doing the same thing? Looking for a specific answer? From the glare in her eyes, he didn't think so. She seemed only to want to end their interaction as quickly as possible so that she could go back to staring at her beloved statue.

It was in Colin's head to turn around and leave her alone. That's what a normal dominant would do. If she wanted him, she knew where to find him. But he couldn't. There was so much that he wanted to tell her, so many things to explain. He took a breath, ready to start, and realised that he didn't know how. This feeling of unease was alien to him. Where was his confidence, where was his cool demeanour?

He was thankful that he'd typed it all into a letter, because ultimately all he had to do was walk forward and hand it to her. She looked as if she might shred it in front of him, but he didn't wait to see if she would. He simply bent to kiss her, once, on the lips, and then hurried from the room.

Chapter Seventy

*L*issa took the letter to the Tuileries Gardens. It was a lovely day and she thought of going to sit on one of the chairs around the fountain, of buying a glass of white wine and sipping it among the tourists, artists and locals enjoying the sun. But as she walked across the street towards the garden, she saw that the ferris wheel was up and running. A first sign of spring.

Feeling slightly giddy, Lissa paid her fare and entered the ride. From the top of the ferris wheel, the view of Paris was breathtaking. It was at this spot that Lissa opened Colin's letter and read what it said. She used two full rides to soak in the meaning of the words, and she found that she was shaking as she comprehended what Colin had written. But at least she understood now, and understanding was somehow better than the not knowing she'd lived with for three days. The surprise of seeing Marcus standing outside the window had been worse than this. So Colin had been little more than a gigolo, a hired hand, someone to stir her passion, to enflame her soul.

The young man running the ride raised his eyebrows as her car came to a stop in front of him. Did she want to go around again? She nodded. The clear, warm air was doing wonders for her, keeping her from freaking out entirely. She no longer wanted a simple glass of wine – a scotch straight up would do her fine.

Down below, she thought she saw a blur of red hair in the crowd gathered around the fountain. Was Colin waiting for her? He could wait as long as he liked, she wouldn't go to him. But even as she thought this, her heart pounded. She hadn't been totally innocent in the relationship either, had she? She had kept it to herself that she was separated from her husband, she had discovered that there was a patron collecting their erotic works of art, and she'd continued with the farce. If she'd known that the patron was Marcus from the start, would that have made any difference?

She didn't know. All she knew for a fact was that she felt angry and betrayed.

The code of the two med school boys, members of the same idiot club. Why hadn't she worked it out before? But then, why should she have? Since Marcus had kept quiet about the club, she hadn't known that it was an international group. How could she possibly have guessed that Marcus and Colin would be friends?

The ferris wheel continued on its rotating route, and Lissa lowered her head into her hands, trying to figure out what to do next. Finally, just as Colin had thought she might do in the museum, she tore his letter into pieces, letting the white confetti trickle out of her fingers and on to the ground far below. It wasn't a decision, but somehow the action made her feel a little bit better.

Chapter Seventy-one

Maybe she would have her computer with her. Marcus didn't want to pour his heart into an e-mail, but what else could he do? There was no way to know if she was even still in Paris. She might have hooked up with Colin again, might have returned to London or even California.

But if she had her computer with her, and if she checked her mail, she would at least be aware that he was trying to get in touch with her. He wanted her to know that. He wondered whether his attempt at a reconciliation had backfired. Had it been smart to thrust his wife into the arms of another lover? It was a risk he had thought he could handle. With her gone, he had plenty of time to worry and second-guess himself. Now, it was obvious to him that Colin's own motivations had run deeper than a simple desire to help out a friend in need.

He stared at his blank screen for several minutes. The 'wallpaper' background on his computer screen was a picture of Lissa from the erotic museum in Hamburg. One of the photos of her as a pony girl, her eyes electrifying to look at. He wondered what the original piece of art looked like, and this made him recall a statement Lissa had made years before. If a picture made you want to learn more, then it had done its job. If a work of art lingered with you after you left the museum, the artist had succeeded.

He wasn't sure if she'd count erotica with regular art, but he was pleased to note that something she had said to him had actually sunk in. If he got her back, he promised himself he would listen more. He would pay attention, be a true partner to her. Not only in the bedroom.

But would she take him back?

She had to give him one more chance.

Lissa read the e-mail again.

His e-mail was concise, much less wordy than Colin's letter. It said that he had embarked on this strange scheme because she had seemed so unhappy. He'd wanted her to experience what the world had to offer, and then come back to him, awake and alive in a brand-new way. By sending her to one of his club brothers, he knew that she couldn't be harmed.

It was ridiculous, and yet it made sense to her. This was the way that Marcus would think. And after finding her journal on a disc, filled with all of the fantasies that had burnt within her for years, he had wanted to make them come true. But why hadn't he had the balls to take care of her himself? She had printed off the e-mail using Gizelle's computer, and she clenched her hand around the letter, not even realising it as she crumpled the paper into a tight little ball.

Then, forcing herself to do so, she spread the letter out to read again.

He wanted to meet her.

Well, everyone had wants, didn't they?

Chapter Seventy-two

*G*izelle didn't want Lissa to leave.

'The men in your life treat you like an object in some video game,' she said, her eyes a darker blue than usual. 'They are trying to make it to the next level, with you as the prize.' Now her voice grew softer and she leant close to Lissa to whisper, 'Only a woman knows how a woman is feeling.'

Lissa sat on the edge of the bed, staring at her flame-haired friend. Without the artistry of cosmetics, Gizelle's face appeared to be much younger, a blank canvas ready for the touch of a master painter. She also looked more vulnerable, and Lissa put one hand out to stroke her cheek, but Gizelle pulled away.

'I appreciate everything you've done for me,' Lissa said softly, aware that her tone had a finality to it that she hadn't heard before, 'but right now I have to sort out the rest of my life.'

Gizelle blinked angrily at the tears forming in the corners of her eyes. Then she turned away from Lissa, throwing herself on to the unmade bed. The satin sheets billowed around her, reminding Lissa of the night of passion she had shared with Gizelle and Roberto, of the way those satin sheets had felt caressing her own naked skin. The memory was powerful and Lissa shook her head to clear it. Then she stood and walked slowly to the doorway, hesitating at the threshold before returning to Gizelle's side.

'It's a new world for me,' Lissa said softly. 'There are no boundaries now, which means that there are no goodbyes. But, if you'll let me, we can say au revoir in a special way.'

Gizelle looked up at her with bleary eyes, then pushed her black satin sheet out of the way and welcomed Lissa back into the bed.

It was a completely unique experience, this time, making love to a woman. Yes, Lissa had been with Gina twice in Amsterdam. And the night of the gallery opening, she had let Roberto and Gizelle include her in their awe-inspiring *ménage à trois*. But this time Lissa was in charge, and this single fact made all the difference.

'Do you like that?' Lissa murmured to Gizelle, nuzzling the redhead under her jaw before kissing in a line along her collarbones. Gizelle made a deep, moaning noise that Lissa took as an assent. 'Tell me what you like,' Lissa continued, and her voice sounded surprisingly like Colin's – even the subtle request had come out like a demand. Gizelle opened her eyes and looked at Lissa, a hint of surprise swimming in the deep, bold blue. Then her eyes took on a glazed glow, and she began to speak in French, telling Lissa exactly what gave her pleasure.

'*Touches-moi ici*' (touch me here), Gizelle whispered. '*J'aime ça*' (I like that), and Lissa quickly followed the request, running the tips of her fingers along Gizelle's lovely body. She traced her fingers over the tattoo of a butterfly on Gizelle's abdomen, as if she could feel the artist's penmanship with her own skin.

As she worked, Lissa tried to discern where the feeling of being in charge had come from. She supposed that she had the power this time because Gizelle wanted her

290

to stay. And with that power, Lissa took her time. She moved slowly, gently, over Gizelle's body. She lingered in all of the most delicate places, drawing her tongue along the underside of Gizelle's jawline. Making her way down the gallery owner's body in long, languid strokes.

Gizelle moaned when Lissa reached the hollow basin of her belly, knowing where Lissa's tongue would go next, and arching her hips to help her. Lissa needed no assistance. She cradled Gizelle's slender hips in her hands and began to eat the French woman's pussy as if she were dining on a delicious feast of something sweet and moist. Melon. Honeydew. Dripping with nectar.

This was different from being in the window in Amsterdam with Gina. Making love to Gizelle made Lissa feel as if they were the only two people in the world. She was doing this because she wanted to, not because of Colin's instructions. Not because of the patron – Marcus. But because of her own wants and desires, and that made it all somehow sweeter when she felt herself growing closer to climax.

Now, she wanted Gizelle's mouth on her, and she manoeuvred her body quickly, placing her sex directly above Gizelle's parted lips. The woman didn't need instructions in any language. She used her hands to part Lissa's pussy lips, and then drew her tongue around Lissa's clit in tiny, rapid figure-eights. Lissa could feel Gizelle's hot breath against her skin, her soft mouth against her clit, and the pleasure radiated through her body. As the climax grew closer, images flashed in her mind – making love to Colin in the Catacombs, fucking in the museum in front of the pictures of herself, doing it in the window in Amsterdam. The memories were tactile, as if she could actually feel them happening again. Gizelle's tongue seemed to unlock a barrier within her, and all the emotions came flooding out.

And then, just as the orgasm hit her and slammed

through her body, she saw Marcus, standing outside the gallery, holding up a glass of champagne to toast her.

Remembering his look, she realised that even as she'd had an awakening, so had he. She'd seen that in his deep brown eyes. There was something different about him, something that she had remembered from long ago, when they'd first met on the campus at the university. A fire in his dark eyes that had been there the very first time he'd kissed her, his arms around her, his strength pulsing through her.

Gizelle spoke in French as she came, and Lissa smiled at the sound of the romantic language.

'*Je viens!*' (I'm coming!)

The words sounded so much more beautiful in French than they did English. Lissa let the waves of Gizelle's climax flood through her own body, and she held on tightly to her female partner until those waves subsided. Then she turned again, to hold Gizelle in her arms, feeling the woman's short hair against the underside of her jaw, feeling the bones beneath Gizelle's skin, and smelling her scent, fresh and clean, like an early morning breeze.

Then it was time to go, and as the sunlight hit the sheets, decorating Gizelle's body in light and shadow, Lissa climbed out of bed, gave the woman a final kiss on the lips and then turned and walked out of the room.

Book Six:

Works of Art

Works of art are indeed always products of having been in danger, of having gone to the very end in an experience, to where man can go no further.

– Rainer Maria Rilke

Chapter Seventy-three

*L*issa felt in control. She had made her decision, and this brought a sense of calm to her that she had never known before. All that remained was for her to clean up the loose ends. Then it would finally be time to move forward.

As she exited the plane back to London from Paris, she felt eyes on her, and she turned, half-expecting to see one of the players in the game: Colin? Marcus? Gina? Gizelle? She scanned the crowd of greeters for a familiar partner. Nobody she knew was waiting for her, but still she could feel both men and women watching her pass. Maybe it was her newfound confidence that drew the gaze of strangers to her.

She ran one hand through her newly shorn hair, then stroked her fingers against the skin at the back of her neck. The cut made her feel naked, unable to hide behind her heavy tresses. But the feeling was positive. She didn't want to hide any longer. Didn't want to disguise her desires.

For this morning's confrontation, she had on a severe black suit, modelled like a man's, and her favourite high-heeled boots. The height of them was important. It helped her keep hold of the powerful feeling that had pumped through her since making her decision. She strode through the airport and hailed a taxi, giving the driver the address and then settling back in the roomy cab.

First, she would deal with Colin. Then she would deal with Marcus.

Then she would get some sleep.

Chapter Seventy-four

When Colin opened the door, Lissa jumped. Behind him, in the foyer, stood a statue of herself. One of the waxworks. He must have contacted the gallery and had Gizelle send over the piece. She realised this as she saw it, staring at herself bent over in a yoga-like position in one corner of the room, her hair falling forward, ass to the doorway. As she took another step into the apartment, she saw the second wax sculpture, the one of her under a blanket, one arm over her head, lips parted in sleep. He had positioned it on the sofa, and the statue was realistic enough to look as if she were simply snoozing away a lazy afternoon.

Lissa bit her bottom lip, staring around the living room. He had bought all seven different versions of herself, and had set the works of art up in the large space, as if decorating a window in a department store. Seeing them gave Lissa a strange, creepy feeling inside.

Colin had snapped.

He lowered his head when she stared at him, and then gave her a puppy-dog look, peeking up under his lashes at her. Something had broken inside him, she sensed it, and she also sensed he knew she was here to say goodbye.

Before she could speak, he ushered her forward, closing the door behind her. She pressed her back to it, not wanting to take another step into the apartment.

'A drink?' he asked, moving quickly to the bar in the corner and pouring one before she could answer. When she shook her head, he drank it for her, downing it all in a single swallow, shaking his head roughly at the burn of the alcohol. 'You read my letter?' he asked next.

She nodded, finally finding her voice. 'Yes.'

'Then you understand?'

'Yes,' she said again, catching a glimpse of the waxwork of her walking, positioned at the start of the hallway as if she were heading towards their bedroom, perhaps going after the paddle at his request. He had dressed this one in her own lingerie, a black merry widow and fishnet garters. It was freaky to see herself all over his apartment while knowing that she was going to leave. In a sense, she'd remain here with him.

'And you've come back?' he asked. His voice quavered with a hopeful tone.

She shook her head. 'Colin, I can't.' She meant to continue, to tell him why, and to ask for several explanations from him as well, but he didn't let her.

'Then fuck you.' He didn't yell it, simply spoke it as if he'd wished her well. But he threw the empty glass against the wall so hard that it shattered. The bits of crystal rained down in the corner, then lay glistening on the floor like tiny diamonds. Colin repeated the words slowly, as if biting each one off and spitting it out. 'Fuck you.'

Lissa stared at him, confused. He had never cursed or sworn at her before. In all their times together, he hadn't even raised his voice. Not even during their most inventive sex play. Now that he was swearing at her, the foul words sounded wrong coming from his lips. It was like watching a badly dubbed movie, one in which she couldn't follow the plot.

'Oh, Jesus, Lissa. Don't fucking leave me –'

That's what didn't make any sense. He was swearing at her, but he wanted her to stay, when everything he'd done seemed as if he had intended to push her away from him. It took an effort to make her feet move, to walk over to where he stood, leaning against the wall and staring at her with weary eyes. She reached one hand out and pushed his bright hair away from his face, but the gesture was false. She should have been the one crying, and he should have played the role of the calming lover. That's how it had always been between them. The shift of power left a sickening feeling inside her.

Colin shook off her hand and it was with relief that she let it fall back to her side.

'Please –' he said again, this time not meeting her eyes. She guessed the problem correctly. He couldn't handle begging. That's what was killing him inside. She understood this and still she felt nothing.

'It was a game,' she reminded him. 'You won. Why can't you accept that?'

He lowered his head in his hands and slid down the wall into a sitting position. Unmoved, she stared down at him, at his wrinkled white shirt, open at the collar, at his unpressed slacks. She'd never seen him in such total disarray. He looked like a sloppily drawn version of his former self.

On the wall behind him was a portrait she'd never seen. Her eyes rested on it, and she brought one hand to her mouth. It was a picture of her, at climax, eyes shut, lips parted in ecstasy. When had he commissioned this? She couldn't understand what was going on, but she felt that Colin was someone she didn't know at all.

'Lissa, please,' he said, then stopped, and she caught the sound of choked sobs. Here he was, her lord and master for the past six months, and instead of him breaking her, she had somehow managed to destroy him. The irony was thick enough to make her smile, but looking down at Colin, she managed to keep a serious expression on her face.

'Please,' he said again, and she could hear the way it sounded in her own voice, an echo in her mind, thought of a medley of pictures of herself in his power, begging him for something. Pleasure. Release. More. *That's* what he wanted. She understood it clearly, as if she'd suddenly been able to decipher a new language. He did not want her. He did not want love. He wanted more.

'I have to go,' she said. She walked past the wax sculpture of herself, seated at the dining-room table. At least, he'd have the works of art to remind himself of her. She could imagine him stroking their waxy skin, pressing his body up against them. The thought made her shudder. Maybe he'd like it, or maybe it would be worse for him, always able to see her when she was no longer there. It didn't matter. She could no longer concern herself with how he felt.

The sculpture nearest the door wore her wedding ring. Startled, she went to it and slipped the ring from its finger, holding the platinum band tightly in her fist. Behind her, Colin made a sound like a wounded animal, a low keening noise from the back of his throat, and it was this that finally tore at her but it didn't slow her down.

Chapter Seventy-five

Marcus waited in the centre of the courtyard, surrounded by the iron figures. In a different situation, he knew that he would find himself pondering the meaning of the work for about a millisecond before deciding that he hated it. He understood this. In fact, he could hear his own voice telling Lissa that the display was unfathomable, that the iron men were no more meaningful than a scattered group of children's toys.

Now, he read the brochure he had picked up at the front desk of the museum. Upon learning that the men were all casts of the artist, he was sure that his normal response would be to chastise the artist for such an egotistical display. Man, how could someone get away with it?

Today, he was different. Armed with a new mindset, waiting to meet her here, at the designated space, he tried to see the work as she might see it. He played her voice from memory, using other situations, remembering the light in her grey eyes when she spoke about a work she particularly enjoyed. Why had he always put her down? Why couldn't he have tried to learn? He had an analytical mind, but that didn't mean he had to be immune to art.

Maybe he'd been afraid to be wrong. Now that he'd nearly lost her, he didn't think that fear was rational. You had to go after what you wanted, no matter the cost, no matter if it could make you look foolish. To hell with false modesty.

As he read over the brochure, he pretended that she was describing the piece to him. Sixty separate casts of the artist, twelve different forms. He looked around. Several of the male figures were suspended upside-down from the roof of the museum. He liked the way they looked. There, *that* was a first. He didn't understand the work, but he had found something in it he liked. Lissa had always said that was the first step to understanding art. Find something that moves you for any reason at all, and take it from there.

The iron men on the ground didn't do that much for him, but the ones hanging upside-down gave him ideas. He could easily picture Lissa hanging upside-down from her ankles, suspended from the cathedral ceiling of their bedroom over their king-size bed. There were so many things that they could do together, now. That door was wide open. He thought of the final pictures Colin had sent him. Each one more obscene than the other. But to him, they were art, more captivating than a Monet or a Matisse. It was all in the eye of the beholder, right? She'd taught him that, as well.

The sound of her steps behind him made him turn. He knew the gait, the quick clacking of her heels against the stone walkway. One thing he had always appreciated about her was the fact that she walked as if she were going somewhere. Even when simply taking a stroll around the block, she didn't meander. She strode. He loved the way she looked in motion, but when she saw him now, she stopped in place and just stared at him.

Why didn't she speak? Was she in love with Colin? Did she want to end things?

He waited. Come to me! he begged her silently. Please.

If you take a step forward it will all be OK. He didn't even berate himself for the mental pleading. For once, it didn't occur to him to do so.

She lowered her head and he focused on the way she stood, head down, eyes refusing to meet his.

'Lissa.' Something in his voice made her raise her head. In her eyes, he saw a light that had been missing for such a long time. 'Lissa.' He said her name again, and now, as if she were terrified that he would run away, she took a hurried step towards him, then came into his arms, pressed her head against his chest and started to cry.

'Not now,' he whispered. 'You don't have to cry now.'

Lissa clung to Marcus, unsure of how to process the feelings that whirled through her. Even after her odd confrontation with Colin, she had been so confident at the prospect of going to meet her husband. But now, seeing him, resting her head against his strong chest, she couldn't contain herself. The tears simply started to flow.

Had she known it was him all along? Maybe. Perhaps some part of her brain had been awake and aware, had intentionally kept the secret within. Since seeing him in Paris, she had worked to figure out the entire plan. Parts of the scheme made sense to her. He'd found her electronic journal, had discovered the fantasies she'd kept private for years. Upon learning what she wanted, Marcus had, in his own way, made each one come true. Still, she had a million questions to ask. Like why had Marcus left after Amsterdam. Why hadn't he told her it was him all along?

She tilted her head to look up at him, preparing to speak, but stopped. She traced her fingertips along the side of his face. His dark eyes flashed at her, and suddenly she didn't need the answers right away. All she needed to know was that meeting him had been the right thing. Now she opened her lips, and said exactly the same words she'd told Colin on their first meeting. 'I'm sorry.'

Was that the first thing Lissa always said? No, Marcus remembered their initial meeting in college. He had seen her on campus before but never spoken to her, although he'd meant to. She had been the one to initiate a conversation, stopping him by the library to ask where a specific hall was. His mind went back further and he smiled. She had apologised then, too. 'I'm sorry, do you know where ...' Instead of 'excuse me'. Continually apologising for things that weren't her fault or weren't appropriate for her to apologise for.

Marcus held her tightly for a moment because he'd missed the feel of her body against his. Then, gripping on to her arms, he pulled her slightly away so that he could look at her. God, he'd missed her face. The lines of it. The silvery sheen of her eyes. Nobody else had eyes like that. Wolf's eyes. Hadn't he called them that when they were at school? Why did it seem so long since he'd looked at her? Really looked at her. In that respect, Colin had been correct. Sometimes you missed things that were right under your nose, missed seeing the needs of someone you took for granted would always be there.

'I'm sorry ...' she said again, and he sensed that she was about to launch into a full confession detailing her past six months with Colin. Of course, Marcus knew it all. He didn't need to hear her describe it. Not now. She could tell him later, tied down to his bed, when he was ready to play the role of her confessor. And her punisher.

'Lissa,' he said softly, 'what a pretty thing you are.'

She swallowed hard, looked down at the ground in the most adorable, most becoming way.

'Don't be sorry now,' he continued, glancing a final time at the sculptures around them before meeting her eyes. A shining, glistening grey, they held all the promises he needed, let him know that it had been the right decision to give her up because it had ultimately brought her back. He pressed his lips against the hollow of her throat and whispered to her, so that she knew he was hers for life. He would give her anything she wanted, everything she needed. From now on, they were a team.

'Don't be sorry now, Lissa,' he murmured again. 'Wait until later.'

When he took a step back from her, she looked up at him, eyes wide. Then her lips curved into a smile and he saw that she understood exactly what he was telling her, that leaving London wasn't the end of their story.

It was only the beginning.

Visit the Black Lace website at
www.black-lace-books.com

LOOK OUT FOR THE ALL-NEW BLACK LACE BOOKS – AVAILABLE NOW!

All books priced £7.99 in the UK. Please note publication dates apply to the UK only. For other territories, please contact your retailer.

THE TEN VISIONS
Olivia Knight
ISBN 978 0 352 34119 8

The moment she starts her doctorate in Oxford, Sarah is beset with mysteries. An old portrait in her rented house bears an uncanny resemblance to her. Her new lover insists he's a ghost. Her attractive, sinister supervisor refuses to let her see manuscripts on witchcraft. An ordinary hill on the meadow fills her with fear – and not just her, but also the man with whom she falls in love. Every time she has sex, she hallucinates strange places and other times.

Through sex magic and orgasmic visions, she must fight betrayal to learn the truth behind the secrets.

THE BLUE GUIDE
Carrie Williams
ISBN 978 0 352 34131 0

Cocktails, room service, spa treatments: Alicia Shaw is a girl who just
can't say no to the little perks of being a private tour guide in London.
Whether it's the Hollywood producer with whom she romps in the
private screening room of one of London's most luxurious hotels, or the
Australian pilot whose exhibitionist fantasies reach a new height on the
London Eye, Alicia finds that flirtation – and more – is part of the
territory.

But when internationally renowned flamenco dancer and heartthrob
Paco Manchega, and his lovely young wife Carlotta, take her on as their
guide, Alicia begins to wonder if she has bitten off more than she can
chew. As the couple unleash curious appetites in Alicia, taking her to
places more darkly beautiful than she has ever known, she begins to
suspect she is being used as the pawn in some strange marital game.

DIVINE TORMENT
Janine Ashbless
ISBN 978 0 352 33719 1

In the ancient temple city of Mulhanabin, the voluptuous Malia Shai
awaits her destiny. Millions of people worship her, believing her to be a
goddess incarnate. She is, however, very human and consumed by erotic
passions that have no outlet. Into this sacred city comes General Verlaine
– the rugged gladiatorial leader of the occupying army. Intimate contact
between Veraine and Malia Shai is forbidden by every law of their hostile
peoples. But she is the only thing he wants – and he will risk everything
to have her.

Coming in September 2007

THE TEMPLAR PRIZE
Deanna Ashford
ISBN 978 0 352 34137 2

At last free of a disastrous forced marriage, Edwina de Moreville accompanies Princess Berengaria and her betrothed, Richard the Lionheart on a quest to the Holy Land to recapture Jerusalem from the Saracens. Edwina has happily been reunited with her first and only love, Stephen the Comte de Chalais, one of Richard's most loyal knights but, although their passion for each other is as strong as ever, the path before them will be far from easy.

After surviving a terrible storm at sea, Edwina and the princess fall into the hands of the cruel, debauched Emperor of Cyprus, Isaac Comenius. He has even more frightening plans for Edwina but, with Stephen's help, she and the princess escape. However, Stephen has an enemy he is unaware of Guy de Lusignan, the King of Jerusalem, who also desires Edwina.

When they reached the besieged city of Acre, their situation becomes more perilous. Guy lures Stephen away from the Christian lines and, with the help of a group of renegade Knights Templar, has him imprisoned in their fortress. When Edwina tries to pursue Stephen, she is captured and enslaved by a Saracen nobleman who desires her for his harem. In the end only one man can help them escape their destiny, the great Saracen leader Saladin. But he also is in danger from the strange sect of assassins, the Hashshashin.

Black Lace Booklist

Information is correct at time of printing. To avoid disappointment, check availability before ordering. Go to www.black-lace-books.com. All books are priced £7.99 unless another price is given.

BLACK LACE BOOKS WITH A CONTEMPORARY SETTING

☐ ALWAYS THE BRIDEGROOM Tesni Morgan	ISBN 978 0 352 33855 6	£6.99
☐ THE ANGELS' SHARE Maya Hess	ISBN 978 0 352 34043 6	
☐ ARIA APPASSIONATA Julie Hastings	ISBN 978 0 352 33056 7	£6.99
☐ ASKING FOR TROUBLE Kristina Lloyd	ISBN 978 0 352 33362 9	
☐ BLACK LIPSTICK KISSES Monica Belle	ISBN 978 0 352 33885 3	£6.99
☐ BONDED Fleur Reynolds	ISBN 978 0 352 33192 2	£6.99
☐ THE BOSS Monica Belle	ISBN 978 0 352 34088 7	
☐ BOUND IN BLUE Monica Belle	ISBN 978 0 352 34012 2	
☐ CAMPAIGN HEAT Gabrielle Marcola	ISBN 978 0 352 33941 6	
☐ CAT SCRATCH FEVER Sophie Mouette	ISBN 978 0 352 34021 4	
☐ CIRCUS EXCITE Nikki Magennis	ISBN 978 0 352 34033 7	
☐ CLUB CRÈME Primula Bond	ISBN 978 0 352 33907 2	£6.99
☐ COMING ROUND THE MOUNTAIN Tabitha Flyte	ISBN 978 0 352 33873 0	£6.99
☐ CONFESSIONAL Judith Roycroft	ISBN 978 0 352 33421 3	
☐ CONTINUUM Portia Da Costa	ISBN 978 0 352 33120 5	
☐ COOKING UP A STORM Emma Holly	ISBN 978 0 352 34114 3	
☐ DANGEROUS CONSEQUENCES Pamela Rochford	ISBN 978 0 352 33185 4	
☐ DARK DESIGNS Madelynne Ellis	ISBN 978 0 352 34075 7	
☐ THE DEVIL INSIDE Portia Da Costa	ISBN 978 0 352 32993 6	
☐ EDEN'S FLESH Robyn Russell	ISBN 978 0 352 33923 2	£6.99
☐ ENTERTAINING MR STONE Portia Da Costa	ISBN 978 0 352 34029 0	
☐ EQUAL OPPORTUNITIES Mathilde Madden	ISBN 978 0 352 34070 2	
☐ FEMININE WILES Karina Moore	ISBN 978 0 352 33874 7	
☐ FIRE AND ICE Laura Hamilton	ISBN 978 0 352 33486 2	
☐ GOING DEEP Kimberly Dean	ISBN 978 0 352 33876 1	£6.99
☐ GOING TOO FAR Laura Hamilton	ISBN 978 0 352 33657 6	£6.99

❏ WICKED WORDS 4 Various	ISBN 978 0 352 33603 3	£6.99
❏ WICKED WORDS 5 Various	ISBN 978 0 352 33642 2	£6.99
❏ WICKED WORDS 6 Various	ISBN 978 0 352 33690 3	£6.99
❏ WICKED WORDS 7 Various	ISBN 978 0 352 33743 6	£6.99
❏ WICKED WORDS 8 Various	ISBN 978 0 352 33787 0	£6.99
❏ WICKED WORDS 9 Various	ISBN 978 0 352 33860 0	
❏ WICKED WORDS 10 Various	ISBN 978 0 352 33893 8	
❏ THE BEST OF BLACK LACE 2 Various	ISBN 978 0 352 33718 4	
❏ WICKED WORDS: SEX IN THE OFFICE Various	ISBN 978 0 352 33944 7	
❏ WICKED WORDS: SEX AT THE SPORTS CLUB Various	ISBN 978 0 352 33991 1	
❏ WICKED WORDS: SEX ON HOLIDAY Various	ISBN 978 0 352 33961 4	
❏ WICKED WORDS: SEX IN UNIFORM Various	ISBN 978 0 352 34002 3	
❏ WICKED WORDS: SEX IN THE KITCHEN Various	ISBN 978 0 352 34018 4	
❏ WICKED WORDS: SEX ON THE MOVE Various	ISBN 978 0 352 34034 4	
❏ WICKED WORDS: SEX AND MUSIC Various	ISBN 978 0 352 34061 0	
❏ WICKED WORDS: SEX AND SHOPPING Various	ISBN 978 0 352 34076 4	
❏ SEX IN PUBLIC Various	ISBN 978 0 352 34089 4	
❏ SEX IN WITH STRANGERS Various	ISBN 978 0 352 34105 1	

BLACK LACE NON-FICTION

❏ THE BLACK LACE BOOK OF WOMEN'S SEXUAL FANTASIES Edited by Kerri Sharp	ISBN 978 0 352 33793 1	£6.99

To find out the latest information about Black Lace titles, check out the website: www.black-lace-books.com or send for a booklist with complete synopses by writing to:

Black Lace Booklist, Virgin Books Ltd
Thames Wharf Studios
Rainville Road
London W6 9HA

Please include an SAE of decent size. Please note only British stamps are valid.

Our privacy policy
We will not disclose information you supply us to any other parties. We will not disclose any information which identifies you personally to any person without your express consent.

From time to time we may send out information about Black Lace books and special offers. Please tick here if you do <u>not</u> wish to receive Black Lace information. ❏

Please send me the books I have ticked above.

Name ....

Address ....

....

....

....

Post Code ....

Send to: Virgin Books Cash Sales, Thames Wharf Studios, Rainville Road, London W6 9HA.

US customers: for prices and details of how to order books for delivery by mail, call 888-330-8477.

Please enclose a cheque or postal order, made payable to Virgin Books Ltd, to the value of the books you have ordered plus postage and packing costs as follows:

UK and BFPO – £1.00 for the first book, 50p for each subsequent book.

Overseas (including Republic of Ireland) – £2.00 for the first book, £1.00 for each subsequent book.

If you would prefer to pay by VISA, ACCESS/MASTERCARD, DINERS CLUB, AMEX or SWITCH, please write your card number and expiry date here:

....

Signature ....

Please allow up to 28 days for delivery.